NATHANIEL S̶̶̶̶̶̶̶̶ ̶̶̶̶̶̶ BURNING CABIN. . .

He saw a man rush out—his clothes and face were blackened with soot. As his family followed, Indians leaped at them from behind the trees and surrounded the house.

It all happened in seconds. The man attempted to fight back. He raised his rifle and fired. But it was too late—he fell, mortally wounded. His young son was next. And two women running into the woods never made it.

This bloody horror paralyzed Nathaniel for just one moment. He could see a warrior holding an infant, and something snapped. He could no longer be a bystander waiting to see what happened next.

Nathaniel raised the flintlock and fired without a second thought. . . .

FLINTLOCK

SIGNET

SAGAS OF THE AMERICAN WEST
BY JASON MANNING

☐ **HIGH COUNTRY** A young man in virgin land. A magnificient saga live with the courage, challenge, danger, and adventure of the American past. (176804—$4.50)

☐ **GREEN RIVER RENDEZVOUS** Zach Hannah was a legend of courage, skill, and strength ... Now he faces the most deadly native tribe in the west and the most brutal brigade of trappers ever to make the high country a killing ground. (177142—$4.50)

☐ **BATTLE OF THE TETON BASIN** Zach Hannah wants to be left alone, high in the mountains, with his Indian bride. But as long as Sean Michael Devlin lives, Zach can find no peace. Zach must track down this man— the former friend who stole his wife and left him to die at the hands of the Blackfeet. Zach and Devlin square off in a final reckoning ... that only one of them will survive. (178297—$4.50)

*Prices slightly higher in Canada

FLINTLOCK

by

Jason Manning

A SIGNET BOOK

SIGNET
Published by the Penguin Group
Penguin Books USA Inc., 375 Hudson Street,
New York, New York 10014, U.S.A.
Penguin Books Ltd, 27 Wrights Lane,
London W8 5TZ, England
Penguin Books Australia Ltd, Ringwood,
Victoria, Australia
Penguin Books Canada Ltd, 10 Alcorn Avenue,
Toronto, Ontario, Canada M4V 3B2
Penguin Books (N.Z.) Ltd, 182–190 Wairau Road,
Auckland 10, New Zealand

Penguin Books Ltd, Registered Offices:
Harmondsworth, Middlesex, England

First published by Signet,
an imprint of Dutton Signet,
a division of Penguin Books USA Inc.

First Printing, August, 1994
10 9 8 7 6 5 4 3 2 1

 REGISTERED TRADEMARK—MARCA REGISTRADA

Printed in the United States of America

Summer 1781

Chapter 1

The whisper of a breeze moving the curtains on the window woke Captain Peter McLeod.

For a moment he thought himself back home in South Carolina. He took in the rustic but comfortable confines of the room with a bleary gaze, disoriented, and in the grip of a peculiarly sharp misery. Accustomed to awakening clear of head and in complete command of his faculties, McLeod found himself on this morning trapped for a disconcerting moment in that limbo between dream and consciousness.

No, he wasn't in South Carolina. This was Virginia, and he had only been dreaming of home, and happier times, prior to this bloody rebellion that had destroyed his life. As he realized where he was, the dream mercifully released him.

It was early, yet already warm. There was a dampness in the air. Through the window McLeod could glimpse a piece of pewter-gray sky. More rain in the offing. McLeod was a cavalryman through and through, and the prospect of more showers to turn these Virginia roads into a morass of mud did little to cheer him.

A sparrow landed on the sill of the open window, then hopped brazenly onto the small roughhewn table that stood beneath the window. McLeod lay quite still. The sparrow pecked at the goat's-milk cheese and black bread laid out on a scrap of linen atop the table. A half-empty bottle of cheap wine anchored one end of the linen. An empty bottle lay on its side on the floor. That explained the cotton in his head.

The woman who slept beside McLeod moaned and stirred. This provoked the sparrow, who took flight through the window. Propped up on one elbow, McLeod stared at a tousled riot of golden hair, the creamy curve of bare shoulder from which had slipped the blanket they shared. He felt the long, warm, silky-smooth length of her.

She was the reason he had awakened out of sorts, with the idea that he was still at home. The sensation of a woman sharing his bed had fooled him, igniting the memory of those nights he had spent with Selene in his arms.

But Selene was dead, and had been for three years now. Taken, abused and murdered by rebels who broke the laws and scorned the king and in spite of all that had the gall to call themselves patriots.

A bitter copper taste filled McLeod's mouth. He had crossed the ocean to America with high hopes for a new beginning. The English laws of primogeniture being what they were, the second son of a

Scottish squire faced lean prospects at home. In the colonies he had done well for himself, raising horses and tobacco, and marrying into a good Charleston family. The future had seemed bright indeed.

Then—the rebellion. Those bloody Sons of Liberty malcontents with their Committees of Correspondence and tea parties and tarring and feathering. McLeod hated them with a passion that grew with each passing day. They had cost him everything. His wife, his land, his future. He did not fight for king and country so much as he fought for vengeance.

Which was one reason he had advanced so rapidly in the ranks of Colonel Bonastre Tarleton's partisan rangers. Most of Tarleton's Tory Legion had been recruited in New York and the Jerseys. McLeod's intimate knowledge of the Carolinas had rendered him invaluable to the dashing Tarleton, and his ruthlessness in battle endeared him to the commander of the Legion as well, for no one knew better than Tarleton that to crush the rebels one had to wage war against the homes and families of the traitors. Only in this way could their spirit be crushed. Quench a man's thirst for war with the blood of his kin and he will not thirst long. So said Tarleton.

McLeod disagreed, but never openly. Tarleton's brutal tactics served only to harden the resolve of the rebels, just as McLeod's resolve had been hardened by the murder of his beloved Selene and the burning of his estate. It mattered not to McLeod whether the fighting dragged on till Doomsday. While others prayed for a speedy conclusion to the conflict, he looked forward to the next fight. While all of his colleagues longed for peace, so that they could return to their homes and families, McLeod dreaded peace, because he had nothing and no one to go back to. He lived for war.

The patriots called Tarleton "the Butcher," because his Legion had massacred Whig partisans commanded by Alexander Buford at the Waxhaws. Rebel propaganda trumpeted the claim that Buford, once cornered, had tried to surrender. McLeod had been present, and he knew that this was so, yet he found no fault in Tarleton's refusal to give quarter. Buford's rangers, along with those who followed Thomas Sumter, Andrew Pickens and the Swamp Fox, Francis Marion, had done their share of raiding and looting Tory strongholds. They had murdered Loyalist civilians and raped Loyalist women. They gave no quarter, and McLeod was of the firm opinion that they deserved none.

McLeod swung long legs off the bed and rose. The woman murmured sleepily and rolled over. Her turning rearranged the blanket, exposing alabaster curve of hip and thigh. Mcleod studied her face and form with ambivalence. He could not recall her name, and spent precious little time trying to, turning to don buckskin britches, a sleeveless waistcoat of white linen, and the short surtout of forest green hue that was the uniform of the Tory Legion.

He was a tall, lean man, with dark good looks, black hair and thick brows over piercing blue eyes, and a cruel mouth beneath a bladed nose. A dangerous-looking man—one that some women found nigh on irresistible—and made even more dangerous looking by the saber scar across the forehead.

As he sat in a chair to pull on his longboots he glanced at her again. No, he could not recall the name. But he did remember the longing in her sleepy violet eyes, the silver of moonlight on her hair, the sweet warmth of her quickened breath through full red lips. She had bewitched him. She worked here in this inn at Hanover Court House. Her husband was a Continental, up north with Washington besieging Sir Henry Clinton in New York. She was petulant as she told him this, deriding the man for going off to fight a "silly little war" and leaving her all alone for so long.

McLeod had given this drivel little credence. The woman was a harlot, and with that in mind he took a crown from a pocket of his surtout and laid it between her breasts, with a silent apology to Selene. He did not often partake of the pleasures of the flesh these days, but sometimes he was weak and betrayed the memory of his dead wife, whom he had loved so fiercely and completely that he knew he would never love another.

She stretched like a contented cat, but did not come fully awake. At any moment her eyes would open, and McLeod did not care to be present when that happened. He hastened to fasten the last of the surtout's nine copper buttons. Grabbing up spurs, saber and webbing, and black leather cap, he was turning toward the door when someone knocked loudly. The woman awoke with a start. McLeod muttered a dark curse and threw open the door to confront Sergeant-Major Angus Mulcahey.

"Beggin' your pardon, Captain," said Mulcahey. His brogue was heavy, his voice a rumbling baritone. "But the Colonel has . . ." He glanced past McLeod, and his eyes widened.

McLeod looked around. She was sitting up in the bed, and was belatedly pulling the blanket up to cover her breasts. The crown had fallen, and was describing a languid circle as it rolled across the floor. Holding the blanket to her bosom with one hand, she brushed tousled golden locks out of her sleepy eyes. She was, mused McLeod, a bonny lass. Turning back to Mulcahey, he saw a twinkle in the sergeant-major's eye.

"Sorry, Captain. I didna mean to interrupt . . ."

"You interrupted nothing, Sergeant-Major."

McLeod realized that word of his romantic conquest would spread like a call to arms through the squadron. Of course, the dragoons would not think less of him for it. On the contrary. They expected their officers to be not only expert handlers of horse and saber, but also masters of the arts of hard drinking and womanizing as well.

"Whatever you say, sir. The Colonel has requested the presence of all squadron commanders at his table this morning."

Mulcahey was a beefy man with a florid, heavy-jowled face. He was a fine noncommissioned officer

who had fought with McLeod all along the Congaree, at the disastrous Battle of the Cowpens, and at
Guilford Court House. A solid, trustworthy subordi-
nate with a good nose for impending action. This latter trait prompted McLeod to ask the question that
had leapt to mind.

"Is this merely a social event, Sergeant-Major?"

Mulcahey beamed. "I wouldna count on it, Captain. There's something in the air. I smell a fine and
dandy fight coming. Rumor has it Lord Cornwallis
sent the Colonel sealed orders. I think we're in for a
ride across this fine Virginia countryside."

"Good!" exclaimed McLeod. "Good! I'll be surprised, Sergeant-Major, if it isn't Charlottesville we'll
be visiting."

"Charlottesville?"

"Aye. The House of Burgesses. We'll capture the
whole bloody lot of traitors and hang them all. With
any luck, we'll bag the biggest traitor of them all into
the bargain, that scoundrel Thomas Jefferson."

Mulcahey glanced at the woman again, and Mc-
Leod, much abashed, realized he had been too loose
tongued, if indeed he had correctly surmised the
contents of Lord Cornwallis's orders to Colonel
Tarleton.

"Be on your way, Captain," said Mulcahey. "I'll see
to matters here."

With a curt nod, McLeod left the room.

As Mulcahey crossed the room, the woman
gasped and shrank back against the headboard of the
bed, fearing for her life.

"Now, now, lass," cooed the sergeant-major. He bent to retrieve the crown, and held it out to her. "I expect you've heard some turrible things aboot us dragoons, but I for one am not a slayer of helpless females. So take this token of Captain McLeod's appreciation, and I'll be on my way."

Greed overcame fear, and the woman reached out to take the coin.

Mulcahey grabbed her wrist. With a shriek, she tried to pull away, but the burly sergeant-major pinned her down on the bed.

"Listen careful, lass. Your life depends on it. You heard nothing that was said here today, d'ya understand?"

She nodded, too frightened to speak.

"You wouldna want to cross Captain McLeod. I remember one night down in the Waxhaws, after we'd cut two hundred of your colonial militia to pieces, a young patriot was brought before the captain in shackles. Why, the lad was only twelve or thirteen years old, but he was full of defiance, that one. The captain liked his spirit, and gave him the chance to serve as his valet. It was that or the horrors of the prison camp. The boy refused."

Mulcahey chuckled, shaking his head. " 'I'll be no slave to a Tory traitor,' said he. He had the gall to curse the captain. The captain, not one to brook disrespect, struck with his saber. The lad was gravely wounded, and hauled off with the rest of the prisoners to rot in the Camden stockade.

"So I'm hopin' you'll get the moral of the story,

lass. So young and winsome—I'd hate to see you after the captain got through with you."

Mulcahey pulled her hand to his lips and kissed it. Then, chuckling, he took his leave without a backward glance at the frightened girl.

Chapter 2

As was his custom when occupying a town, Bonastre Tarleton chose the best house for his own quarters, giving assurances to the occupants that he would be a responsible guest, and making certain they understood that as long as they were good hosts their property would be left intact. There would be no looting. Not a single piece of silverware would turn up missing.

In this case the occupants were the wife and daughters of the Honourable Henry Blevins, a lawyer and Virginia burgess who was at the moment in Charlottesville with the rest of the colonial assembly. They had no choice but to accept Tarleton under their roof. For his part, Tarleton acted the perfect gentleman. Mrs. Blevins was not deceived by his impeccable manners. She had heard all about his notorious exploits down south, and believed everything she heard. Her two daughters were impressed by Tarleton's boyish good looks and natural charm, much to Mrs. Blevin's consternation.

That night Tarleton slept in the parlor downstairs,

having gallantly announced that the upstairs of the Blevins home was strictly off limits to himself and all of his staff. The next morning he politely asked Mrs. Blevins and her daughters to prepare breakfast for himself and his officers, after which they would have to temporarily vacate the premises, making sure that all their servants went with them.

"You dare run me out of my own home?" gasped the outraged Mrs. Blevins.

Tarleton's smile was a disarming one. He shrugged apologetically. "Alas, dear lady, I must, but only for an hour or two. My officers and I will be engaged in a council of war. The matters we discuss must remain confidential."

So it was that as Captain McLeod arrived, Mrs. Blevins and her two daughters were departing, trailed by a brace of house servants. McLeod touched the brim of his plumed leather cap at the Blevins daughters, who smiled and giggled behind their hands. Already in a huff, the doughty Mrs. Blevins glowered at McLeod while sternly rebuking her offspring, then led the way up a street clogged with dragoons.

The two sentries posted at the front door snapped to attention as McLeod entered the house. One of the colonel's aides-de-camp met him in the hallway and directed him to the dining room. This McLeod entered to find Tarleton and the other squadron commanders just finishing breakfast. Several orderlies stood around the long table.

"Ah, McLeod," said Tarleton. "We were wondering

what had become of you. I fear your breakfast is cold. The ham is delightful."

"I'm not hungry."

"Just as well." Tarleton took a last bite, sipped his tea, touched his lips with a napkin, and told the orderlies to clear the table, oblivious to the fact that several of his subordinates had not yet finished eating.

The dishes cleared away, Tarleton summoned an aide with an imperious snap of the fingers. The aide carried a map, which was spread out on the table, and anchored with a saber on one side, a pistol and a bottle of sherry from Henry Blevins's well-stocked wine cellar on the other.

Studying the map, which included the Carolinas and Virginia in good detail, from Savannah in the south to the Potomac River in the north, McLeod mentally reviewed the campaigns of the past year.

In the spring of 1780, Sir Henry Clinton had sailed south with 10,000 men from New York and blockaded the rebel general Benjamin Lincoln and his army in Charleston. Having served until then with the Tory Legion in the Jerseys, that siege had marked McLeod's return home. He had fought with distinction at Monck's Corner, when the Tory Legion smashed Isaac Huger's mounted partisans and closed the trap on Lincoln. In May, Lincoln was forced to surrender his 5,000 Continentals unconditionally—a disaster for the so-called patriots, and a move that many had assumed would lead to the swift conclusion of the war.

Clinton then sent the Tory Legion on military excursions up the Congaree and Wateree Rivers. In May, Tarleton cornered Buford and butchered his troops at the Waxhaws. Houses were torched, livestock slaughtered, as the Tory Legion faithfully executed Clinton's "scorched-earth" policy.

In June of '80, Clinton had turned command of the southern theater over to Lord Cornwallis and sailed back to New York. "There are few men in South Carolina who are not either our prisoners or in arms with us," Clinton confidently wrote Lord George Germain in London. But the colonists weren't giving up. A new Continental army under the command of Horatio Gates was on the march to recapture Charleston.

The majority of Gates's men were not battle tested, a fact that became apparent that August at Camden. Tarleton's Legion was in the thick of that fight, breaking the backbone of the Continentals by smashing Gates's right wing, the Delaware and Maryland veterans under the command of the stalwart soldier of fortune, Baron de Kalb, the only strong resistance to the British onslaughts.

The rebels were routed, and the Tory Legion pursued vigorously, cutting down the fleeing colonists left and right—a slaughter that continued until darkness and exhausted mounts forced Tarleton to call a halt to it. McLeod remembered that day as a particularly splendid one.

Horatio Gates had led the retreat, being one of the first to depart the field of battle. As a result, he was replaced by Nathaniel Greene, a crafty and courageous fighter handpicked by George Washington himself for the task of saving the South.

And the tide began to turn.

At King's Mountain, Major Patrick Ferguson and one thousand Tory partisans ran afoul of overmountain men led by Isaac Shelby and Jack Sevier. Ferguson was killed and his force annihilated by the rough-hewn frontiersmen. Meanwhile, with raiders like Marion and Sumter and Pickens harassing his supply lines, Cornwallis fell back to winter quarters, postponing his grandiose plan to conquer the southern colonies until the following year.

Greene knew he was too weak to attack Cornwallis head on, so he adopted a daring plan, splitting his small army in the hopes that Cornwallis would divide his own force. It was risky business, for if Cornwallis kept his units together and struck first one and then the other wing of Greene's army, the British would win the war in the South.

Cornwallis played into Greene's hands, dispatching Tarleton's Legion, along with the 7th Royal Fusiliers and the 71st Highlanders, to come to grips with the "Old Wagoner" Daniel Morgan and his 600 seasoned Delaware and Maryland Continentals. Morgan and Tarleton clashed at the Cowpens, lightly wooded meadows in the shadow of King's Mountain where drovers had traditionally grazed cattle destined for markets on the coast. Morgan's front line pulled back after firing a few volleys, luring Tarleton into a trap. The 71st Highlanders,

completely surrounded and caught in a deadly en-
filade, surrendered. Tarleton furiously tried to rally
his dragoons, to no avail. Ninety percent of the Legion was killed or captured. McLeod fought his
way clear of several rebel horsemen, receiving the
saber cut across his face. Blinded by his own
blood, he nonetheless managed to cut his way
through the enemy and make good his escape.

Defeats as disastrous as King's Mountain and the
Cowpens would have rendered a lesser commander
paralyzed with indecision, but Charles Cornwallis
was a daring and imaginative leader. Burning all sur-
plus wagons and supplies, he set out to catch
Nathaniel Greene. If he could reach the fords of the
Dan River before Greene, he would have the Continentals in a trap of his own.

So began the race for the Dan, in the bitter cold
of a February that brought an unusually heavy
amount of snow and sleet to the Carolinas. Mc-
Leod recalled uncounted gallop-and-hack skir-
mishes with the rebel cavalry in muddy fields and
blackjack thickets as Greene hurled his sabers at
the British in a desperate attempt to slow Cornwallis down.

Greene and his Continentals won the race and
crossed the Dan to arrive safely in Virginia. Cornwallis could take some small comfort in reporting to
London that the rebel army had been chased out of
the Carolinas. Of course, there were still the partisan rangers following men like Francis Marion—the

man Tarleton declared that not even the devil could catch.

And then, much to the surprise of the British, Greene, having been reinforced, crossed the Dan again, back into the Carolinas, and Cornwallis marched to clash with him at Guilford Court House, a bitterly fought contest. Cornwallis won the field but was so badly mauled he had to retire to Wilmington to be resupplied and reinforced by the Royal Navy. Unable to hold the Carolinas, Cornwallis had moved north into Virginia.

"As you gentlemen may know," said Tarleton, "Lord Cornwallis intends to effect a conjunction with Major General Phillips, whom Sir Henry has dispatched from New York to the mouth of the James River.

"We have fought in the north. We have fought in the south. We have fought the rebels to a draw. I believe the final act of the play will be performed here, in Virginia.

"Virginia is the key to victory. It has supplied the rebel armies with provisions since the outbreak of hostilities. Her tobacco has provided the Continental Congress with credit abroad, with which to purchase French munitions."

"Aye," grumbled a captain across the table from McLeod. "And now the flamin' frog-eaters themselves have come over to join the fight."

Tarleton smiled. "Ah, yes. The boy general, the Marquis de Lafayette, is flittering about north of the

Rapidan. But Lord Cornwallis has wisely declined to dance."

Rough laughter filled the room.

"Instead, Lord Cornwallis will hold fast near the James River, at Yorktown, until sufficiently reinforced. That does not mean, however, that we will be inactive."

"We could use some reinforcements," opined another officer. "I have less than twenty-five able-bodied dragoons left in my command."

Tarleton made a dismissive gesture. "We have suffered grave losses. But we have sufficient numbers for the task at hand. This morning I received orders from Lord Cornwallis to strike west to Charlottesville. Our mission is twofold. Our spies inform us that stores of powder, clothing, and muskets destined for Greene's army are located there. We are to destroy those supplies."

He scanned the grim, weathered features of the green-coated officers around the table—and flashed that deceptively boyish grin of his.

"The second part of our mission is to capture the governor of Virginia, the author of that damnable Declaration of Independence, Thomas Jefferson."

A murmur of surprise followed on the heels of this announcement.

"The effect of the governor's capture on rebel morale would be, it is safe to say, monumental. Lord Cornwallis has bestowed a great honor upon the Legion by entrusting us with this assignment. Are we up to the task?"

"Aye!" came a gruff chorus.

"Good. Then let us be on our way. To your squadrons, gentlemen. We ride within the hour. We must strike swiftly. Let nothing come between us and Mr. Jefferson."

Chapter 3

Having bagged two hares and a turkey in the grove of oak and hickory near the medicine springs two miles south of Louisa, Nathaniel Jones was heading home when he ran afoul of the Tory dragoons.

The sixteen-year-old Nathaniel was aware that there was a war being waged, but he had no thought of it coming to Louisa, the town of his birth. He had thrilled to the tales told by travelers staying over at his father's inn, and knew quite a lot about the Boston Tea Party and Bunker Hill, Trenton and Ticonderoga. But not a lick of fighting had occurred in this country, and while the locals had been somewhat alarmed by the arrival of Lord Cornwallis in Virginia, the consensus was that the redcoats were far to the east and would remain there, along the James River. For a boy who had never ventured more than twenty-five miles in any direction from Louisa, the James River might as well have been on the moon.

Though not well traveled, Nathaniel was a wanderer of sorts, and he liked nothing better than to tramp through wood and dale, exploring. As a result, few knew the countryside in the vicinity of Louisa better than he. This was one of the reasons he was so successful as a hunter. Joshua Jones relied on his only son to provide meat for the table at the inn, and scarcely a day passed, come rain or shine, that young Nathaniel wasn't out searching for game.

The other reason for his success was his uncanny proficiency with the flintlock rifle.

It was common knowledge in the county that Joshua's boy was the best shot around, bar none. They said it was God's gift. There was no other explanation. Nathaniel Jones had been blessed with the eye and the skill. Sure, experience counted for something. But experience was one thing; a lad who could drop a bird on the wing at fifty yards with a pistol at the age of six was quite another.

His almost daily excursions into the woodlands around Louisa were preferable, in Nathaniel's opinion, to the chores he was obliged to perform at the inn: bringing in firewood, tending to the horses of the guests, cleaning boots, countless other duties. Joshua Jones employed a woman from town to do the cooking and some of the cleaning, and the woman's daughter helped some, too. Joshua's wife, Nathaniel's mother, had perished years ago—so long ago, in fact, that Nathaniel scarcely remembered anything about her.

Nathaniel did not care at all for innkeeping. His favorite guests were those few hardy souls bound for the wilderness on the far side of the mountains. Somehow Nathaniel just knew that one day he would see that country with his own eyes. He longed to strike out on his own. Not a day passed that did not find him gazing with longing at the nearby ridges. Beyond those hazy blue heights lay his future. He couldn't put into words how he knew this—he wasn't very good with words—but he felt it with an unshakable conviction.

Problem was, his father depended on him to help at the inn. The inn was his father's whole life, and he took tremendous pride in it, and he had every expectation of passing it down to his son. Nathaniel just did not have the heart to tell his father that he had absolutely no desire to be an innkeeper. He didn't know how to explain that he didn't want to be anything in particular. He simply wanted to live free in wild country, to live as he imagined the Indians lived. Not a very lofty ambition, and certainly not one of which his father, a man of industrious Scotch-Irish stock, would approve.

With rabbits and turkey dangling by rawhide strings from his belt, Nathaniel broke out of the woods into a meadow adorned with wildflowers. On the other side of the meadow ran the tree-lined road to Hanover Court House, which passed through the tiny hamlet of Louisa on its way to Charlottesville. Nathaniel bent his steps toward the road, flintlock rifle shoulder-racked, taking long strides through tall grass wet with last night's rain. The sky was still overcast, and Nathaniel could smell more rain coming.

He was tall for his age, and whipcord lean, with an unruly shock of chestnut-brown hair and piercing green eyes. Broad shoulders testified to his strength. His narrow hips and long legs were clues to speed and agility—no one in the county could best him in a footrace. But once he reached the road Nathaniel shortened his stride and sauntered, in no hurry to get home.

Even distant thunder could not prompt him to quicken his pace. The prospect of being caught in a downpour was preferable to the drudgery that awaited him at his father's inn.

Belatedly, he realized that this roll of thunder did not end. He felt the ground vibrate beneath his feet. Brows knit, he stopped and turned. At that moment a column of green-coated horsemen appeared at the top of the road. Startled, Nathaniel froze in his tracks as the riders bore down upon him, their lathered horses at the canter. At the last moment he collected his wits and jumped to the roadside for fear of being trampled.

The green coats fooled him. He knew they were soldiers, but assumed them to be patriots since, as far as he knew, the British wore red coats. He did not realize his mistake until the six horsemen had sharply checked their horses, surrounding him, with one pointing a pistol at him.

"Put doon that rifle, lad," growled Sergeant-Major Mulcahey.

Stunned, Nathaniel just stood there and stared up the barrel of the pistol aimed at his head.

"Are you daft?" asked Mulcahey. "Put doon the rifle or I'll blow your bloody brains oot."

It suddenly occurred to Nathaniel that he was very close to the death, and that scared him so much he could scarcely breathe. But he wasn't so scared that he would mistreat the flintlock rifle, his prized possession. He bent to lay the weapon gently on the ground at his feet.

"What's your name, laddie?"

"Nathaniel. Nathaniel Jones." The boy gulped down the lump in his throat. "What's yours?"

One of the dragoons laughed. A scowl darkened Mulcahey's beefy face.

"I'll ask the questions, if you don't mind. Where are you from?"

"Louisa."

"Ah. And the town would be right down this road, would it not?"

"Yes, sir."

"Are there any soldiers posted in Louisa?"

"No, sir."

"He could be lying," remarked one of the dragoons.

"Thank you, Private Dunston," said Mulcahey, acerbic. "I'm well aware of that." The sergeant-major dismounted, handing his reins to one of the dragoons. He leaned forward, his face very close to Nathaniel's. "Do you know who we are, laddie?"

"No, sir."

"Tarleton's Tory Legion."

Nathaniel's eyes widened. He had heard of Butcher Tarleton's rangers. Who hadn't? These men delighted in slaughtering innocent women and children. They were far worse than the infamous Hessian mercenaries King George had employed to augment his forces in the colonies. The Tories were traitors, notorious for looting and pillaging, and the fact that they were fellow Americans just made it worse.

Nathaniel was very much afraid that these men planned to kill him. He considered begging for his life. But only briefly. He was too proud for that.

"Ah," said Mulcahey, chuckling. "I see by your expression that our fame has preceded us. Good. Then you should know better than to lie to us. I'll ask you again. Would there be any soldiers in Louisa?"

"No, sir." Nathaniel was surprised and pleased by the steadiness of his voice.

Mulcahey belted his pistol and picked up the flintlock rifle. He turned it this way and that, admiring the weapon.

"A fine work of art. Now how is it that a poor hardscrabble son of a dirt farmer like you can have a fine weapon like this? Did you steal it, by any chance?"

"I did not!" said Nathaniel, offended. "I never stole

anything in my whole life. I won that rifle last year at the turkey shoot."

"Did you now? You're a good shot, then."

Nathaniel shrugged. "Pretty good, I guess."

"Well, then, I'd better be taking the rifle. You might get it into that thick skull of yours to start shooting Tories."

"I want my rifle back."

Mulcahey was surprised by Nathaniel's sudden change in attitude. He'd thought the boy completely cowed. Now he realized he had misjudged young Nathaniel Jones.

"What did you say, lad?"

"You heard me." Nathaniel stood with chin tucked and fists clenched. "I'm not going to let you steal my rifle. Sir."

Mulcahey struck without warning, driving the stock of the rifle into Nathaniel's midsection as hard as he could. Nathaniel doubled over, wheezing, and dropped to his knees, hugging himself.

"I'm not a thief, boy," said Mulcahey coldly. "I'm confiscating this weapon."

Nathaniel felt the earth tremble beneath him again, and managed to lift his head and looked down the road. The dragoons were looking that way, too. A whole column of green-coated Tory rangers came over the hill.

"What's going on here?" asked Tarleton, as he brought his prancing charger to a stop and waved the column on.

Mulcahey had remounted. "We came across this

lad. He comes from Louisa. We were questioning him."

"Any rebels up ahead?"

"He says no."

Tarleton's features were a cold, inscrutable mask as he looked down at Nathaniel, who was slowly and unsteadily getting to his feet. Then he turned his frosty gaze on one of the dragoons in Mulcahey's advance party. The colonel's eyes, noted Mulcahey, seemed curiously lifeless.

"Take him into the field and do away with him."

The dragoon grimly saluted. "Yes, Colonel."

"Sergeant-Major," said Tarleton curtly, "assume your place in advance of the column."

As the others spurred their horses down the road, the dragoon who had been ordered to "do away" with Nathaniel grabbed the boy by the arm and kicked his horse into motion.

The horse plunged into the tall grass of the meadow. Nathaniel tried to shake free, but the dragoon's grip was like iron. He half-dragged, half-carried Nathaniel a stone's throw from the road before letting go. Nathaniel hit the ground, rolled, and came up running. The dragoon rode him down, planting a boot between Nathaniel's shoulder blades. Nathaniel sprawled in the wet grass. The dragoon executed a nimble running dismount, drawing a pistol from his belt. Nathaniel got up and, aware that he could not outrun a bullet, turned in desperation and launched himself at the dragoon. The latter knocked him down with contemptuous ease. Then he straddled Nathaniel, aimed, and fired.

The bullet missed Nathaniel's head by inches. The dragoon stepped on his heaving chest to pin him to the ground and leaned over.

"Stay down," rasped the dragoon.

Nathaniel just gaped at him. He couldn't believe his ears. The man had spared his life.

But why?

The dragoon fired a quick glance toward the road. The end of the column was just now passing. He turned back to Nathaniel.

"I haven't a mind for murder today," he said, his voice harsh. "Kill them all and let God sort them out—that's the colonel's way of doing business. Well, not today. Not today. Stay down, Nathaniel Jones, until you're certain it's all clear."

With that the dragoon wheeled, ran to his horse and leaped into the saddle to gallop back to the road.

Nathaniel lay there staring up at the pewter sky and thanked God he was alive. When his heart was beating more or less regularly, he sat up and peered cautiously around. The Tories were gone. He stood, trudged back to the road, his mind a blank. The purple shadows of dusk were lengthening. Collecting his wits, he began to worry about his father. Joshua Jones had been active in a Committee of Correspondence, and he was quick to make it known that he was a patriot to all who cared to listen.

A Tory invasion of Louisa would not sit well with him.

Filled with apprehension, Nathaniel left the turkey and the hares by the wayside and began to run down the road toward town.

Chapter 4

The common room at the inn of Joshua Jones was the favorite meeting place of the Louisa menfolk. The food was good, and Joshua's buttered rum was renowned. Apart from that, the common room, or "ordinary," was the place to go to hear all the news that was worth hearing, since the post riders dropped their mail off there, and most travelers intending to spend the night in Louisa chose to stay there.

At any time during the afternoon or early evening, one might find a half-dozen of the locals taking their ease in the common room, with its trestle tables and split-log benches, big stone hearth and heavy beams across the ceiling.

So it was that Dr. Benjamin Stowe left his office in his two-story home on High Street at dusk and headed along the cobblestone street in the direction of the tavern. The sun had slipped behind the mountains. Dr. Stowe exchanged greetings with Charles Bendix, who was lighting the streetlamps at the intersection with Main. With his gold-ferruled hickory walking stick, Dr. Stowe menaced a stray dog who growled at him in passing. He touched the brim of his tricorner to two ladies heading home from the farmers' market.

Crossing the bridge that spanned the creek at the end of High Street, he continued on past the grist mill to the inn at the crossroads just beyond. The first drops of rain were stirring the red dust of the road as he reached his destination and entered.

The inn was a large house built of square-cut logs, painted white, with a stables and kitchen behind it, the latter connected to the main house by a covered walk. One would pass through a large pantry where another door led to the stairway that descended into the basement, and from the pantry into the common room, which took up most of the first floor. Adjoining the common room was Joshua's office-bedroom, and another small room where Joshua's son Nathaniel slept. The second floor, attainable by means of a steep staircase, contained four spacious rooms for overnight guests.

Dr. Stowe was a man in his seventies. His bent, reed-thin body testified to his advanced years. But his mind was still keen and his heart still strong, and he remained active in his practice. In forty years as Louisa's physician, he had brought virtually the entire community into the world. He liked nothing better than to engage in intelligent debate. His talent lay in playing devil's advocate, and so vast was his knowledge, and so wide-ranging his interests, that he could discourse in a learned fashion on either side of almost any issue. So it was with delight that he entered the common room to find Joshua Jones in a heated discussion with John Lessing, one of Louisa's two lawyers.

"I'm telling you," said Joshua, rather passionately, "those men in the Continental Congress are muddleheaded fools. It's a disturbing thought indeed that they are our only government."

"Now, Joshua, that kind of talk could get you into trouble," admonished Lessing.

Joshua scowled. "Trouble? What kind of trouble might you be referring to, John?"

"Some patriots might think it seditious."

"Seditious!" roared Joshua. "By Jehovah, isn't that what this war is all about? The right to say what you think and do what you want? If I can't voice my opinion of our so-called leaders, then I might as well go back to being a subject of the Crown."

John Lessing chuckled good-naturedly. As a good lawyer, he sought to consistently straddle every fence. "Well, you still are, in fact, since the outcome of this little squabble is yet in doubt. Ah, doctor, how do you fare?"

"I am well. And you?"

Lessing shrugged heavy shoulders. "I cannot complain." The attorney was something of a dandy in Stowe's opinion, and this evening he wore a plum-colored coat and cravat that, to the doctor's austere eye, was ostentatious.

"And you, Joshua? Your business is slow."

"There's a storm brewing. It's kept some home. And the coach from Hanover is late."

"That's certainly not out of the ordinary. It has just begun to rain, by the way."

"Your boy's not yet back from his hunting, Joshua?" asked Lessing. He was accustomed to young Nathaniel's presence in the common room, raptly soaking up everything that was said.

"Not yet. Would you care for something, Doctor?"

"A brandy would do nicely, thank you."

"Amanda!" roared Joshua, loud enough to rattle the chimneys on the common room's lamps.

A girl appeared from the pantry door, a willowy child with hair the color of cornsilk and bright blue eyes in a pert, heart-shaped face. Amanda Roberts was the daughter of Joshua's cook and house-keeper.

"Fetch a bottle of brandy and a glass for the good doctor, girl."

"Yes, sir." With a shy smile Amanda vanished to do Joshua's bidding.

Dr. Stowe settled across the table from John Lessing. "So what is all this talk about the Continental Congress?"

"Joshua is waxing indignant about our political leaders," said the lawyer, smiling. "He considers them shallow, selfish, small-minded men more concerned with their own aggrandizement than with the welfare of the colonies."

"My, my," murmured the physician, rubbing his

gnarled hands together with ill-concealed glee. "A rather harsh assessment, Joshua, I must say."

"Not at all. Look at what they've done. Giving command of armies to their kind, with no thought to experience or competency. They forced Schuyler from the army. They gave the southern command to that coward, Horatio Gates. Worst of all, they bear the responsibility for Benedict Arnold's defection to the British."

"No excuse is sufficient to justify such betrayal," rejoined Lessing. "Arnold is a traitor, and that's that."

"The Continental Congress is to blame," insisted Joshua. "No one can say that Benedict Arnold was not a brilliant strategist and courageous leader. His soldiers were devoted to him.

"Those who knew him knew a kind and generous man. Are you aware that when Joseph Warren perished at Bunker Hill, Arnold petitioned the Congress to procure the funds to see to the schooling of Warren's motherless children? An altogether proper gesture to the offspring of a man who gave the ultimate sacrifice for our liberty and was such an inspiration to so many.

"Yet the Congress refused, and Arnold provided the money out of his own pocket. The Congress would have you believe he is a thief, a braggart, and a coward. The irony of it all is that he is none of these things, while the Congress is filled with creatures of such description."

Amanda arrived with brandy and glass. Dr. Stowe

beamed fondly at her. Having delivered almost all the children of Louisa, he thought of them as his own, in a way, being a man who had lost his wife and child thirty years ago to cholera.

"Thank you, my dear. How are you doing?"

"I am well, sir."

"And your mother, bless her heart?"

"She is well, too. Thank you, sir."

"Good, good. Run along now. We seem to be embroiled here in a discussion of politics, and when Joshua gets the bit in his teeth on that subject, well, there may be language used which is entirely unsuitable for a young lady's ears."

After Amanda had left the room, Joshua said, "The worst of it is this unholy alliance between the Congress and the French."

"Well, I would have to say that without French assistance we would be in dire straits indeed," said Dr. Stowe.

"Have you forgotten that not too many years ago, the French were giving powder and shot to the Indians, who in turn were murdering our friends and families?"

"No, I haven't forgotten," replied the physician, who had the infuriating habit of smiling in an ever more kindly fashion, and speaking in an ever more gentle manner, in direct proportion to the rising anger of the person with whom he was engaged in debate. "Nor have I forgotten that in those dark and bloody times we fought side by side with the British."

"Makes no sense," said Lessing, shaking his head, as he packed tobacco into a clay pipe.

"I'll tell you what makes no sense," barked Joshua. "Any French officer who wants a commission from Congress need only ask to receive his heart's desire. Meanwhile, they turn away deserving American officers on a whim. My God, look at Lafayette. He's scarcely older than my own son, yet he is in command of the army assigned to protect Virginia from Cornwallis!"

"Actually, I believe the marquis is twenty-three years old," remarked Dr. Stowe.

"Oh, that's comforting," said Joshua dryly. "He was seventeen when they commissioned him. Meanwhile, they refuse to give Arnold the major general's commission he so amply deserved. Why? Because he was forthright in denouncing Congress for what it was."

"Forthright, perhaps. Reckless, certainly."

"He spoke his mind, as was his right."

"Quite so. A man has the right to cut his own throat, but it is still not something I would recommend."

Joshua fumed. "I fear for our country, assuming we win our independence from England, with such men at the helm as those who now serve themselves while claiming to serve us in the Continental Congress."

"Well, Joshua, one crisis at a time. There are a few good men we can trust to have our best interests at heart. Messrs. Washington, Jefferson, and Madison, to name a few."

"Good Virginians, all," intoned Lessing.

Dr. Stowe cocked his head. "I believe I hear the coach coming."

The sound of horses on the road reached Joshua. He got up and headed for the door. "Mark my words, Benjamin," he said. "We may well find ourselves under French rule once this is over. And then we will have traded one brand of tyranny for another."

Dr. Stowe chuckled. "Really, Joshua. At the risk of offending you, I must say you remind me of a British bulldog—once you sink your teeth into something you can't be shaken loose."

Joshua started to say something in response as he opened the door, but Sergeant-Major Mulcahey stormed across the threshold, plowing into the innkeeper and sending him reeling into a table. Dragoons poured into the common room on Mulcahey's heels, leveling pistols at Lessing and Stowe. The pipe slipped from Lessing's hands as he made a strangled noise and turned white as a sheet. Dr. Stowe shot to his feet.

"What's the meaning of this?"

A dragoon advanced, prodded him in the chest with the pistol.

"Sit down."

Dr. Stowe sat down.

Amanda Roberts appeared in the doorway leading to the pantry. A startled cry escaped her lips, bringing her to Mulcahey's attention. She turned and fled.

"Get that girl!" roared Mulcahey.

A dragoon started after Amanda.

"Leave the child alone!" bellowed Joshua.

Mulcahey struck with a backhanded blow that snapped Joshua's head back.

"I'll give the orders here, sir, thank you."

Eyes ablaze, Joshua wiped blood from a split lip. Then his gaze dropped to the flintlock rifle in Mulcahey's hands.

"My God," he breathed. "That's my son's rifle. *What have you done to Nathaniel, you bastard!*"

"Joshua, no!" yelled Dr. Stowe.

But Joshua wasn't listening. He launched himself at the burly sergeant-major. He was quick, but Mulcahey was quicker. He swung the stock of the flintlock rifle as hard as he could at the innkeeper's head. Joshua heard a very loud crunching sound—the sound one hears when he bites down on a celery stalk, only magnified a hundred times. Then Joshua's world turned black.

He fell heavily at Mulcahey's feet.

Dr. Stowe was up again. The dragoon grabbed him roughly by the arm and pinned him against the table.

"Good God, man! I am a doctor. Let me see to my friend."

The impassive dragoon glanced at Mulcahey, who nodded curtly. Released, Stowe rushed to Joshua's side.

"How is he, Benjamin?" asked a shaken Lessing.

"Badly hurt," replied Stowe flatly, ruthlessly tamping down his emotions. "His pulse is quite faint." He glared at Mulcahey, who loomed over him. "You cracked his skull. You may have killed him."

Mulcahey shrugged. "In war, people die."

Chapter 5

As he neared Louisa, Nathaniel Jones was quick to realize that the Tory Legion had occupied the town. He easily avoided detection by the pickets stationed out on the Hanover Road, cutting through a grove of trees and then crossing Simon Marcy's tobacco field to reach the creek. Down the creek he stole, keeping to the bottom of the rocky ravine, working his way up toward the bridge at the end of High Street.

Nearing the bridge, he dived into a pile of deadwood as a squad of mounted dragoons galloped across the span, not a stone's throw away. It was dark now, and drizzling. In the creek up to his calves, and with his soaked clothing clinging to his skin, Nathaniel was uncomfortable, but he thanked God for the night and the rain because they were his allies. His chances of getting to the inn, past all these troops, would have been slim indeed without them.

Nathaniel crouched in the deadwood for a few minutes after the squad had passed. He was shivering, but not because he was wet and cold. It was the adrenaline, and the fear. His heart seemed to be pounding at his ribcage. He was alive only by the grace of God and because of the compassion of a single dragoon. There was no doubt in his mind that all the rest of these Tories would kill him without a second thought if they caught him lurking about in the darkness.

Eventually moving on, he reached the bridge. Hiding beneath the stone span, he heard voices. A sentry was stationed at one end of the bridge, and an officer of the guard had joined him. Nathaniel ventured halfway up the bank, hoping to get close enough to hear what they were saying. Pressed against the cold stone of the bridge, he strained to hear.

"A bloody bad night for guard duty," growled the officer.

"Yes, sir."

"Have you seen anything?"

"No, sir. Nary a thing."

"Well, keep your eyes peeled. Remember, the colonel has established a strict curfew. Anyone on the streets is to be arrested. Anyone trying to leave town is to be shot. We must keep them bottled up here. Can't have one of them trying to be a Paul Revere and warning the burgesses in Charlottesville."

"Yes, sir, Lieutenant. I understand."

"Let's see . . . three more hours by my watch, Jeffries, and we'll have you relieved and quartered in some nice, warm house."

"Yes, sir."

The lieutenant crossed the bridge, passing directly above Nathaniel, and proceeded down High Street.

What he had overheard confirmed Nathaniel's worst fears. If he were discovered he would be shot on sight. But he had to get home. His father would be worried sick about him. And, of course, there was Amanda Roberts.

Nathaniel couldn't bear the thought of any harm coming to her.

Gulping at the lump in his throat, he returned to the creek bottom and continued on, past the grist mill with its slowly turning, loudly creaking wheel. Circling behind the mill, he descended down into and clambered up out of a brush-choked gully, crossed a meadow dotted with stately sycamores, and finally reached the vicinity of his father's inn.

From his vantage point in a clump of bushes, he could see the rear of the main house and the kitchen. Yellow lamplight poured through the open doorway of the latter structure, to spill out onto the ground where a single sentry paced. Through one of the tall open windows on this side of the main house Nathaniel could see two more dragoons standing and talking together, and by the sound of it there were several other soldiers in the common room as well.

It looked like there was a light on in every room of the house. No doubt there were sentries in front, too. Nathaniel began to despair of getting inside and reaching his father. Maybe his father wasn't even here. By the looks of things the Tories had taken over the inn.

Nathaniel didn't know what to do.

Then he saw Mrs. Roberts emerge from the door leading out of the pantry. She was carrying a large wooden bowl overflowing with blood-soaked rags. There was blood on her hands and lower arms. Her face was puffy, her eyes red and swollen from crying. She entered the kitchen, hurrying past the stoic guard.

Nathaniel circled around to the rear wall of the kitchen, and was gratified to find open the small window located in that wall. Pressed against the wall directly beneath the window, he could hear everything said within the kitchen.

What he heard froze the blood in his veins and almost wrenched a cry from his throat.

"The doctor needs more hot water, Amanda." This was Mrs. Roberts. Her usually cheerful tone of voice had been replaced by hollow, weary despair. "Hurry it long to him, please."

"Is Mr. Jones going to live, Mother?"

Mrs. Roberts sighed. "I don't know, dear. It is in God's hands. All we can do is pray."

"Why? Why did they hurt him?"

"Because that is the kind of men they are," replied Mrs. Roberts, anger injecting some iron into her voice. She spoke loudly, wanting to guarantee that the sentry just outside the kitchen door could hear. "Cruel, vicious, Godless men. Now, hurry along with . . . no, wait. I'll take it, Amanda."

"I can do it, Mother. I don't mind. You're tired. Just sit there and rest yourself."

"No, you stay here. Whatever you do, do not leave this place. It isn't safe."

"I'm not afraid of these Tories," said Amanda, defiant.

"*I* am. Now you mind me, child."

"Yes, ma'am."

Mrs. Roberts left the kitchen, returning to the main house.

Nathaniel reached high to grab the windowsill and haul himself up. He wasn't sure what he was going to do. But he had to find out what had happened. And the only person he could reach was Amanda.

But when he peered over the sill into the kitchen, the first person he saw was the dragoon who had been, just moments before, standing guard outside the door.

Fortunately for Nathaniel, the dragoon was too busy looking at Amanda, who stood near the hearth, where water was boiling in a flame-blackened iron kettle dangling from a big hook above a crackling fire.

Startled by the presence of the dragoon, Nathaniel let go and dropped to the ground, his heart racing.

"You're not supposed to be in here," he heard Amanda say. "Get out."

"That's not very hospitable."

"You better get out of here before my mother comes back."

"Oh, she will be gone for a while. You're an awfully pretty lass. How old are you?"

"Fifteen. What do you want?"

"A drink of water. And perhaps a little kiss."

Nathaniel moved, circling the kitchen.

"Get away from me!"

It was Amanda, her voice shrill with fear.

Nathaniel crossed the threshold of the kitchen doorway to see the dragoon advancing on Amanda, who had backed into a corner. She tried to slip past him, but he grabbed her, and pushed her back into the corner.

Nathaniel snatched up an empty bucket on the floor just inside the door and rushed forward.

The dragoon heard him coming and whirled, raising an arm as Nathaniel swung the bucket with all his might. The bucket's staves shattered; the impact staggered the dragoon but did not fell him. A saber appeared in his hand. Nathaniel tripped over a three-legged stool as he desperately avoided a sword stroke that missed by inches gutting him. He hit the hard-packed dirt floor and rolled away, fetching up close to the fireplace, grabbing an iron poker that was leaning against the hearthstone.

"Amanda, run!" he yelled, as he parried another saber-stroke with the poker. Steel clanged and sparked against iron. The force of the blow almost knocked the poker out of Nathaniel's grasp. He kicked out with one leg, trying to trip the dragoon— and, to his astonishment, succeeded.

As quick as Nathaniel was in bouncing to his feet, the dragoon was quicker. Snarling, he swung the saber. Nathaniel ducked under, lashing out blindly with the poker, catching the dragoon in the back. The dragoon fell forward. His head struck a sharp edge of hearthstone, and he crumpled, falling partially into the fire. Nathaniel dropped the poker, grabbed the man's ankles, and pulled him out of the fire. The stench of burning flesh and hair reached him. He turned away, stumbled, dropped to one knee and dry heaved.

Feeling a cool hand on his cheek, he jerked away, startled, and looked up to find Amanda standing there.

"I told you to run!" he exclaimed.

"I-I just couldn't seem to move," she replied, contrite. "Are you hurt, Nathan?"

"No. No, I'm fine." He glanced at the dragoon. His stomach performed a slow roll, and he tasted bile. "We've got to get out of here."

He rushed to the door, peered cautiously out, expecting to find that the fight in the kitchen had made such a racket that all the Tories in and around the main house had heard. He was amazed to find that such was not the case. Faintly he could hear voices from the common room, but no alarm had been raised.

Turning, he found Amanda standing close behind him, her arms folded, her eyes bright with fear.

"Let's go," he said. "It's all clear."

"Go? Where?"

"We can't stay here, Amanda."

"I'm afraid."

"I'd die before I'd let anything happen to you," he declared.

He took her by the hand and slipped out into the night, heading for the nearby ravine.

Chapter 6

It was so dark down in the brush-choked ravine that Nathaniel could scarcely see an arm's length in front of him. Nonetheless, he and Amanda stumbled and thrashed their way to the bottom before stopping.

"Nathan, I—"

"Ssh."

He listened a moment, expecting to hear a clamor from the inn, perhaps the sounds of pursuit. Surely the injured dragoon had been discovered by now. But he heard nothing except the chorus of countless crickets in the brush.

His voice was shaky when he turned to speak to Amanda. "My father . . . what happened?"

"One of the soldiers had your rifle. Mr. Jones started for the man, and the man hit him, really hard, in the head. It must be very bad. Oh, Nathan, we thought you were dead!"

She put her arms around him, and laid her head against his chest, and Nathaniel's whole body was tingling from head to toe at her touch.

It amazed him that, even in the midst of such danger and anguish over his father, he felt this way. For years he had known he loved Amanda Roberts. Someday they would be married—that was something both of them instinctively understood. They had held hands, and even kissed a couple of times, but she had never embraced him like this, and Nathaniel was rendered utterly speechless.

"Nathan," she breathed, "what are we going to do?"

"I don't know," he said lamely.

"Mother will be sick with worry. Somehow I must let her know that I am unhurt."

"I will. I've got to go back to the inn."

"But you can't! They'll catch you."

"I've got to, Amanda. I must see my father. And I'll find your mother, and tell her that you're well. You wait here. You'll be safe. I'll be back."

She clung to him. "I'm afraid, Nathan. Afraid, most of all, for you. Aren't you afraid?"

"No," he lied. "Well, maybe a little."

Amanda cupped his face in her hands and brushed her lips against his. The darkness was so thick he could hardly discern her features face-to-face. But he could taste her tears. The kiss, and her warm sweet breath, was so intoxicating that it made Nathaniel dizzy.

"Be careful," she whispered.

"Where do they have my father?"

"Upstairs. The back room on this side. Dr. Stowe and Mr. Lessing are with him. I think that's why the

Tories made them take Mr. Jones upstairs, though he was in no condition to be moved. They were afraid one of the others would try to climb a window and get away."

"They're trying to keep everyone penned up," said Nathaniel.

"Why? Why did they come here?"

"They're going to Charlottesville. They don't want anyone getting out to spread the alarm."

"How will *we* get out, Nathan?"

"We will. I'll come back and take you out of here. I promise."

"But . . . but what if you don't come back?" Apprehensive, Amanda looked around at the dark woods, imagining a Tory dragoon lurking behind every rock and tree. The thought made her shudder.

"If I don't, you've got to slip out and get to Charlottesville somehow."

"You must come back, Nathan Jones. You promised."

Nathaniel gave her hand a squeeze, and left her there in the rocks and brush of the ravine.

Approaching the inn, he found all was quiet around the kitchen. He wasted no time moving to a big oak. This tree was the solution to getting into the inn. He'd known it the moment Amanda had told him his father was in the upstairs room on the southwest corner of the house.

Leaping, he grabbed the lowest bough, swung his legs over another, and muscled his way up into a fork. He had climbed this tree countless times.

Studying the limbs above him, he traced the route he would take—the route that would bring him to the stout limb that reached to within a few feet of one of the windows to the room where his father lay injured.

Upward Nathaniel climbed, strong and agile and sure. In a matter of minutes he was on the limb, almost thirty feet above the ground, inching further and further out, clinging tightly with his arms and legs, not looking down, but rather keeping his gaze fixed on the window. The curtains were drawn. He could not see inside, and hoped Amanda was right about the people in that room.

The further out he crawled on the limb, the more it began to sway. When he was as far as he could go, the window was still beyond his reach. Heart in throat, he wrapped his arms as tightly as he could around the limb and slid off, swinging his legs, trying to reach the windowsill. The limb was bowing now under his weight—there was little chance of his getting back up on it. It was all or nothing. If he fell, and the fall didn't kill him, the dragoons standing near the open window of the common room would surely capture him. His life wouldn't be worth a Continental dollar after that.

Getting one foot anchored on the sill, Nathaniel tapped on the glass with the toe of his other foot. The curtains were swept aside. Wearing a startled expression, Dr. Stowe raised the window.

"Good heavens! Nathaniel! What . . . ? John, come and help."

The husky lawyer arrived at the window. Alarmed by the vision of Nathaniel dangling precariously from the limb, Lessing reached out to grab him by the belt and lifted him bodily into the room.

"Nathaniel!" gasped Lessing. "We'd given you up for dead. When we saw that dragoon with your rifle—"

"*Father!*" Nathaniel rushed to the bed where his father lay.

Joshua Jones was unconscious. His complexion was ashen. His head was swathed in a dressing spotted with blood. The manner of his breathing—short, sharp inhalations—scared Nathaniel most of all.

Dr. Stowe put a hand on Nathaniel's shoulder. "He lost his head when he saw that sergeant-major with your flintlock."

"I know."

"You do? How do you know?"

"Amanda told me."

"Amanda?!"

"Is he going to die, Dr. Stowe?"

The physician sighed. It was his rule to be honestly candid in such instances, believing it morally wrong to lie for the sake of another's feelings. That only led to greater hurt.

"I can't tell you, Nathaniel. We know so little about injuries to the head. I've done all that I know to do, which is damnably little, I must confess. It rests in God's hands."

Nathaniel's eyes burned with hot tears. He fought them back.

Shouts outside lured John Lessing to the open window. He leaned out and looked down.

"What is it, John?" asked Dr. Stowe. "What is happening?"

"I'm not sure. But something has got these Tories worked up."

Nathaniel could have enlightened them as to the source of all that turmoil, but he scarcely heard them. He just stood there, staring at his father, oblivious to all else, consumed by dread and grief and a growing rage.

Then Mrs. Roberts burst into the room, shutting the door quickly and leaning against it, breathing heavily, fear in her eyes.

"Amanda . . ." she gasped. "My child . . ."

Hearing the panic in her voice, Dr. Stowe rushed to her.

"Calm yourself," he urged. "Take deep breaths."

She clutched at his arm. "My daughter is gone!"

"Gone? What do you mean, gone?"

"She's disappeared. And there's a . . . there's a dead soldier in the kitchen."

"Dead? How? Who?"

"I did it," said Nathaniel.

"You?" queried Lessing, incredulous.

"Yes." Nathaniel turned to Mrs. Roberts. "It was right after you left the kitchen. The guard was . . . well, he was bothering Amanda. I had been right outside, listening beneath the window. I rushed in.

We fought. I . . . he . . . it was an accident. He was trying to kill me. I hit him with the poker. He stumbled and fell. Hit his head on the hearthstone. I didn't know he was dead."

"Amanda," said Mrs. Roberts. "Where is she?"

"She's safe, ma'am. Hiding in the gully."

Mrs. Roberts covered her face with her hands. "Thank the Lord," she sobbed.

"This is very grave," said Lessing, anxiously wringing his hands. "A dead soldier . . ."

"I fear they will reach the conclusion that Mrs. Roberts or Amanda did the deed," said Dr. Stowe.

That jolted Nathaniel. It was an aspect of the situation that had not occurred to him. There was only one solution.

"I'll turn myself in," he said. "I'll confess to it."

The others were grimly silent. Everyone knew what the consequences would be for Nathaniel Jones.

"Someone must ride to Charlottesville," said Nathaniel. "I overheard two soldiers talking. Charlottesville is their destination."

"The House of Burgesses!" exclaimed Lessing.

"The governor, too, no doubt," said Dr. Stowe. "They must be warned. You're the one to do that, Nathaniel."

"No. I must surrender to the Tories."

"You're the only one who can do what must be done," insisted the physician. "We are prisoners. You are not. Assuming you can get out of here the same way you came in. And you are young, energetic, and clever."

"If you went to Simon Marcy's farm," said Lessing, "he will loan you that blood bay of his. Fastest horse in the county. Then you could ride to Charlottesville and raise the alarm."

"And you must take Amanda with you," said Mrs. Roberts, suddenly calm.

"But then they will think you or Amanda killed that soldier," protested Nathaniel.

"I will *tell* them that I did it," she said.

"Good Lord!" said Lessing. "Confess nothing."

"She's right," said Dr. Stowe. "Your being a woman will not save you from a firing squad. These Tories do not play by the rules."

They heard heavy footsteps in the upstairs hall.

"They're coming," breathed Dr. Stowe, and whirled to face Nathaniel. "Go, boy! Hurry!"

Mrs. Roberts turned and threw the bolt on the door. The dragoons hit it hard enough to shake the very walls—so hard that Mrs. Roberts jumped back with a small cry, half-expecting the door to collapse inward.

"Open up in there!"

Nathaniel raced to the window. Lessing was leaning out over the sill, looking down.

"All clear," he said. "Godspeed, Nathaniel Jones."

"Take care of my daughter, Nathan," said Mrs. Roberts, silent tears streaming down her cheeks.

"Break down this door!"

"I will," promised Nathaniel, perched on the sill.

He spared his father a last glance. Somehow he knew that he would never see him again. Knew this with anguish so profoundly deep in his soul that it took him beyond the point of tears.

"Goodbye, Father," he whispered, and was gone.

Chapter 7

Evading the Tory pickets in the darkness and drizzling rain was no easy matter, and a somewhat harrowing experience besides, as the word had spread swiftly through the Legion that one of their own had been murdered. But eventually Nathaniel and Amanda reached Simon Marcy's tobacco farm.

The farmer answered Nathaniel's knock on the door with a flintlock rifle in his fists. The weapon primed and hammered back, he threw open the door and shoved the barrel in Nathaniel's face. Seeing the bedraggled pair on his doorstep, Marcy breathed a gusty sigh of relief, lowered the rifle, and called to his wife that they had company.

"I can't stay." Nathaniel said. "I must get to Charlottesville. Mr. Lessing said you would make me the loan of a horse, Mr. Marcy."

"A horse? Why, yes. Yes, of course. But first, you must tell me what is happening in town. I've seen Tory dragoons on the road. They didn't see me, thank the Lord."

"They've taken over the town."

Mrs. Marcy was trying to herd Amanda into the other room. "Come, child, you must get warm."

"I want to stay with Nathan. Nathan . . ."

"Go on, Amanda."

"You won't leave without me, will you?"

"No."

Amanda reluctantly accompanied Mrs. Marcy into the next room. Simon Marcy was stirring up the fire. While Nathaniel warmed himself at the hearth, he told the farmer what had transpired at his father's inn.

"So I must ride to Charlottesville," he said. "The Tories are marching there. I need a horse."

Simon Marcy nodded grimly. "They're after the assembly, then. The governor as well. A bold plan indeed. Worthy of that bastard, Butcher Tarleton. Yes, you'll have your horse. But first, you must have some hot food. I'll warrant you've missed your supper."

"There's no time, sir. I must—"

"Tarleton will not leave Charlottesville until first light. Not in this weather. You have time."

Nathaniel wasn't hungry. He didn't think he'd ever be hungry again. But when he began to smell the stew warming in the kettle Mrs. Marcy set over the fire, he changed his mind.

Amanda came out of the next room clad in one of Mrs. Marcy's flannel nightgowns, which was about five times too big for her, and a blanket draped over her shoulders. She sat at the table next to Nathaniel. While they ate stew and bread washed down with hot tea, Simon Marcy ventured out into the rainy night to saddle a horse.

All through the meal Amanda was silent. Nathaniel could tell she was worried, and he thought he knew why. They had grown up together, and for the longest time now it seemed like he could tell exactly what she was thinking without her having to say a word. Right now she was afraid—terrified, really—that he was going to leave without her. And he was afraid she would take it badly when she found out she was right.

"There is rain picking up now," announced Marcy when he came back inside. "A bad night for a ride. And across country, at that. You'll have to stay clear of the roads, Nathaniel, at least until you're much closer to Charlottesville. But I didn't name that blood bay out there Jumper for nothing."

"Thanks, Mr. Marcy." Nathaniel knew that the blood bay was Simon Marcy's pride and joy. No squire in the county had a better horse. Marcy was making quite a sacrifice.

"Yes, sir."

"I notice you're unarmed."

"The Tories took my rifle."

"Well, I have a pistol you can carry, just in case."

"And you, my dear," said Mrs. Marcy, addressing Amanda. "You will stay here with us."

Amanda just stared at Nathaniel.

"You can't go," he said. "You'll be safe here. And besides, your mother will be sick with worry. When the Tories leave tomorrow, you can go back to her."

With a quiet, heart-wrenching sob, Amanda fled to the next room.

Nathaniel jumped up. "Amanda!"

She slammed the door behind her.

"She'll be all right," said Mrs. Marcy reassuringly. "She's tired and frightened, and the two of you are such close friends."

Nathaniel could only nod.

Simon produced a greatcoat and tricorner. "You'll need these, son. The rain won't be lettin' up anytime soon."

Nathaniel donned hat and coat, and accepted the flintlock pistol proffered by the farmer.

"Good luck, Nathaniel. Everything depends on you, lad."

"I know," he said, somewhat dazed by it all. A few hours ago he had been out hunting, and all had been right with the world. Now his world had been turned upside down.

The ride ahead of him, through a night filled with enemies, was a daunting prospect. He was weary, and scared. Only the thought of his father gave him the will to continue. He would do everything within his power to stop the Tories.

With grim resolve, he said his goodbyes to the Marcys and, casting a last glance at the door to the room into which Amanda had fled, stepped out into the rainswept night.

When Captain McLeod entered the small office-bedroom of Joshua Jones, he found Tarleton pacing the length of the room, through the narrow straits between the innkeeper's desk and bed. The colonel's hands were clasped behind his back, and worry creased his high forehead. His spurs sang against the puncheon floor. So deep in thought was he that he failed to hear McLeod enter.

McLeod cleared his throat. "You sent for me, sir?"

Tarleton glanced across the room at him. McLeod snapped to attention, plumed leather cap under one arm.

"Ah, Peter. I suppose you've heard what has happened here tonight."

"I am told a scully maid killed one of our men, sir."

"So she says. So she says."

"Is it not so, Colonel?"

"I cannot help but think that there is more to this than meets the eye."

"An old campaigner's instinct, perhaps, sir."

"Hmm." Tarleton moved to the room's only window. It was open, and the soothing song of the rain relaxed him. "Perhaps so, Peter. My instincts tell me that all will be lost if we remain here until morning."

"Lost? How?"

"The woman's daughter is nowhere to be found. The entire town has been searched."

"What does the woman say about that?"

"She claims our man was making untoward advances to her daughter. Now, you tell me, Peter. Does that sound like a dragoon of the Tory Legion?"

McLeod could see the cold smile flicker across Tarleton's profile.

"The woman says she assaulted our man with an iron poker. That she was compelled to do it to protect her daughter's honor. In the mêlée, her daughter fled into the night."

"Sounds plausible enough, sir."

"No. She didn't do it. She lied. I could see it in her eyes. I know when I'm being lied to. Someone else killed that dragoon, Captain. And since everyone else in this bloody town is accounted for, that means there is a man running loose out there who probably knows quite a bit more about us than we do of him."

McLeod considered what Tarleton had said. The Tories had posted at least one man in every house upon arriving in Louisa, and in most cases a number of dragoons were quartered in each home. All the horses had been rounded up. Every weapon that could be found had been confiscated. There were pickets on the roads leading out of Louisa. And there were patrols roaming the streets.

"He would have to be a pretty crafty fellow," decided McLeod.

"Oh, indeed," Tarleton concurred. "Crafty—and clever enough to divine our purpose."

"You think word of our presence is on its way to Charlottesville, then."

"My gut tells me it's so. This damned rain," muttered Tarleton, peering bleakly out into the blackness of the night. "With better conditions we could have pressed on without tarrying here. But these bloody Virginia roads are quagmires by now. And if we attempt to cut across country we could very well lose our way, without the stars, or a dependable guide."

He moved to the desk, leaned over a map, and stabbed it with a finger. "Here we are. Here's Charlottesville. And right about here, I believe, is Monticello."

"Jefferson's estate."

"Correct. Do you think you can get from here to there without relying on the roads? Do you know of anyone in the Legion who comes from this area?"

"No, sir."

"Alas. Neither do I. Must be a breeding ground exclusively for traitors, then, eh?"

"But I can get there, Colonel."

"I was hoping you would say as much. Take twenty men. Avoid Charlottesville. Leave the assembly to me. I will move on them at first light. But if we capture one man it should be—it must be—the governor."

McLeod nodded. Twenty men could move quickly, avoid detection, and yet remain a force large enough to capture Jefferson, even if his family members and retainers put up a resistance. But twenty men could not ride into a city the size of Charlottesville and seize a hundred burgesses.

"When do I leave?" asked McLeod.

"Immediately. If you capture Jefferson, remain at Monticello and wait for me. I'll be along with the rest of the Legion by midday tomorrow."

McLeod saluted smartly and spun on his heel to leave the room.

At the door he paused and turned around. "What will you do, Colonel, about the soldier who was killed?"

Tarleton had resumed his place at the window. "You mean in the way of retribution?"

"Yes, sir."

"An example must be made. I'm sure I'll think of something appropriate."

McLeod was certain of that. And it would be something the town of Louisa would not soon forget.

Chapter 8

The storm just wouldn't let up.

It was a harrowing ride for young Nathaniel Jones. For one thing, he wasn't a good rider. The son of an innkeeper who did not even own a horse, Nathaniel had been afforded few opportunities to acquire even the most fundamental equestrian skills.

Simon Marcy's prize blood bay was a spirited animal that required a firm hand. As a result, the first time Jumper sailed over a split-rail fence, Nathaniel flew out of the rain-slick saddle. He had the wherewithal to hold onto the reins. His landing was painful, but the saturated ground was a boon. Jumper galloped another ten yards, dragging Nathaniel through the muck, until finally slowed by the human anchor clinging tenaciously to the leathers. Covered with mud from head to toe, Nathaniel got to his feet, remounted, and kicked the horse into a gallop.

A few hundred yards further on the horse plunged headlong down into a ravine, and Nathaniel lost his seat again. The saddle's pommel caught him in the chest and knocked the wind out of him. He almost slipped off, but caught himself and hung on for dear life as the blood bay leaped up the other bank of the ravine and stretched out again.

And so it went. Twice more Nathaniel was thrown. The third time he jumped to his feet, mad as a hornet, and punched the horse in the shoulder. Unaccustomed to such rough treatment, the horse jumped sideways, snorting. Holding onto the reins, Nathaniel was yanked off his feet and landed flat on his face. He got up, spitting mud and grass, and wiping the rain out of his eyes.

"I've got to warn the governor!" he yelled, utterly frustrated. *"Don't you understand, you ignorant nag?"*

Jumper just looked at him and whickered.

Nathaniel climbed back into the saddle. Barely tapped with his heels, and they were off again.

The storm raged on. Lightning flashed in the mountains straight ahead. Thunder rolled across the angry sky. Driving sheets of rain and gusting winds lashed at the trees. Before long, Nathaniel had lost Mr. Marcy's hat. But he was thankful for the greatcoat. The rain was chilling.

He tried to stay close to the road that connected Louisa and Charlottesville, keeping always to the south of the thoroughfare. Every few miles he turned north, knowing he would come to the road, getting his bearings when he did. This procedure was time consuming, but he knew of no better way to insure his arrival in Charlottesville. The road itself was virtually impossible. He tried it once, and Jumper sank down to his hocks in the mire. As bad as cross-country travel was, with countless gullies, fences, and creeks for obstacles, at least Jumper could run.

Speed was of the essence. It was over twenty miles to Charlottesville. Under these conditions that added up to a six- or seven-hour ride.

Nathaniel was soon exhausted. Being a poor rider, he was one solid ache from head to toe after an hour in—and out of—the saddle. But even though his strength was ebbing, he hung on by dent of sheer willpower.

Then, after what seemed like several days rather than a few hours, disaster struck.

A bolt of lightning struck so close that Nathaniel was momentarily blinded. He could feel the heat. Then, a split second later, he felt the impact of a limb. The low-slung bough swept him out of the saddle, knocking him cold before he hit the ground.

When he came to he had no idea how long he'd been unconscious. It was still pitch black, still raining. He was lying flat on his back. He'd been lucky. Had he landed face down in the mud of the soggy field, he might have drowned. He lay there a moment, gingerly testing his legs and arms, making sure nothing was broken.

Jumper!

With a sick feeling in the pit of his stomach, he sat up sharply.

He had lost his horse! And Virginia had lost her governor!

But Jumper was standing nearby, watching him—

and as he sat up, the blood bay whickered and seemed to nod.

Laughing, almost hysterical with relief, Nathaniel got to his feet, a little shaky. Jumper stepped up to him, and Nathaniel managed to climb, laboriously, into the saddle.

A little further on he came to a creek running too deep and fast to chance crossing. Nathaniel wheeled Jumper to the right and headed north until coming to the road. A covered bridge spanned the creek. He crossed, and returned to the firmer ground of a tobacco field. Proceeding parallel to the road, he had gone but a short distance before hearing a sound similar to thunder. Similar—but not quite.

He looked back. An opportune flash of lightning illuminated a scene that sent a chill down Nathaniel's spine.

A column of at least a dozen dragoons was pouring through the covered bridge. The sound he had heard were the hooves of twenty horses reverberating against the timbers of the bridge, and echoing off the planks of the roof and walls.

The lead dragoons whipped their struggling mounts through the muck of the road, veering off to the opposite side of the thoroughfare. Nathaniel almost panicked. He was caught out in the open with no place to hide. But then, without benefit of the lightning flash, he could scarcely make them out in the darkness. So they could not see him. In fact, they were abreast of him now, on the other side of the road, a stone's throw away. Then they had passed his position.

Nathaniel knew what they were after—or rather, who.

Thomas Jefferson.

And now they were ahead of him in the race to reach Monticello first.

Nathaniel had only seconds to make a decision. Then he drew Simon Marcy's flintlock pistol from under the greatcoat and thumbed the hammer back, praying that the powder was dry.

He pointed the pistol above the treeline and pulled the trigger.

The pistol shot had a remarkable and immediate effect on the dragoons. For a moment there was confusion in the ragged ranks as they checked their horses and searched the night to locate the source of the gunfire.

Nathaniel had no extra powder or shot. He shoved the empty pistol into a pocket of the greatcoat and kicked Jumper into a gallop, riding straight at the dragoons.

One of the Tories spotted him and gave a shout. Nathaniel wheeled Jumper sharply and made a run for it. The dragoons gave chase. Some of them fired at him. Muzzle flashes were flame blossoms in the darkness. Nathaniel bent low in the saddle, his face in Jumper's mane.

As they raced across the soggy tobacco field, he threw a few over-the-shoulder glances, and was pleased to note that his pursuers—scarcely discernible shadows in the gloom of the stormy night—were not gaining on him. Nathaniel decided then and there that Simon Marcy had every reason to be proud of his horse. After an all-night run, Jumper still had something left. Meanwhile, the mounts of the dragoons seemed to be wearing down.

Nathaniel's destination was a line of trees several hundred yards from the road, on the other side of a field. He reached them well in advance of the dragoons. Checking his horse, he tarried a moment, wanting to be certain that the dragoons were still after him. They were. Nathaniel turned west, guiding Jumper through the trees, staying low in the saddle to avoid branches—he had learned his lesson.

His hope was that the dragoons would waste valuable time combing the woods for him. Meanwhile, he would work his way through the trees and eventually swing back closer to the road and continue on his way.

When Nathaniel eventually ventured out of the woods he faintly heard a bugle sound and figured that the officer in charge of the Tory detail had realized the search was futile and was trying to recall his men. There was no time to waste. Nathaniel tapped his heels and Jumper responded with a gallop.

A few miles farther on he came to yet another creek. This one was about to crest. The only way across was another bridge, this one not covered. Nathaniel returned to the road, preparing to cross the span. But the ominous sound of creaking wood gave him pause. The angry torrent was undermining the bridge supports. Nathaniel couldn't be certain in the darkness, but it looked like the whole bridge was wobbling! Any minute would find it washed away. When that happened there would no crossing this creek. He would fail in his mission. What was he to do? Would the bridge sustain the weight of a horse and rider? Nathaniel was afraid to try. But what choice did he have?

With a fear-strangled "Hiya!," he kicked Jumper into a leaping gallop. The brave horse flew across the bridge. A rending crash made Nathaniel's heart skip a beat, as a section of the bridge behind him collapsed. But they were almost across. Just a little farther.

Then the bridge tilted sharply beneath them and abruptly disintegrated.

Nathaniel gasped as he hit the cold waters. Submerged, choking, he floundered, lost to panic, bobbed to the surface, only to be struck a stunning blow by a piece of shattered timber and driven under again.

He came up again. The wreckage of the bridge was swirling around him. The current was carrying him downstream at a frightening rate of speed. The heavy greatcoat was dragging him under. He tried to squirm out of it. It was then that he saw rein leather. *Yes, there was Jumper, straining to reach the bank!*

With one arm out of the greatcoat, Nathaniel grabbed for the reins and climbed up them, hand over hand, until he could reach the saddle's pommel. He clung to this with all the strength remaining to him. He knew it was up to Jumper whether they lived or died. The powerful horse fought the current to reach the bank, seeking purchase in the treacherous mud, failing once, again, but still fighting—and all the half-drowned Nathaniel could do was hold on for dear life.

Suddenly they were out of the water. Exhausted, Nathaniel let go of the pommel and collapsed into the mud. He still had a grip on the reins. Jumper reached the top of the bank and just dragged Nathaniel along with him. Nathaniel rolled over and threw up a bellyful of creek water. He lay there for a while, catching his breath. Somehow he mustered up the strength to get to his feet. He hauled himself into the saddle. The greatcoat was gone, but he hardly noticed.

Lifting his head, Nathaniel looked around. The mountains were dead ahead. He could see them now, shrouded in white mist, by the murky gray half-light of the hour before the sunrise. The rain had died down.

The fact that it was nearly daylight stirred Nathaniel's inner strength. He urged Jumper into a canter, aiming west, relocating the road. An hour later, he arrived at the outskirts of Charlottesville.

Chapter 9

The first person Nathaniel saw was a shopkeeper sweeping the walk in front of his store. The shopkeeper stopped sweeping when he saw the mud-caked apparition coming down the still-sleeping street, and just stared. Reaching the store, Nathaniel dismounted. His legs betrayed him, and he fell to his knees. The shopkeeper dropped his broom and rushed to Nathaniel's side, helping him up.

"My word, boy! What's happened to you? Come inside and dry yourself—"

"No!" Nathaniel urgently clutched the man's arm. "Tories . . . Tories in Louisa."

"What?"

"Butcher Tarleton's Tory Legion," croaked Nathaniel. "They are coming this way. They are—"

Another man appeared, tall, elderly, severe in black broadcloth, brandishing a walnut walking stick as though it were a sword.

"Here now, Collins. What's the meaning of this?"

The shopkeeper, Collins, relayed to this man what Nathaniel had said.

"The Tory Legion!" exclaimed the second man. He turned to Nathaniel. "Who are you, lad?"

"Nathaniel Jones. My father is Joshua Jones. He runs the inn at Louisa. He's badly hurt, sir. I fear the Tories have killed him."

The old man's eyes flashed fire. "And they are coming here, are they?"

"No doubt for you, Mr. Randolph," said Collins, "and all the rest of the burgesses."

"No doubt."

"I must warn the governor," muttered Nathaniel, and stumbled back to Jumper.

"You won't reach Monticello on *that* horse," predicted Collins. "Look at the poor beast, Mr. Randolph."

"*I will!*" was Nathaniel's fierce reply.

"Let him go," said Randolph, and the dry rasping sound Nathaniel heard was his chuckle. "I daresay neither hell nor high water could keep this lad from his destination."

Nathaniel summoned every last shred of strength left in his body and pulled himself up into the saddle. Jumper's head came up. The horse whickered and fiddle-footed.

"Aye," said Randolph, admiringly. "There's some fire yet. Good luck, Nathaniel Jones."

"Thank you, sir. There's a bridge washed out a few miles down the road. That ought to slow them down."

"Praise God. With His help, those damnable Tories will leave Charlottesville empty handed. You've done Virginia a great service, lad."

The small house that Thomas Jefferson had designed for himself was located on a high hill. The road that led to it ascended sharply through a stand of trees. Nathaniel was surprised to discover the four "roundabouts"—lanes that circled the hill, the first at the base, the second some distance above the first, the third at a higher elevation than the third, and the fourth girdling the crest of the hill. The purpose of these roundabouts escaped Nathaniel, though he was too fatigued to give them much thought.

He was further surprised to find the house itself unfinished. The bases and capitals for four columns were in place on the east portico, but only one of the white columns was in place. The foundation and basement had been fashioned from unhewn field-stone, the ground level of red brick.

Extending from the main house, with its prepossessing white dome and bowed sides, were L-shaped wings where the "dependencies"—kitchen, store-rooms, pantry, smokehouse, laundry, carriage house, pavilions, stables, and privy were located. Work was still in progress at points along these wings. The workers paused in their labors as Nathaniel arrived, and his disheveled appearance piqued their curiosity, as did the condition of his horse. It was as clear as a mother's milk that the blood bay and its rider had been through hell and high water to get here in a hurry.

Reaching the unfinished portico, Nathaniel checked Jumper and slumped forward, too weary even to dismount. A husky black man emerged from the house and peered at him askance, ham-sized fists planted on his hips.

This was Great George, Jefferson's most loyal and trusted retainer, and the man most feared and respected in the Monticello slave community, which numbered over a hundred souls. His wife, Ursula, was a cook and laundress. George made sure the house was run efficiently, and he kept the other slaves in line. He had an independent streak, which antagonized some whites, who were not accustomed to a slave who acted like an equal in their presence, but Jefferson was fond of George, and tolerated even his most surly moods. For his part, George had one primary concern, apart from his family, and that was the well-being of Thomas Jefferson.

"Who are you, boy?" he rasped, "and what you doing coming up here like this?"

"The governor," gasped Nathaniel. "I must see the governor."

"Not just any ol' body can ride up here and demand to see the governor," replied George. "You need a good reason to—"

"The Tory Legion . . . Tarleton's Tories are on their way here to capture Mr. Jefferson."

George rushed forward to help Nathaniel dismount. He cast a quick look at the laborers, converging from all points of the compass. "Come on inside, boy. What you gots to say might be best heard only by the governor."

Nathaniel was hustled into the large entrance hall. George ordered another house servant to stand fast at the door and keep everyone out, then led Nathaniel to Jefferson's library-study, rapping his knuckles on the door. The door swung open immediately, and Nathaniel was confronted by a tall man, with a ruddy, freckled face and untidy sandy hair. The man's features included a patrician's nose, a wide but firmly set mouth, a strong and stubborn jaw. But the eyes, a startling blue, were the most arresting feature of all. They were frank, intelligent, and friendly.

"Ah, George. So, is this the fellow I saw riding up?"

"Yessuh."

"I fear you may have ruined that splendid horse, young man, in your haste to get here."

"He's not ruined," said Nathaniel, with some heat. At some point during his harrowing night ride a bond had been forged between him and Jumper, and he felt obliged to leap to the blood bay's defense. "He could run another week if I wanted him to."

"I see," said Jefferson, merriment twinkling in his eyes. He stood with arms crossed, and looked Nathaniel over. "You've had a rough ride. Where are you from? What is your name?"

"Louisa. My name is Nathaniel Jones. Last night, Tarleton's Tory Legion took the town. They're on their way here."

Alarm flashed across Jefferson's face. "My God, George," he breathed. "The Butcher's men. Your wife, your infant child, everyone is in jeopardy."

"It's you they be after, suh," said George.

"Someone must warn the assembly."

George shook his head. "That's just like you, suh. Worried 'bout everybody else when it's your own life that's at stake."

Jefferson smiled. "Dead, I become a martyr. No, George, they would prefer to take me alive, as a hostage."

"I've already warned the folks in Charlottesville," said Nathaniel.

"The debt we owe you cannot be readily measured, Nathaniel. Come in and rest yourself. George, bring our friend some food."

Nathaniel gaped at the room into which he was led. The chamber was of a half-octagon shape. Shelves of books, reaching from floor to ceiling, covered every available inch of wall space. Between this room and the next was an open alcove, in which a narrow bed was located. The adjacent room was two stories high, with a skylight. All in all, the architecture was quite unusual—and certainly unlike anything Nathaniel had ever seen.

Jefferson bade Nathaniel to be seated in a richly upholstered wing chair at one end of a large plain desk. Nathaniel was reluctant to do so, his clothes being wet and muddy. Jefferson laughed softly.

"I daresay you will do much less damage to that chair than the Tories shall. Sit, sit." He looked about the room, and dismay flashed across his features. "Strange," he said. "I find myself wondering what fate will befall my books?"

In short order George arrived with a plate of biscuits, grits, and ham, which he placed on the desk in front of Nathaniel, accompanied by a glass of still-warm milk.

"Would you want a horse or carriage, suh?" George asked Jefferson, who was gathering papers from the drawers of the desk and shoving them into leather panniers.

"Oh, a horse, I would think. The roads are unsafe."

"Isaac will ride with you, then."

"Yes, that will be fine. I charge you, George, with the responsibility of getting everyone else safely away. Do not concern yourself with personal belongings, especially mine. Our lives and our freedom are the most important thing."

"Yessuh."

George left the room, and Jefferson glanced at Nathaniel, who was ravenously attacking the food that had been placed before him.

"As for you, Nathaniel Jones . . ."

"Yes, sir," mumbled Nathaniel, over a mouthful of biscuit.

"You must conceal yourself in the woods until it is safe for you to return home. The Tories won't linger long. They'll do some looting and be on their way. I know your father must be concerned about your welfare."

"My father is bad hurt. He may die."

"The Tories?"

Nathaniel nodded, and all the pent-up grief and rage came welling up inside him, bringing tears to his eyes. He blinked them away.

Jefferson circled the desk and placed a hand on the boy's shoulder.

"My heart goes out to you, lad. Balanced against the harsh realities of life and personal loss, such abstract notions as liberty seem to bear little weight. I know that it is small consolation to you now, but the nation we forge with our blood and our tears will be a proud and noble and enduring legacy to patriots like your father."

"I believe that, sir," said Nathaniel, feeling better.

"I do not like running before the enemy," confessed Jefferson, moving to one of the windows and gazing out across his estate. "Indeed, it rankles, being chased out of one's own home. But I must go. Would that I were not the governor. Ah, well. The governor must put aside his own pride and do what is best for all. Ironic, isn't it, that the capture of a single humble farmer could be so damaging to the cause of freedom." He turned back to the desk and draped the bulging panniers over a broad shoulder. "I must go. Eat quickly, then depart as well. When the crisis has passed, we will meet again. I am sure of it. Until then, good-bye."

With long strides, Thomas Jefferson left the library.

Nathaniel forgot the food and rose to go to a window, in time to see the governor climb aboard a long-legged stallion held by George. Jefferson and the burly slave had a brief but intense exchange of words, and then Jefferson was off.

Now that he had accomplished his mission, Nathaniel was suddenly lethargic, at a loss what to do. A wave of exhaustion swept over him. He sagged onto the window seat. All he needed was a moment of rest. Then he would go on his way. He lay down . . .

And woke with a start. George was shaking him.

"Rise and shine," George said grimly. "Them Tories are here."

Chapter 10

Nathaniel's first inclination was to make a run for it, but George responded with an emphatic head-shake when he asked for his horse.

"Nossuh, you can't do that. Them Tories are comin' up the hill right this minute. They'd see you, sure as night follows day, and then I wouldn't give a bent horseshoe for your chances. Nossuh, we gots to hide you away."

The slave hustled Nathaniel out onto the east portico. A couple of the floorboards had been pulled up, to reveal a space beneath. Another slave was hastily concealing silverware, china, portraits, and various other items beneath the floor. A tall black woman stood nearby with a blanket-wrapped infant child in her arms. George went to her, kissed the baby on the forehead and the woman on the cheek.

"Get on down there, Ursula," he said. "You gots to keep the chile quiet, now."

"What about you?"

"Me and Martin here are going to stay and welcome our guests."

"Be careful, George. Don't anger them or they'll kill you."

"Tell that to Martin. He's the troublemaker, you know."

Looking at Martin, Nathaniel believed it. He was young, muscular, scowling, with a distinct sullenness in his eyes and the set of his mouth and the way he stood on the balls of his feet, as though he were about to pounce like a catamount.

Ursula descended into the hideaway. George turned to Nathaniel.

"You get on down in there, boy. We'll let you know when it's all clear."

Nathaniel reluctantly complied. The floorboards of the portico were about three feet above the hard-packed ground. It was dark—the only illumination was daylight leaking through the floorboards. Nathaniel crawled past the pile of possessions to the nearest wall and settled down as comfortably as possible to wait.

In no time he felt the ground tremble beneath the hooves of galloping horses. Shouted orders. The heart-stopping clamor of booted feet pounding the floor-boards overhead. Nathaniel peered through the dusty gloom at Ursula, afraid that the baby would start squawling and give them away. But Ursula was gently rocking back and forth, humming ever so softly, with her lips near the infant's head—so softly that Nathaniel could only just hear her, and he knew the loud men a few feet above them would not be able to hear her.

"Where is the governor!"

It was one of the soldiers standing on the portico, and the sound of the voice jolted Nathaniel, because he had heard it before. This was the man, the sergeant-major, who had struck him, yesterday on the road into Louisa. The man who had taken his flintlock rifle.

Since that was so, it followed that this was the man Nathaniel's father had seen with the flintlock. Did that mean also that this was the man who had gravely wounded Joshua Jones?

"He's gone to the mountains," George spoke.

"Give me all the keys to this house."

"You won't find no silver," said George, matter-of-factly. "Mistuh Jefferson done took it all with him up into the mountains."

Captain Peter McLeod dismounted and stepped up onto the portico to stand next to Sergeant-Major Mulcahey. Stripping the gauntlets from his hands, he gave George and Martin, who stood blocking the door, a cold appraisal.

"So you say the governor has fled, eh?"

"Yessuh."

"Now how did he know to do that? Who told him we were coming?"

George shrugged. "I dunno, suh."

"You're a smart nigger," said McLeod. "Too smart, I think."

"He could be lying," suggested Mulcahey. "Jefferson might be cowering under his bed."

"I doubt it. The colonel was right."

"About what?"

"Never mind, Sergeant-Major. Suffice it to say that Jefferson was forewarned. Commence searching every room of this house. Every outbuilding. Every foot of ground. We must at least be able to report a thorough search."

"Yes, sir."

Mulcahey stepped off the portico and dispatched the men. Two of them followed him into the house. George stepped aside to let them pass. Martin wouldn't. So Mulcahey shouldered him roughly out of the way. No sooner had Martin recovered his balance than he found Captain McLeod's pistol aimed at his heart.

"So why don't you tell me where Mr. Jefferson was going?"

Martin just glowered at him.

McLeod prodded him with the pistol. "Tell me what I want to know or I will shoot."

"Fire away," said the defiant Martin.

But McLeod didn't shoot. He put the pistol away. "You two are free to go."

"We gots nowhere we want to go," said George. "We live here."

"Not anymore. You are free men, I tell you. Slaves no longer. It is the policy of His Majesty's army that all slaves of rebels are to be freed. So I hereby emancipate you."

George and Martin looked at each other.

"This is our home," said George. "If we're free to go then I reckon we're free to stay, too."

"Stay and be damned," snapped McLeod. "Just keep out of my way or I'll send you to hell."

With that he stalked angrily into the house.

Several hours passed before the Tories left Monticello. Those hours seemed like a lifetime to Nathaniel. He felt like he was buried alive, and it was all he could do to keep still.

Not once in all that time did the baby cry. Ursula breast-fed her child, and seemed not the least bit ashamed of baring herself in Nathaniel's presence.

When finally George pulled up the floorboards and let them out, the sunlight blinded Nathaniel. The slaves went inside. He followed, wandering aimlessly through rooms filled with smashed furniture. Paintings had been slashed with sabers. In Jefferson's library-study, books and papers were strewn across the floor. The Tory vandals had done their dirty work.

Nathaniel wrongly assumed that Great George had forgotten all about him, but the slave found him in the library and informed him that his horse was ready.

"They didn't take Jumper?" Nathaniel was astonished by the news.

"Way he looked, mebbe they didn't figure he was *worth* taking."

Nathaniel was vastly relieved. Having already lost Simon Marcy's hat, greatcoat, and flintlock pistol, he had been wondering how best to break the news to the farmer that his prized possession, the blood bay, was lost as well.

"But he's all set to go," continued George. "Been fed and watered and cleaned up some. Reckon you're ready to get back home, aren't you?"

"I hope I have a home to get back to."

"Just keep fightin', boy, no matter what happens."

Taking his leave of Monticello, Nathaniel avoided Charlottesville, assuming it was full of Tarleton's dragoons. He also stayed away from the roads, except when he had to cross the rain-swollen creeks.

Since the bridge was out on the Louisa–Charlottesville road, he had to make a long detour to Keswick. The journey back took the entire day. But at least it wasn't raining. The storm had passed. The hot sun quickly dried the soggy fields.

Nathaniel didn't push Jumper. The horse had earned a respite. Besides, Nathaniel was dreading his return to the inn, fearful that he would find his father dead. He had taken his leave with the premonition that he would never see Joshua Jones alive again, and that premonition was still very much with him.

His worst fears were realized.

John Lessing was waiting for him in the inn's common room. As soon as Nathaniel saw the lawyer's stricken expression he knew the truth.

"Nathaniel!" said Lessing. "Your father . . ."

"I know." Nathaniel sagged onto one of the split-log benches at a trestle table.

"He died during the night, lad. I'm terribly sorry. He passed away without regaining consciousness."

Nathaniel didn't say anything.

Uncomfortable, Lessing cleared his throat. "Dr. Stowe wanted to be here when you got back. But, well, several people were injured by the Tories, though no one else, save Mrs. Roberts, was killed."

"Mrs. Roberts!"

"Aye, lad. The bastards shot her in retribution for the killing of that dragoon."

"But *I* killed him!" cried Nathaniel.

"Now, Nathaniel, don't—"

"She died for something I did. Why didn't she tell them the truth?"

"She wouldn't. A brave and defiant woman was Mrs. Roberts."

"Why didn't you tell them?"

"I didn't know their plans until it was too late to save her."

Nathaniel covered his grime-blackened face with his hands. Neither he nor Lessing said anything for several minutes.

Finally, Lessing softly spoke. "Did you reach the governor in time, Nathaniel?"

"Yes, he got safely away," replied Nathaniel dully.

"Thank God for that at least."

Nathaniel stood up suddenly.

"Mr. Lessing, will you undertake the sale of this inn?"

"But why! Your father worked hard to make a success of this venture. He did it for—"

"I don't want it. I never did. I'm going over the mountains."

"Over the mountains! Hold on, lad, you—"

"Will you sell it for a commission, or shall I find someone else to represent me?"

Lessing thought it over. He could tell that Nathaniel had made up his mind and would not be swayed from his decision.

"Yes, I will do as you wish. Do you have any money at all?"

"Father had a strongbox—"

Lessing shook his head. "The Tories found it, broke it open, took all of its contents. I tell you what I'll do, Nathaniel. I'll give you fifty pounds sterling in advance of the sale."

"No, I couldn't."

"Of course you can. You'll need to purchase supplies. I insist."

Nathaniel nodded, telling himself that it was a fool who let pride come before necessity. He turned for the door.

"Don't you want to see your father? His mortal remains are still upstairs."

"No. I must go see Amanda."

"She is safe?"

Again, Nathaniel nodded. "Thank you, Mr. Lessing."

"But . . . but where will you go? How will I find you?"

"I'll let you know."

"Tell poor Amanda that Mrs. Lessing and I would

be more than happy to take her into our home. The child has nowhere to go now."

"I'll tell her," said Nathaniel, "but I don't think she will take you up on that kind offer, sir."

"Indeed? And why not?"

"Because I'm going to ask her to go with me."

"The wilderness is no place for a young girl."

"Maybe not. But I don't think there'll be any stopping her."

And he hurried out, eager to leave Louisa and the nightmare of the past two days behind him, looking forward to the mountains and the dream that lay waiting beyond them.

Chapter 11

Nathaniel was right about Amanda Roberts.

She wept quietly upon the news of her mother's death. While Mrs. Marcy tried to console her, Nathaniel regretfully announced to Simon Marcy the loss of the farmer's pistol, hat and greatcoat. Marcy brushed it off as of no consequence.

"Important thing is you saved the governor."

"I don't know about that . . ."

"Nonsense, Nathan. You did it, and no one else. What I lost is a small price to pay for what you did for Virginia, and our country. And you brought Jumper back to me safe and sound, as you promised."

"You have every right to be proud, Mr. Marcy. He's a fine horse, Jumper is."

"And how is your father, lad?"

"He's dead," said Nathaniel flatly, willing himself to be strong.

"You're made of stern stuff," observed a shocked Marcy.

"It came as no surprise."

"What are your plans?"

"Over the mountains."

"What about the inn?"

Nathaniel relayed to him the arrangement he had made with John Lessing, and showed the farmer the pouch bulging with gold coin. He had accompanied the lawyer to his home to receive the fifty-pound advance.

"I'd like to make you an offer on Jumper, sir."

"You would, eh?" Marcy rubbed his chin. He fetched a jug from the cupboard and brought it to the table. Pulling the cork with his teeth, he offered the jug to Nathaniel.

"What is it?"

"Corn likker. What else? I make it a habit of pullin' a cork when I conduct business. Smooths out the deal."

"Simon Marcy!" scolded Mrs. Marcy, returning from the other room. "He's but a boy."

"A boy!" Marcy guffawed. "If so, he's done a job most men couldn't bring off."

"How's Amanda?" asked Nathaniel.

"She'll be fine. Poor child." Mrs. Marcy dabbed at her puffy eyes with the corner of the apron she was wearing over a plain brown gingham dress.

"I always break out the jug when I'm cuttin' a deal," Marcy told his wife.

"Business?" she asked.

"Nathan wants to buy Jumper."

"Good! You pay more attention to that horse than

you do to me, Simon, so I'd just as soon see him gone."

Marcy grimaced. "And you think I paid too much for him, too, don't you?"

"Indeed I do, now that you mention it. I'll be happy if we get some of that money back, so's we can put it towards something more practical."

"Well, we won't," said Marcy, in triumph. "I'm giving the horse to Nathan."

"Oh, no, sir," said Nathaniel, stunned. "I can't—"

"Yes, you can, and you will. You'll be in need of a good horse to get you where you're going."

"And where is that, pray tell?" asked Mrs. Marcy. Simon explained the situation to her.

Standing in the doorway to the next room, unnoticed by the others, Amanda heard it all, and when the farmer had finished, she stepped forward and spoke up.

"I'm going with Nathaniel."

Mrs. Marcy voiced the same objections as John Lessing. But Amanda would not be swayed. Nathaniel didn't tell her that Lessing had offered to take her in, just as the Marcys were doing now. For one thing, he didn't think it would change her mind. For another, he didn't want to take the chance. He wanted her to go with him. He wasn't all that certain he could leave without her, and he didn't care to find out if he could.

He didn't have to.

Before long they were on their way, riding double on Jumper. The Marcys provided them with a burlap sack filled with provisions: flour, salt, sugar, beans, sidemeat, jerked venison, coffee, a pot and a pan, a length of rope, a good blanket. And Simon tendered Nathaniel yet another gift: a flintlock rifle.

"It isn't as fine as the one those damned Tories took from you," admitted the farmer, "but it shoots straight. And here's some powder and shot."

Again Nathaniel protested. Again it was to no avail. Simon had made up his mind. His heart filled with gratitude, Nathaniel managed to slip the pouch of gold into the Marcys' cupboard when the farmer and his wife weren't looking.

They did not go far that day, as Nathaniel deemed it wise to have mercy on Jumper. As night fell they made camp in a secluded meadow deep in a grove of trees, near a gurgling brook. He staked Jumper on the rope so that the horse could graze. Then he gathered some wood and built a small hot fire. Amanda made a batch of biscuits while he went down to the creek, stripped naked, and washed himself as well as his mud-caked clothes. Donning the wet clothes, he returned to camp and hunkered down close to the fire, shivering a little.

"You should get out of those wet clothes," said Amanda.

Nathaniel blushed furiously.

"We have a blanket," she reminded him.

"Just the one. That's for you to sleep in. I'd get it all wet. No, I'll be all right."

"You're just shy."

"No, I'm not."

"When we were little we swam together in the pond. I've seen you without clothes before, Nathaniel Jones."

"Amanda!"

"Well?"

"We were just children then."

"You'll catch pneumonia, is what you'll do."

Something about the way she said it made Nathaniel smile.

"What's so amusing?" she asked, a little put out because she assumed his amusement was at her expense.

"You sound like Mrs. Marcy scolding her husband."

Amanda smiled at that. Turning back to her biscuits, she said, "I guess I did, didn't I? And we're not even married . . . yet." She looked up at him shyly as she uttered the last word.

Nathaniel's heart skipped a beat, and he found himself blushing all over again.

The biscuits were just as Nathaniel liked them, crisp and brown on the outside, fluffy on the inside, and he ate like a starving man, tackling some of the jerky besides. Belatedly he realized that Amanda was scarcely eating.

"Aren't you hungry?" he asked.

"Not 'specially."

"Don't you want to try some venison?"

"No. I've had a biscuit."

"The biscuits are mighty good."

"Well, I've been cooking for you for years," said Amanda, "so I guess I know what you like."

And then the tears came again, as she recalled the many hours spent in the kitchen of Joshua Jones's inn, helping her mother prepare meals.

Nathaniel jumped up and went to her, putting an arm around her shoulders. Sitting there, with her face nestled in his chest, he listened to her cry, and it almost broke his heart. Eventually the tears subsided, and she fell into exhausted sleep. Rather than disturb her, Nathaniel sat there the whole night through, gently rocking her, and watching the fire burn down to ashes gray as ghosts.

In spite of the tragedy they had suffered, both Nathaniel and Amanda felt a strange, almost giddy exhilaration as they headed west. They were starting a new life, and they had each other. The great unknown that lay before them did not frighten either one; Amanda Roberts had a spirit of adventure as true and strong as Nathaniel's.

South, down through the verdant cradle of the Shenandoah they traveled, making for the Cumberland Gap, the natural gateway from Virginia and the Carolinas to the wilderness across the mountains.

They fell in with a man named James Hurley. He was a peddler, and a veteran of several trips into the frontier, and he seemed a friendly enough sort. Tall, lanky, black bearded, he chewed tobacco incessantly and talked like there was no tomorrow. He was headed over the mountains and invited them to come along.

But Amanda didn't like him, and when the opportunity to do so out of Hurley's hearing presented itself, she urged Nathaniel to let the peddler go on his way alone.

"Why?" asked Nathaniel, who was eager to hear all about the overmountain country, and figured the peddler was just the man to tell him. "He seems to be a nice fellow."

"Appearances can be deceiving."

"But what's wrong with him, exactly?"

"I don't know," said Amanda hotly, frustrated precisely because she couldn't put her finger on exactly what it was about Hurley that bothered her. "I just don't trust him."

Hurley carried his goods on two packhorses. Among his treasures: tinware, wooden bowls, iron cooking utensils, needles and combs, two pairs of spectacles, axes, gingham and calico, knives, a few pistols and rifles, powder and shot, even a fiddle and a few books. He told Nathaniel that he always fared well in the selling of these goods.

"Aye, I make out like a bandit," he boasted. "Not to say that I overcharge, mind you. I could, since there aren't many peddlers with grit enough to risk going up the Warrior's Path. But I like the settlers. And they treat me like family. That's on account of I'm just about the only white man some of 'em ever lay eyes on."

"What's the Warrior's Path?"

"It's a trail through the mountains, used by the Injuns for many a year. But it wasn't too long ago that no white man knew of it."

"It will take us to Kentucky?"

"Aye. You know, the Injuns call Kentucky 'the dark and bloody ground.' On account of there's been many a fight twixt tribes waged there."

"Why is that?"

Hurley chuckled. "Yore full of the questions, ain't ya, Nathaniel Jones?"

"I figured you're the man to ask."

"It's true. I am. You see, thing about Kentucky is, a lot of different tribes consider it sacred ground. You've got the Cherokees and Chickasaws down south. Then there's the Wyandots and the Shawnees up north of the Ohio River. None of 'em lives in Kentucky. In fact, they get riled when anybody but their own steps foot on that sacred ground. So natcherly when a Shawnee comes up on a Cherokee on Kentucky soil, there's a ruckus. And it works the other way around, too. They been killin' each other for generations over that land. So, it's called the dark and bloody ground."

"I guess they don't cotton to our kind settling there."

"No, not at all. There ain't a settlement out there what hasn't been attacked several times. You won't find a farmer in his field without a rifle tied to his plow." Hurley's eyes flicked to Amanda, who rode behind Nathaniel. "And the Injuns like to steal young white girls, too, by the way."

Nathaniel felt Amanda's arms tighten around him.

"Are you brother and sister?" asked Hurley.

"No," said Amanda. "We're going to be married."

"Is that so? What you aimin' to do, Nathaniel Jones?"

"I . . . I'm not sure. Hunt, I reckon."

"Hunt? Well, you can make a little money off of furs and such, true enough. But you'll have to leave your purty bride-to-be alone at home for long spells."

"Maybe I could farm. Is land cheap in Kentucky?"

"Cheap? Cheap as land can be. If you can drive a few stakes into the ground, you can have yourself a legitimate claim. But you don't look much like a farmer. And that mare don't look like no plow horse. Nossir." Hurley gazed admiringly at the blood bay. "Looks like a racer. You ever raced that horse, Nathaniel Jones?"

"Yes, I have," said Nathaniel. "Once."

"I'll wager you won, on that horse."

"I did."

Hurley nodded. "I know a good horse when I see one, and I been known to bet on a race or two. Well, Nathaniel Jones, you ain't got much in the way of worldly goods by the looks of it, but you got the three things a man truly needs in life: a good gun, a good horse, and a good woman."

All that day, as they climbed the foothills to reach the Cumberland Gap, the garrulous peddler filled their ears with a wealth of information about Kentucky. It was music to Nathaniel's ears, even the parts about Indian massacres.

Kentucky was a hunter's paradise, to hear Hurley tell it. Wild turkeys so abundant a man tripped over them every time he took a walk in the woods. Passenger pigeons, too—millions of them. So many, swore Hurley, that he had seen them blot out the sun for two whole days and part of a third. There were buffalo, herds of shaggies so vast a man had to go a whole day out of his way just to get around them.

There were precious few white settlements in Kentucky. After the Shawnee chief, Cornstalk, had agreed to the treaty of peace ending Lord Dunmore's War, in 1774, Harrodsburg was raised, named after its founder, the intrepid James Harrod. About fifty men lived there now, most of them with families, including the famous scout, Daniel Boone. In 1777, breaking Cornstalk's solemn promise that the Shawnees would never again cross the Ohio River to pester the whites, the Shawnees had attacked Harrodsburg. A terrible fight ensued, and some of the settlement was burned, but Harrodsburg survived.

The Shawnees had been pests since then, declared Hurley. On every overmountain trip he had come across at least one burned-out cabin. It never failed. He carried a pick and shovel because he knew he would need them to bury the dead. He couldn't figure out why some men were such hardheaded fools, insistent on living miles from anybody, off by their lonesome, putting their wives and children at such risk. They said they hankered after "elbow room." Like as not, all they found was a horrible death and an early grave.

They shared a camp that night only a few miles below the gap. On the other side, said Hurley, was the Warrior's Path, which would take them through the rugged mountains to the promised land of Kentucky. The Warrior's Path was not easy to find. You had to know where to look for it. Hurley knew, and he would show them.

"Get a good night's sleep, Nathaniel Jones," advised the peddler. "This'll be the last one you get for a spell. Startin' tomorrow we got to keep our eyes peeled for Injuns. We're safe enough here, though. They don't never come across the gap. But once we're on the other side, look out!"

They ate, and Hurley played a little tune on the fiddle. Nathaniel went to sleep with Amanda in her blanket close by his side. A lot closer than on previous nights. Nathaniel figured that was on account of Hurley's presence, and he made no objection. In fact, he kind of liked her close.

He dreamed of Kentucky, of being out hunting, with a herd of buffalo like a sea of brown passing in front of him, and millions of passenger pigeons passing across the sky, turning day into night.

He woke with a start.

Amanda was shaking him. The pearly light of dawn was just now reaching through the trees.

"He's gone!" she exclaimed. "So is Jumper!"

Nathaniel lunged to his feet, looked wildly around

the camp. It was so. There was no sign of the peddler—or the blood bay.

Hurley had stolen Jumper!

And all of their provisions, too!

The only thing he hadn't taken was the flintlock rifle, which had been under Nathaniel's hand all night long.

Nathaniel felt sick. Then he got mad. He snatched up the rifle.

"Come on, Amanda," he said grimly. "He can't have gotten far. We'll catch him."

Chapter 12

Nathaniel was a better-than-average tracker, and he had no difficulty following James Hurley's trail, at least until they reached the Cumberland Gap. Once in the notch it was another story. The path was rocky, the ground hard packed. There was a confusing abundance of signs of recent activity on the prominent horse trail.

The ascent to the gap was steep and strenuous. All that morning they climbed. By noon Amanda was exhausted. Worse, her small white feet were bruised and bleeding. Nathaniel was horrified by his own failure to even consider the fact that Amanda was barefooted.

As he gently washed her feet in a spring-fed rock pool, and watched the water tinged pink with her blood, he felt awful, and apologized so often that Amanda had finally heard enough.

"It isn't your fault," she said. "I could have spoken up."

"Why didn't you?"

"I didn't because you want to catch Hurley. You want to get Jumper back."

"Yes, but . . . but, you're more important. I don't care about that old horse."

"Of course, you do. And you should. We need a horse if we hope to make it to Kentucky. Leave me here, Nathaniel. Go on. You can come back for me once you've got Jumper back."

"No. I won't leave you."

"I'll be safe until you get back."

"No." Nathaniel was adamant. "I'll carry you."

"You can't."

"Sure, I can."

"You can't carry me all the way to Kentucky, Nathaniel."

"I can try."

He gave her the flintlock to hold, and swept her up into his arms.

Through the V-shaped cleft they passed, and at the point where they could see westward for some distance, the fog-wreathed and tree-cloaked mountains seemed to roll on forever. It was a discouraging sight. Nathaniel wondered how he could carry Amanda and make it through this rough country. It was all up and down—there was scarcely a level spot to be found.

Fighting his doubts, he trudged on. The muscles in his arms and legs screamed for mercy. But he showed himself no mercy. It became his goal in life to carry Amanda until at least the sun went down.

Naturally, the sun seemed to hang motionless in the azure sky, just to spite him.

As the interminable day dragged on he began to stumble, and Amanda insisted he put her down, that she could walk, but he didn't believe it. She was just saying that to spare him, and she would try to go it on her own even though it caused her great pain. Pain was something Nathaniel never wanted her to experience. Besides, he was too stubborn to give in now. He had set a goal for himself, and it was vitally important, in a way he could not really define, for him to win.

When he came to a fork in the trail he wasn't even thinking about looking for signs of activity anymore. He was too exhausted, and in too much pain himself, to think about anything beyond the next step. He staggered down the left fork.

"Let me down!" cried Amanda, and started fighting him.

He couldn't hold her, and dropped to his knees rather than let her fall. She got to her feet and tried to walk, but her feet were too swollen, and the pain wrenched a whimper from her lips, and she sat down hard. He crawled to her on his hands and knees.

"I can carry you," he said.

"You stubborn . . ." She was crying. Then she was laughing. Crying and laughing at the same time, as she flung her arms around his neck and kissed him hard on the mouth.

"Amanda!" he gasped. "What's got into you?"

"I love you, you fool."

Nathaniel was flabbergasted. "You never . . ."

"No, I never. And you never, either. But I do. Do you?"

He nodded.

"Say it, Nathaniel. Tell me. Please."

"I love you."

She laughed and cried some more. "You know, some men carry their brides across the threshold into their new home. It just struck me—you carried me across a whole mountain."

"To our new home."

She looked around her at the darkening woods. The obstinate sun had finally yielded the sky to its sister, the moon, a pale orb perched on the tip of a mountain, against the purple heavens.

"I'm sorry, Amanda."

"Sorry? For what?"

"I should have listened to you about Hurley. But I didn't, and now we don't have anything."

"We have everything," she said.

"Amanda! Look!"

Nathaniel pointed down the path.

She looked, down through the woods, and saw the flicker of light. A campfire, or a lantern—she couldn't tell which.

Nathaniel stood up, retrieved the rifle. "Come on, Amanda. I'll carry you. It isn't far."

She took the rifle from him, and he took her up in his arms again.

The light proved to be produced by a lamp in the window of a ramshackle cabin on the banks of a fast-

running river. As they approached the cabin they
failed at first to see the woman sitting in the dark
shadows of the porch. When she spoke it startled
Nathaniel so that he almost dropped Amanda.

"Who are ye and what do ye want?"

She rose from her rocking chair and moved to the
edge of the porch, so that they could make out her
features by the threads of moonlight filtering down
through the trees. She was very old, with stringy
iron-colored hair and wizened features. She wore an
old linsey-woolsey dress, belted at the waist, and a
battered flop-brim hat set back on the crown of her
head. She plucked a corncob pipe from her nearly
toothless mouth with a gnarled hand and used it to
point at them, jabbing at the air as she talked.

"I'm talkin' to ye. Are ye daft? Who ye be, and
state ye're business." Nathaniel noticed that her
other hand was resting on the butt of a pistol stuck
into her belt. "I'll shoot ye iffen ye don't answer."

"Nathaniel Jones, ma'am."

"And ye?" She stabbed the pipe stem in Amanda's
direction. Nathaniel had put her down, and now she
stood close beside him, clinging to his arm.

"Amanda Roberts."

"Why, ye're just children." She stepped down off
the porch and came closer. Amanda shrank back as
she drew near. The old woman cackled in laughter.
"What spooks ye, gal? Are ye skeered? I won't bite."
She reached out and pinched Amanda's cheek. "Aye,
ye're real flesh and blood. Fur a minute there I
thought ye were ghosts."

"Ghosts?"

"Aye, gal. There be ghosts in these woods, don't ye know. Have ye lost yer way?"

"No," said Nathaniel. "We're going to Kentucky."

"Ye are? Just the two of ye? No horse? No possibles? You won't git fur."

"A man named James Hurley stole our horse and possibles. Do you know him? He's a peddler. Did he pass this way?"

The old woman shook her head. "Naw. Never heard the name. And nobody passes this way no more."

"Isn't this the way to Kentucky?"

"It's one way. But don't nobody come this way no more. Did ye not see the fork? Folks go down to Pilcher's ferry now. Used to be, we had the only ferry crost this here river, my husband and I. But then Pilcher come along a few miles upriver."

"Your husband?" asked Nathaniel.

"Rest his soul."

"He's dead?"

"Smart lad. Gone ten year now. Left me all by my lonesome. I tried to keep the ferry goin'. Hired a man to work it. But he run off, and stole dang near ever'thing I had that was worth spit. So Pilcher's got all the ferryin' business, damn his Dutch eyes." She cocked her head and gave Nathaniel a sidelong appraisal, feeling his upper arm. "Ye're a fine strappin' young lad. How'd ye like to stay here with me and work the ferry? Pilcher's gone up on his toll, now that he's got the only crossin'. We'll undercut him, and steal away his business, same as he stole ourn years back."

"I can't. We're bound for Kentucky."

She looked them up and down, shook her head with a snort. "You'll never make it up the Wilderness Road, chillun."

"Yes, we will," said Nathaniel.

The old woman laughed again. "Ye got the spirit, at least. C'mon in and rest the night at least. Kilt a rabbit yesterday. Got some stew." She turned and went inside.

Nathaniel took a step to follow, but Amanda tugged fiercely at his sleeve.

"What is it?" he asked. "Aren't you hungry? I could eat a horse."

"Nathaniel . . . do you think . . . could she be a witch?"

"She's just an old woman, Amanda. Maybe a little addled from being alone for so long."

Reluctantly, Amanda accompanied him inside.

While they sat at a rickety table partaking of the old woman's rabbit stew, their host mixed up a poultice in a wooden bowl, and plopped it down in front of them when they had finished eating.

"This here's fur yer feet, gal," she told Amanda. "It'll work wonders. Take the swellin' right down."

"What's in it?" asked Amanda, a little leery.

The old woman shrugged bony shoulders. "A pinch of this. A dab of that. Mustard, poke root, bear grease. Other stuff. Go on, use it. Ye'll be right as rain come sunup."

"I'll do it," said Nathaniel.

Amanda propped one foot and then the other in his lap, and he gently applied the poultice. The old woman sat across the table from them, watching as she puffed on the corncob pipe.

"Why do you stay here all alone?" Amanda asked her.

"Where else would I go?"

"You have family anywhere?"

"Gal, my husband was my only family. Oh, we had two sons. One drowned in that there river when he war just a pup. T'other died of the consumption."

"I'm sorry."

The old woman shrugged again. "Nothin' to be sorry fur. It's all part of life. Some good times mixed in with a heap of bad times. This here's my home. It's all I got. I ain't about to leave. I'd have to leave all my memories behind. My family's buried out yonder. I like to stay close to 'em. When my time's comin' I'll know it, and I'll dig me a hole out there next to my husband. Then I'll just crawl down in that hole and pass on." She grunted, cocked her head in an attitude of listening. "Night wind's pickin' up. You all kin bed down in here. I'll fetch some blankets."

They spread the blankets out near the dying fire in the blackened hearth. The old woman retired to the other room of the cabin. Nathaniel used his hunting knife to cut the sleeves out of his deerskin hunting shirt. Then he cut the sleeves open longways and wrapped Amanda's feet and ankles, using some of the long fringe off his leggins to secure the wrappings.

"You won't ever leave me alone, will you?" asked Amanda.

"Never."

"Promise?"

"I promise."

"I don't want to end up like that old woman. And I would, if anything ever happened to you. I could never love anyone else, Nathaniel. Never." She smiled. "I was so afraid all this time to tell you that I loved you. Afraid just to say the words. Isn't that funny?"

"So was I," he confessed.

"But now that I've said it I want to keep saying it. I want to say it every minute."

He kissed her on the cheek and lay down, groaning as he stretched his aching body, more tired than he had ever been in his life. Amanda snuggled up beside him, an arm thrown across his chest. Nathaniel figured it wasn't very proper, their sleeping together like this. But, on the other hand, it seemed like the most natural thing in the world. Of course, having her so close stirred desire within him. He tried to keep it tamped down. There was a time and a place for that and this was certainly not the place; as for the time, it would have to wait until they were married. Their understanding of that was unspoken.

He drifted off to sleep.

A creaking floorboard woke him.

The fire had burned down to orange embers embedded in mounds of gray ash, so the cabin was quite dark. The wind was howling beneath the eaves. Propped up on an elbow, Nathaniel searched the darkness, his hand on the flintlock rifle beside him. There was someone else in the room, on the other side of the table. Amanda was sleeping soundly next to him.

Then the door burst open, thrown back violently on its leather hinges by the gusting wind, and Amanda woke with a start. "Stay down!" said Nathaniel as he leaped to his feet, the rifle in his grasp.

With an unearthly shriek the old woman flew across the room, making for the door, her arms outstretched, as though she were reaching for something. Confused and frightened, Nathaniel started toward her. "What's wrong?" he yelled. "What is it?" She turned on him, then, framed in the doorway, her iron-gray hair streaming in the wind that whipped the long white gown against her frail frame. Her eyes blazed with an odd, wild light.

"My husband!" she cried. "My beloved husband is calling me! Don't ye hear? Don't ye hear?" She gestured out into the night. "He comes fur me on nights like this . . ."

Icy fingers of dread clutched at Nathaniel's spine. Speechless, he watched her leap across the porch and disappear into the darkness.

"Nathaniel!"

Unnerved, he rushed to Amanda's side.

"Can you walk?"

"I think so."

"Then walk. No, run. Run as fast as you can. I'm right behind you."

As they fled the cabin, racing up the trail, Nathaniel looked back. At the end of a path of moonlight he saw the old woman in her white gown, straddling a mound of dirt and clutching at a wooden cross.

He ran on, pursued by the mad shrieks of the old woman carried on the howling wind.

Chapter 13

They spent a sleepless, nerve-wracking night in the woods. Sitting with his back to a tree, Nathaniel kept one arm tightly around Amanda. The flintlock, primed and ready, lay across his knees. He didn't sleep a wink.

Much to her surprise, Amanda discovered the next morning that the swelling in her feet had subsided, and she was able to walk without much pain. They found the fork in the trail and by midmorning arrived at Pilcher's crossing.

Pilcher turned out to be a pleasant man, not at all the evil cutthroat Nathaniel had pictured, thanks to the calumny heaped upon the Dutchman's head by the crazy woman downriver. When Nathaniel explained to him that they had no means of paying for the crossing, Pilcher shrugged it off. And when Nathaniel told him that James Hurley had stolen their horse and provisions, Pilcher nodded, believing every word.

"Your horse vas a blood bay, maybe?"

"Yes. You've seen him?"

"I have seen him. Hurley crossed yesterday. I didn't think dat horse vas his. I have alvays thought dat Hurley is a scoundrel and a thief. I vas vondering who he had stolen dat horse from."

"Do you know where he was headed?"

"Up dah Wilderness Road to Harrodsburg or Boonesboro, I guess. He thinks he vill make much money racing dat blood bay. By dah looks of dat horse, I think maybe he vill."

"Then we'll be going to Harrodsburg," Nathaniel told Amanda.

The amiable Dutchman studied Nathaniel's sundarkened features, hardened with grim resolve. "Vat you do den?"

"Get my horse back, of course."

"You vill have to kill dat Hurley."

"I hope not."

"Oh, you vill," said Pilcher, convinced.

"If that's what I have to do, then so be it."

"Hah! I believe you vill, at dat, by Gott. Come on, I vill take you across. The sooner Hurley gets vat is coming to him, the better."

Pilcher and his son ferried them across. On the other side, the Dutchman warned Nathaniel to keep both eyes peeled for Indians, and wished them all the luck.

Later that day they came upon a cabin in a clearing beside the trail. This turned out to be an inn, of sorts, run by a kindly gray-haired woman named Cogburn. Her two sons helped her run the place, and the adjacent forge. Nathaniel was quick to notice a profusion of bulletholes and a few scorch marks on the log walls of the cabin.

"Injuns," one of the Cogburn boys told him. "We get hit once or twice a year." He said it in an offhand way, as though Indian raids were as ordinary as mosquito bites. "But all of us Cogburns are good shots. Ma's almost as good a shot as I am, and that's saying something. We hold our own agin them heathens. They skulk around this here road quite a bit, hoping to pick off travelers. It's the damned redcoats what supply them with muskets and shot, you know."

"Where you all headed?" asked Ma Cogburn.

"Harrodsburg."

"You all ought to stay here until another bunch of settlers pass by. Then you could join up with them. Be better off. There's safety in numbers. You're welcome to stay here with us."

Nathaniel declined. He wanted to catch Hurley and get Jumper back. Apart from that, he wasn't too happy with the way the Cogburn boys were looking at Amanda.

Ma Cogburn persuaded them to at least stay for a meal. Nathaniel confessed that he could not pay. Like Pilcher, Ma Cogburn just shrugged it off.

There was a fourth Cogburn, a white-bearded codger, older than dirt, who watched the world go by from a bench on the cabin's porch. The Cogburn boys called him Gramps, and warned Nathaniel that he had appointed himself the official historian of Kentucky, and would talk any stranger's ear off, given half a chance.

That suited Nathaniel right down to the ground, and he offered himself as a willing audience for the garrulous tale-teller, while Amanda helped Ma Cogburn put a meal together. In an hour's time Nathaniel learned much more about the trans-Allegheny frontier than he ever had from occasional visitors to his father's inn, or the peddler Hurley. In spite of his age, Gramps Cogburn's mind was as sharp as a tack, and he had an encyclopedic memory when it came to names and dates.

According to Gramps, Daniel Boone and five other intrepid souls had started the ball rolling back in 1769 by venturing into the Kentucky wilderness from the Yadkin Valley on a hunting expedition. Boone and his brother-in-law, John Stuart, were captured by Shawnee Indians, escaping after seven days of harrowing captivity. This discouraged their companions sufficiently to send them packing, but Boone and Stuart stuck it out, and were later joined by Boone's younger brother, Squire.

Boone persuaded several Yadkin Valley families to sell their farms and resettle in Kentucky with him. Boone's younger son James was killed by Indians, which gave the settlers cold feet. They got as far as the Clinch River country and would go no further.

That same year, 1773, James Harrod and thirty other men were beginning to build a settlement which in time would be called Harrodsburg, while the McAfee brothers were surveying the lands in the vicinity of the falls of the Ohio.

Virginia's Governor Dunmore, learning that the

Shawnee were planning an all-out war to purge the Middle Ground of all white interlopers, sent Daniel Boone and Mike Stoner to warn Harrod and the McAfees. Boone reached Harrodsburg in time to help Harrod fend off a fierce Indian attack. Harrod's party abandoned the half-finished town, only to return a year later, after Cornstalk's signing of the treaty that ended Lord Dunmore's war.

Meanwhile, Judge Richard Henderson devised a scheme to buy land from the Cherokees and establish his own sovereign kingdom in the wilderness, which he planned to call Transylvania. The Transylvania Company signed up 200 colonists and paid the Cherokees $50,000 for a vast tract of land south of the Kentucky River.

Once again, Daniel Boone was in the thick of things. He set out with thirty men, including brother Squire, to blaze a trail for the rest of the Transylvania colonists. Despite an Indian attack that claimed the lives of three of the pathfinders, they pushed resolutely on. Reaching the Kentucky River near a buffalo lick, they staked out the site for Transylvania's capital, Boonesboro.

But Henderson's dream of ruling a wilderness empire was short lived. Representatives from Harrodsburg—one of them being George Rogers Clark—petitioned the Virginia Assembly to claim Kentucky as part of the Commonwealth. As a result, in 1776, Virginia created Kentucky County.

When war broke out the British agitated the northern tribes to attack the colonists in the trans-

Allegheny region. Rumor had it that the British commandant at Detroit was offering a bounty for the scalps of colonists, and even paid handsomely for live captives. In 1778, George Rogers Clark and 200 volunteers, including Simon Kenton—at 23, already a legend among the Long Knives—marched on the British outpost at Kaskaskia and captured it. Clark pressed on to take the fort at Cahokia without a shot being fired. Stunned by the success of the Kentuckians, the Indians began to talk peace.

But the British weren't finished yet. General Henry Hamilton and his redcoats were marching on Vincennes. And over 400 Shawnees under Black Fish laid siege to Boonesboro. Since trouble usually comes in threes, Clark should not have been surprised when his most trusted scout, Simon Kenton, was captured by the Indians.

But George Rogers Clark was not one to give up. He led 130 hardened frontiersmen on a seventy-day trek in the middle of a harsh winter to reach Vincennes and capture a surprised Hamilton. It was a tremendous victory that won the whole of the Old Northwest for the Americans. The Shawnees abandoned the siege of Boonesboro. And Simon Kenton finally escaped the clutches of the British in Detroit, to whom he had been given by the Shawnees, after ten grueling months in captivity.

The defeat of the British split the powerful Shawnee nation in two. Those seeking peace, some four thousand in all, most of them from the septs of the Kiskopothas, the Peckuwes, and the Thaweligas, moved to new lands across the Mississippi River. Those who remained, the Chalahgawthas and Maykujays, swore to fight the Shemanese—the whites—to the last man. These were the Indians who persisted in making life miserable for the Kentuckians.

Virginia wasn't much help, either. True, the Old Dominion had problems of its own with the British, but Kentucky County had been left to sink or swim on its own stick from the very start, and Kentuckians had only themselves to thank for having survived the British and the Shawnees. There was talk of becoming a separate and sovereign state. Of course, that all depended on whether independence was won from Great Britain. If it wasn't, Kentucky was doomed. Those who had ventured into the frontier tended to be entirely too independent for British tastes.

"A feller kin do well fur himself in Kaintuck," opined Gramps Cogburn over dinner, "iffen he's got the gumption, and kin shoot."

"I'm the best shot in these parts," declared one of the Cogburn boys.

"Second best," said the other.

"That's a black lie," countered the first. "Last time we had us a turkey shoot, who shot the most tail feathers off that gobbler?"

Nathaniel grimaced. He could tell that the Cogburn boys were bragging on themselves just to impress Amanda. Not that he could really blame them for trying to catch her eye. They were young men in their prime, and there was obviously a grave shortage of young women around these parts. Such was the curse inherent in loving a pretty girl.

"You boys just eat," said Ma Cogburn.

"Kin you shoot?" Gramps asked Nathaniel.

"Some."

"He's the best shot in Louisa county," said Amanda proudly. "If not the whole of Virginia."

Nathaniel scowled at her.

"Well, we ought to have us a little shootin' match," exclaimed one of the Cogburn brothers.

"I don't think so," demurred Nathaniel.

"Aw, come on. Ain't you the best shot in Virginia?"

"I've got nothing to wager."

"Who said anything about a wager? We'll just shoot for fun."

Nathaniel knew there was more to it than that. The Cogburn boys, secure in their perceived superiority with the rifle, just wanted to show off for Amanda's sake. There was nothing in it for Nathaniel. If he lost, they would crow at his expense, and if he won there would probably be hard feelings. The Cogburns didn't look the type to be good losers. But there was no way out of it. Nathaniel couldn't back down from a challenge.

So after dinner they all stepped outside. Ma Cogburn, Gramps, and Amanda stayed on the porch, while Nathaniel and the Cogburn boys got ready.

Their targets were pine blocks, cut into roughly six-inch squares, and crosshatched. These were lined up on a split-rail fence, a dozen of them. Then the three sharpshooters walked to the far side of the clearing to toe their marks at a range of about a hundred yards.

Each contestant would fire four times, and then retrieve his pine blocks. The Cogburns insisted that Nathaniel go first, since he was their guest and all. That was fine with him. Almost casual in his movements, he took his stance. He brought the flintlock to his shoulder, aimed and fired in one quick, smooth motion. He scarcely seemed to aim. Yet he sent all four of his pine blocks spinning. He retrieved them and walked over to the audience on the porch. Gramps examined each block. Four times Nathaniel had hit dead center in the cross-hatch.

"How'd he do, Gramps?" called one of the Cogburn boys.

Impressed, Gramps squinted at Nathaniel. "Kin you do that ever' time?"

Nathaniel shrugged. "I reckon. It really wasn't much of a shot."

He was trying to downplay his accomplishment, but realized too late that it came across as bravado.

The Cogburn boys fired away. Not once did they miss the pine blocks. But close inspection revealed that between the two of them they had managed to hit dead center only three times.

They were not poor losers, after all. In fact, they praised Nathaniel, and shook his hand, and looked at him as though he had just walked on water. It was clear they put great store by a man's prowess with a rifle.

"What's your name agin?" asked Gramps.

"Nathaniel Jones."

Gramps nodded, storing the name away in his mental encyclopedia, certain that he would hear more of this young man.

A while later, Nathaniel and Amanda took their leave, with some biscuits and jerky provided by the generous Ma Cogburn. The Cogburn boys returned to their chores. Gramps resumed his post on the bench, where he watched the world go by. And when he told subsequent passersby all about Kentucky he invariably spoke of a young man from Virginia who was the best shot with a flintlock rifle that God had ever made. Just about everybody who crossed the Cumberland Gap and turned up the Wilderness Road for the Middle Ground of Kentucky heard tell of a man named Flintlock Jones.

Chapter 14

Nathaniel and Amanda did not see another living soul the rest of that day and all of the next. The first night they slept in the woods, after dining on some of Ma Cogburn's biscuits and venison jerky. Game was plentiful—Nathaniel could have shot a deer and a whole passel of wild turkeys. But all the talk he had heard of late about Indians on the prowl along the Warrior's Path made him think better of firing the flintlock. A gunshot would travel a long way in these quiet mountains, and might attract unwanted attention. He did not even build a fire, though the night was cool at this elevation.

The next morning they struck out early. The mountain mists were heavy until the sun rose above the forested heights and burned it away. All day they walked the Wilderness Road. They finished off the biscuits and most of the jerky for their noonday meal, so that by nightfall both of them were starved. Nathaniel took a chance and shot a turkey. Amanda plucked and cleaned the bird while he built a small hot, smokeless fire in a clearing carpeted with clover. They ate well, and slept even better.

On the third day they began to emerge from the mountains. They were making pretty good time, by Nathaniel's calculations. Amanda's feet were much better, and she was scarcely limping at all by the third day from the Cumberland Gap.

Nathaniel was impressed by the vistas stretching out before him—the magnificent hardwood forests and the inviting expanses of open and gently rolling country, the grass a sea of blue caressed by a breeze laden with the sweet aroma of wildflowers. The game was every bit as abundant as James Hurley had said it would be. A hunter's paradise, indeed. Nathaniel decided that, for himself at least, living the carefree life of a nomad in this country would be the second best thing to residing in heaven.

But of course, a nomad's life would not suffice for Amanda. She deserved better than that. He would build her a cabin with his own two hands on the most beautiful plot of land in Kentucky, and he would farm that land, and learn to like being a farmer. Hurley's words—about his having to leave Amanda alone for days on end if he tried to make a living as a hunter—stuck in his mind. He couldn't do that. He had promised her he never would leave her, and he fully intended to abide by his word.

It was on the third day that they heard the shooting. It came from some distance up the trail. They clambered to the top of a ridge and found a vantage point on the rim of a limestone escarpment from which they could survey the full reach of the valley that lay before them. A plume of dark smoke rose from the woods about a mile away.

"What is it?" asked Amanda. "What do you make of it, Nathaniel?"

He shook his head. "I don't know. But whatever's happening, it looks to be right in our path."

"Could it be Indians?"

Nathaniel looked at her. She was scared, and trying to conceal it. Scared, but not just of Indians. She was afraid of what Nathaniel was about to do.

"I have to go find out," he told her, aware that he wasn't telling her anything she didn't already know.

"Then I'm going with you."

"Not this time. It's too dangerous."

"Well, if it's too dangerous for me, then it's too dangerous for you."

"I . . . don't you see, Amanda? There could be some folks down there in need of help."

"Don't leave me."

"I can't stand by if there are people in need of help."

She looked down, trying to hold back the tears. "I have a bad feeling, Nathaniel. Like if you leave me here you won't ever come back. That I'll never see you again."

"I will come back. I promise."

He expected her to remind him that he had promised never to leave her, too, and was presently breaking that promise. But she didn't.

"I'll wait here for you, then," she sighed.

"I'll be back," he said, and the distraught look on her face almost made him choke on the words.

Making his way back down to the trail, he broke into a ground-eating lope, and ran the mile without stopping. All the while the shooting continued. When he was quite near, he ducked into the woods, and proceeded with more caution. Then, through the trees, he saw the flames. A cabin in a clearing not far from the trail was ablaze.

The woods in front of him were crawling with Indians.

They wore leggins and breechclouts. Their faces and bare torsos were painted. Their heads were shaved but for a roach cut. Some of them wore tails of horsehair attached to the hair at the back of the head. They were dodging from tree to tree, never firing twice from the same spot. Nathaniel saw seven warriors in the woods in front of him. There were more lurking in the cornfield on the east side of the cabin. They would come to the edge of the field, fire at the cabin, and duck back into the rows of shoulder-high corn to reload. One warrior lay sprawled face down between the cornfield and the cabin.

The people in the cabin were returning fire. Nathaniel saw the barrels of rifles slide out through the gunslots in the sturdy wooden shutters over the windows. The barrels spit flame and then disappeared, to appear again a moment later.

Nathaniel couldn't see how they were able to remain in the cabin. One whole side wall was engulfed in flame. The fire was licking across the shingled roof. Dense black smoke was pouring out of the gunslots and leaking through chinks in the log walls. The people in there could not last much longer. And when they emerged it would be finished. That was what the Indians were waiting for.

Nathaniel wasn't sure what to do. He could drop one, maybe two, of the Indians before the rest were on him. And then Amanda would be alone and defenseless in the middle of the wilderness. He couldn't do that to her. She depended on him as much as he depended on her. And yet he could not bring himself to turn his back on the people trapped in the cabin.

The cabin door opened.

A man rushed out. His clothes and face were blackened by soot. The Indians in the woods and the cornfield let loose a ringing, triumphant chorus of whoops and cries that chilled Nathaniel to the bone. It was a sound savage and terrible—one he would never forget.

Right behind the man came two women, an older and a younger. The latter was about Nathaniel's age. The older woman carried an infant in her arms. Last out was a boy, some years younger than Nathaniel, but old enough to wield a rifle.

Seeing their prey, the Indians leaped forward from their places of concealment in the woods and the cornfield. There were ten of them. The man raised his rifle and fired. One of the Indians crumpled, shot through the heart. The man turned and shouted something at the boy. In that instant he was struck by three bullets, and fell, mortally wounded. The boy cried out. He too fired. Another Indian hit the ground, writhing as he clutched at his leg. The boy dropped to his knees beside his father as the warriors converged. The warriors closed in. They used tomahawks and the butts of their muskets to finish off the man and kill the boy.

The two women were running for the woods to the west of the house, toward the trail. They didn't get far.

Four Indians broke cover to block their path. The older woman drew a flintlock pistol from beneath the baby cradled in one arm, and fired point-blank at the nearest warrior. The Indian's face dissolved in a bloody mist. The older woman fell an instant after he did, her skull cleft in two by a tomahawk. The warrior who killed her snatched up the screaming infant and held it aloft. The young woman lunged at him, reaching for the baby. The warrior laughed and pushed her away. His two cohorts grabbed the girl and bore her to the ground.

All of this transpired in a matter of seconds. The bloody horror of the scene momentarily paralyzed Nathaniel. His insides were twisted with rage, grief, fear, disgust. But when the warrior hurled the infant against the flaming wall of the cabin something snapped inside him. He raised the rifle and fired without a second thought. His bullet caught the warrior in the head and felled him like a cut tree.

He ducked down immediately, flat on the ground

behind the roots of a tree, and reloading as fast as he could, which wasn't as fast as usual, because his hands were shaking.

Did they know where the shot had come from? Had one of them glimpsed the muzzle flash in the speckled shade of the woods? Or a wisp of white powdersmoke? Were they all coming for him now? Slipping through the woods, with muskets and bloody tomahawks ready to deal him death?

Nathaniel had a strong urge to run. But then he also had an equally strong urge to stay put, because if he got up to run they would see him for sure. He listened hard, but for a moment heard only the crackle of the flames.

He couldn't bear not knowing his fate, so he raised his head slightly above the gnarled roots of the tree.

Several of the Indians were loping toward the woods that concealed him. They were spread out, moving in a running crouch, looking this way and that, trying to find him. That offered Nathaniel a little encouragement. At least he wasn't quite done for.

Beyond them, a warrior approached the two who were pinning the girl to the ground. Just by the way he moved Nathaniel could tell he was the leader of this bunch.

"*Tschi squithetha,*" he barked at the two Indians, and made a curt downward gesture. Clearly he was giving an order.

"*Ni-la-weh* . . ." began one of the other Indians, in protest.

"Mattah!" roared the leader. *"Ni-la-weh wehpetheh. Tschi!"*

One of the warriors looked down at the girl . . . and raised his tomahawk.

The girl screamed.

Nathaniel jumped up and fired. It was the fastest, truest shot he had ever made. The warrior with the tomahawk fell sideways off the girl, who struggled free of the second Indian's grasp and got to her feet to run.

The leader buried his tomahawk in the back, between the shoulder blades.

A snarl escaping his lips, Nathaniel turned and ran for his life.

The three warriors gave chase, converging on him through the woods, yipping like bloodhounds who have picked up the scent. One of them paused to fire his musket. The bullet smacked into a tree a foot away from Nathaniel's head as he raced by. A splinter gashed his cheek. He sped through the forest, reloading as he ran. Leaping a ravine, he spun around, dropped to one knee, aimed, and fired. One of the Indians clutched at his chest and toppled. Nathaniel was up and running before the dead warrior struck the ground.

He could see the trail now, up ahead. If he could just reach the trail maybe they would not follow him out into the open. A frail hope, certainly, but it was all he had, and he clung to it.

Then he tripped over a root hidden in the thick carpet of leaves, and fell, sprawling.

A war whoop so near it froze the blood in his veins got him back on his feet in a hurry. He whirled. One of the Indians, more fleet of foot than the other, was right on him, charging forward with tomahawk raised.

Nathaniel raised the empty flintlock and blocked the downward stroke of the hatchet. The warrior's impetus carried him past Nathaniel. He turned . . . in time to take the stock of the flintlock square in the face. The stock shattered. The Indian fell, his face a bloody mask. Nathaniel hurled the useless rifle away, wrenched the tomahawk from the grasp of his stunned foe, and with an animal sound welling up out of his throat, buried the hatchet in the warrior's chest.

Another war cry—behind him!

Nathaniel snatched up the dead Indian's musket. Turning, he saw the third warrior stop dead in his tracks, twenty yards away. Nathaniel checked the musket's firing pan. The weapon had been discharged. It was empty! That made his nape hairs crawl.

But it didn't matter. The last Indian looked at his slain colleague at Nathaniel's feet, then at Nathaniel. He shook a fist. *"Wahpahkeh, Shemanese!"* he yelled, by the sound of it a taunt. With that he turned and loped away, heading back to the cabin.

By the time Nathaniel reached the trail he was weak in the knees. He wanted to sit down and be sick. But he forced himself to keep going at a jogging trot.

Amanda saw him coming up the trail from her vantage point on the rimrock, and ran down to meet him. She threw herself into his arms, and he kissed her, squeezing the breath out of her.

"What happened?" she gasped, touching his gashed cheek.

He shook his head. He couldn't speak of it. Not now.

Leading her deep into the woods, he found a good hiding place at the base of the limestone escarpment, in a plum thicket. A spring trickled out a crevice in the rock. There they spent the remainder of the day.

Much later he was able to tell her all that had transpired.

She was silent for a while. Then she said, "Tomorrow we must go bury them."

"No."

"They deserve a decent Christian burial, Nathaniel."

"Leave them where they lay," he said, his voice hollow.

The gray-purple fingers of twilight reached through the thicket. Nathaniel sat with his back against the limestone, arms draped over pulled-up knees, head down. He kept seeing the warrior hurl the infant into the flames, and the girl falling with the tomahawk in her back. He squeezed his eyes shut but the terrible, vivid images would not go away.

"Nathaniel . . ."

He looked at her—looked deep into her eyes, and

as she reached for him he knew what she wanted. It wasn't right, wasn't proper, but he wanted it, too. Kentucky had lost none of its allure, but he realized that there was nothing to be gained by living for tomorrow in this untamed land. Tomorrow would never come for that settler and his family. *And it might not come for me or Amanda*, thought Nathaniel.

They made love there, in the deepening gloom of a summer twilight, and as their young bodies were fused together in a passionate embrace, her soft cries reached into his mind and merged with the echoes of the screams of the dying, and the savage war whoops of the Shawnee warriors.

Chapter 15

They made it the rest of the way to Boonesboro without mishap.

Not far from the settlement they were startled by a lusty voice halloo-ing them from somewhere in the forest. Having not yet fully recovered from the shock of witnessing an Indian massacre, Nathaniel almost jumped out of his skin, and came close to shooting the buckskin-clad man who emerged from the trees.

"Ease down that hammer, friend," said the stranger. "I may be burned red by the sun—it's that dad-blamed Irish complexion of mine—but I'm no redskin, though I've had the great misfortune of living amongst them, against my will, on more than one occasion."

He ventured closer as Nathaniel lowered his musket. He was a tall, broad-shouldered man with a shock of unruly sandy hair, a strong-boned face, and a ruddy complexion, and the clearest shamrock-green eyes Nathaniel had ever looked into.

The man proffered a hand. His grip was like an iron vise.

"The name's Dan'l Boone."

"Daniel Boone!" breathed Nathaniel. "I've heard an awful lot about you, Mr. Boone."

Boone laughed. "Call me Dan'l. *Mister* Boone makes me feel older than I am, which is pretty old. And don't go believin' everything you hear, particularly where it concerns me. I haven't done half the big things they say I have. Wish I could say the same about the bad things. Who are you, if you don't mind my asking?"

"Nathaniel Jones."

"Where you from, Nathaniel?"

"Virginia."

"And your lady friend?"

"Amanda Roberts," she said. "Also from Virginia."

"A good place to be from, if you get my meaning. 'Course, any place east of the mountains is a good place to be from, since there just isn't any elbow room over there nowadays. I never liked livin' where I could see the smoke from my neighbor's chimney, and you can't hardly help that back East, can you?" Glancing at the musket in Nathaniel's possession, he abruptly changed the subject. "Run into Injuns down the trail, by any chance?"

"How'd you know?"

Boone shrugged, grinning. "It's written all over your face, for one thing."

"A few days back. They slaughtered a settler and his family."

Boone's grin faded. "Cabin near the trail?"

"Yes."

"I s'pose that would be Sam Kennedy. All dead? Let's see. Sam had a wife, son, and daughter."

Nathaniel nodded bleakly. "And an infant child."

"Well, I hadn't been by Sam's place for a spell. I reckon it was Shawnee what done it."

"I don't know."

"It was Shawnee," nodded Boone, certain. "How'd you get clear of them?"

Nathaniel told him what had happened, beginning with their seeing the smoke and hearing the sound of the guns. "I killed three of them," he said, in conclusion. "Then I ran like the devil was after me."

"And he was. You did all you could do, by the sound of it, Nathaniel."

Nathaniel morosely shook his head. Doubts still plagued him.

"Yes," said Boone, "and more than most would have done, had they been in your moccasins The musket—can I see it?"

Nathaniel handed it over.

Boone examined the weapon closely. "Where'd you get this?"

"Off one of the Indians. I broke my flintlock over his head."

"This is English made," said Boone grimly. "Were all of them so armed?"

"I think so."

Boone was grim. "This is solid evidence of what I've been saying all along. The bloody British in their forts up north of the Ohio are supplying muskets—powder and shot, too—to their Shawnee allies. Then they pay a bounty for Kentucky scalps. It's a damned dirty way to fight a war. Where you headed, Nathaniel Jones?"

"I'm looking for a man named Hurley."

"James Hurley? The peddler? I know him."

"Have you seen him of late?"

"Only yesterday. He's in Boonesboro as we speak. What's your business with Hurley?"

"He stole our horse."

"A blood bay, by any chance?"

Nathaniel nodded.

Boone chuckled. "That's the horse Hurley is racing today. He came into Boonesboro two days back and commenced to trying to drum up a horse race. Finally found a couple of takers. That's a good-looking thoroughbred. Don't recall when I've seen better. Scared off some folks. But Hurley finally got the odds right. What do you aim to do?"

"Get my horse back."

"Hurley will call you a liar."

"Then we might have a scrape."

Boone laughed at that. "Come on, Nathaniel, I'll walk with you."

Just outside of Boonesboro they passed a man, woman, and two children in a wagon. They had just left the settlement.

"Why the long face, Lucius?" Boone asked the man. "Did you bet against Hurley's racer?"

"Aye. Call me a gold-plated fool if you want to, Dan'l." Lucius glanced at the woman beside him on the wagon seat. "You won't be the first. But the odds were twenty to one."

"A hundred to one would still be poor odds."

"Aye." Again Lucius looked sheepishly at his unhappy wife. "I reckon it's clear enough in hindsight. I thought just maybe I'd get lucky, once in my lifetime. Should've known better."

"Hurley still here?"

Lucius nodded. "In Grinder's place, be my bet. Countin' his ill-got gains."

Boone, Nathaniel, and Amanda pressed on.

They arrived soon in a vast clearing. There were several cabins scattered among fields of corn and tobacco. A pleasing pastoral scene. On the far side of the quarter-mile clearing stood a stockade, with two blockhouses. They bent their steps that way. Passing through the gate, they found the stockade filled with people.

Children were running hither and yon, chased by barking dogs. Laughing men, women visiting with each other—a lot of bustle and tumult. It made Nathaniel long for the tranquil solitude of the forest, Indians and all.

Through the throng they made their way, Boone taking the lead. Almost everyone exchanged greetings with the frontiersman for whom the settlement had been named. Boone asked after Hurley, and several men directed him to the tavern. The race had just been won. Hurley's blood bay had beaten the other two horses by a country mile. The peddler had lured many a man into an ill-advised wager with odds that were hard to resist. Nathaniel looked for the blood bay. But all he saw was a blur of strange faces.

"It's a shame Hurley didn't lose," Boone told Nathaniel. "He'd have lost all his wares, and probably the shirt off his back besides, trying to pay up at twenty to one."

Grinder's tavern was full of frontiersmen. Boone had to shoulder his way through the blocked doorway. Nathaniel turned to Amanda.

"Best wait out here," he said, and followed Boone.

He failed to notice that Amanda didn't heed his advice.

"James Hurley!" called Boone, pushing through the press to one of the split-log tables lined up in the center of the common room.

The peddler was seated at the table, collecting the last of his winnings. He looked up at Boone with a smile of recognition.

"Dan'l, you missed the race!"

Boone smiled affably. "Met a feller on the trail, Hurley. He's come a long way to find you."

Hurley looked past Boone. When he spotted Nathaniel, the smile vanished from his face.

There was shock, then fear mixed with anger in his expression. He stood up quickly. The crowd in the common room fell suddenly silent. Those closest to Hurley could read on his face that something was amiss, and when they looked at Nathaniel they could tell that violence was imminent. Only one man failed to appreciate the sudden hush in Grinder's tavern. In a corner, he was singing a sailor's chanty, and his slurred baritone testified to the fact that he had partaken of too much ale. Someone shut him up in midverse.

"I want my horse back," said Nathaniel, his voice ringing strong and clear.

"I don't . . ." Hurley changed his tack in midsentence. "It's my horse."

"You're a dirty liar."

The tension in the crowd went up a notch. Those were fighting words.

"I bought that bay fair and square in Virginia," said Hurley.

"Got a bill of sale?" came a query from the rough-hewn throng.

"Why, yes . . . somewhere. Truth is, this boy's a thief. He waylaid me on the Wilderness Road. Tried to steal the blood bay. I'm just lucky he didn't cut my throat in the bargain."

"Simon Marcy of Louisa gave me that horse," said Nathaniel.

"Why'd he go and do that?" wondered another spectator.

"Because when the Tory Legion came to Louisa, Nathaniel rode that horse to Charlottesville and warned Governor Jefferson," said Amanda.

Nathaniel whirled. "Amanda, I told you—"

"I'm not your slave, Nathaniel Jones," said Amanda hotly. "So don't bother ordering me around."

A chuckle rippled through the crowd.

"Thanks to Nathaniel, the Tories didn't capture

the governor. But they did kill his father, and my mother. So Mr. Marcy gave Jumper to Nathaniel when he found out we were going overmountain."

There was an excited buzz of discussion among the frontiersmen.

"When did this happen?" asked one doubting Thomas. "I ain't heard nothing about it."

"I'm bringing you the news," said Amanda.

Something about the way she said it made Nathaniel smile. And no one else ventured a comment that sounded like they questioned her word.

"He's a common thief, I tell you," said Hurley. "You should grab hold of him and throw him into the guardhouse."

"I think you and I should settle this between ourselves," said Nathaniel, through clenched teeth. He did not much like being called a thief, least of all by Hurley. "Guns or knives or fists. Your choice."

Boone looked around at the crowd, judging its mood. Two things were immediately apparent to him. One was that the frontiersmen were impressed by what they had seen and heard of Nathaniel Jones.

And there was no love lost in this bunch for James Hurley. It wasn't just because Hurley had won hard-earned money off many of them. Nor was it entirely the fact that some of those present resented Hurley for gouging them with prices on his wares. The peddler took advantage of them, and could get away with it because there were few of his ilk who went to the trouble to cross the mountains. Despite his oft-repeated declaration to the contrary, he charged double what a man would pay for comparable goods back East.

No, the main reason the crowd was inclined to take Nathaniel's side in this matter was that they just plain didn't like Hurley's I'm-better-than-you attitude.

"This is crazy," said Hurley, who had no desire to fight Nathaniel. He was a man who relied on guile, not guns, and he was suddenly afraid of dying. Checking the faces of the buckskin-clad men surrounding him, he found precious little sympathy.

"I have a better idea," said Boone pleasantly. "You just hand that horse over to young Nathaniel here. I think we all know the truth of the matter."

The crowd murmured assent.

"Then you can just be on your way," continued Boone. "But don't come around here anymore."

"I say we tar and feather him," growled someone in the crowd.

A chorus of enthusiastic agreement followed this suggestion.

Boone held up a hand, and the men quieted down.

"We'll let him go. But he leaves the winnings behind. I reckon, it being Nathaniel's horse and all, that money belongs to Nathaniel."

"Now just a minute—!" protested Hurley.

"It's that or accept the man's challenge," snapped Boone.

Hurley looked at Nathaniel. Then he lowered his gaze and nodded acceptance of Boone's conditions.

"I don't want the money," said Nathaniel. "I just came here to get my horse back. You men take your money. Seems to me Hurley took it from you under false pretenses, anyway."

And so it happened. Hurley left Boonesboro in a hurry, leaving Jumper and the money behind.

Daniel Boone talked Nathaniel and Amanda into settling near Boonesboro. He took them to a high meadow not far from his own place—but not too close, either. The soil was rich, there was a creek and year-round spring handy, good timber, and there was a view that in Nathaniel's opinion rivaled the one Thomas Jefferson enjoyed at Monticello. Nathaniel knew the minute he laid eyes on the land that this was what he had in mind.

The good people of Boonesboro showed up in force to help him raise a cabin. It had two rooms with a loft, and both Nathaniel and Amanda were very pleased with it.

A traveling preacher man showed up a fortnight later and presided over their marriage. The preacher was an eccentric character named Luther Brashears, who mumbled to himself constantly in Latin. Boone said it was on account of his experiences as a Shawnee captive—Brashears was a little addled from the torture he had suffered at the hands of those heathens. Nowadays he wandered the wilderness with impunity, the Indians having decided he was touched and keeping their distance as a result.

A couple of months after that, Boone arrived at Nathaniel's door bearing a gift.

A flintlock rifle.

Not just any old rifle. This one was every bit as fine as the one Nathaniel had won in that Louisa county shooting contest—the same one the Tory sergeant-major had taken from him.

"She's got a good pedigree," said Boone. "Made by Henry Leman of Lancaster, 'specially for those what deal with Injuns."

"I can't accept," said Nathaniel.

"Sure, you can. We all pitched in to get it for you. You're a fine shot, Nathaniel. I been out huntin' with you enough to know that's the gospel truth. But that ol' English musket you carry doesn't do you justice. And besides, I've had my eye on that musket."

"You? For what?"

"I want it for evidence that the redcoats are arming the Shawnees. We're gonna win this war, Nathaniel, and when the time comes for treaties and such our leaders have got to know what the British have been doing out here. They've got to make sure the redcoats leave all those forts they've got north of here. Otherwise, the war will *never* end for Kentucky."

Nathaniel accepted the flintlock, and gave Boone the musket.

Boone stayed for dinner. He liked to partake of Amanda's vittles, claiming that next to Rebecca, his wife, she was the best cook west of the Alleghenies. He and Nathaniel talked about the crops Nathaniel would put in. And Amanda took the opportunity to inform Boone that she was expecting. Boone was delighted, and doubly so when they asked him to stand in at the christening as the baby's godfather.

Taking his leave, he turned to wave before plunging into the woods, now aflame with autumn's glorious hues, and seeing Nathaniel and Amanda standing in the doorway of their sturdy cabin, arms around each other, he smiled and nodded to himself.

He figured that with folks like these putting down roots in the dark and bloody ground, there were great things in store for Kentucky.

Winter 1806

Chapter 16

Jonathan Groves arrived at the Executive Mansion very early in the morning. Dawn was slow in coming. The day promised to be overcast, damp, and cold. Jonathan had walked the several blocks from Conrad and McMunn's tavern, where he had stayed the night, and noted with some amusement that Pennsylvania Avenue, designed by L'Enfant and others to be a grand boulevard, was really nothing more than a muddy quagmire.

In fact, he was not at all impressed by the young republic's new federal city. He had expected more . . . well, grandeur. Washington was a swampy village, a collection of several wretched hovels, with the exception of the President's House. He remembered reading that Gouverneur Morris had remarked, with tongue firmly planted in cheek, that Washington was the best city in the world for *future* residence, since all that was lacking were well-built houses, well-stocked kitchens, well-informed men, amiable men, and other trifles.

The climate had something to do with it. Though

Jonathan had never been here before, he had heard that the summers were miserable and the winters even worse. During the former, oppressive heat and swarms of mosquitoes rising up out of the miasmic marshes made life perfectly awful. The winters were singularly cold and wet. It being the end of October 1806, Washington winters evidently came early. It was still a balmy autumn in his southern homeland.

So why had this swampland on the banks of the Potomac been chosen in the first place? As Jonathan, a well-educated young man, understood it, a deal had been struck between Alexander Hamilton, Thomas Jefferson, and James Madison. That was back when Hamilton had been the nation's first secretary of the treasury, and Jefferson its first secretary of state. Hamilton had wanted Virginian support for his Bank of the United States, and the price of getting that support had been his backing of the Virginian proposal that the federal city be located on the Potomac, of considerable commercial and symbolic advantage to the Old Dominion. It was a case of *quid pro quo*. Climate and comfort had played no role in the scheme, apparently.

Reaching his destination, the slender young North Carolinian noticed with dismay that, as circumspect as he had tried to be, his trouser legs below the knees were splattered with black, viscous mud. One tried to be as well groomed as possible when calling upon the president of the United States. Jonathan had donned his best civilian clothes for the occasion. He felt much more at ease in his naval uniform, but had sacrificed personal comfort out of respect for the president's express wishes. Mr. Jefferson did not want it known that a military man was calling on him. Jonathan had no idea why this was. In fact, he hadn't a clue as to why he had been summoned to the President's House.

Since there was nothing he could do about the mud on his trousers, Jonathan consoled himself with the knowledge that the president himself, it was said, did not put much store by appearances. There were some who complained that Jefferson's refusal to attire himself in a presidential manner proved that he had no respect for the high office that he possessed, albeit reluctantly. At least Washington and Adams had recognized the importance of pomp and ceremony, especially in the performance of affairs of state, in enhancing the dignity of the office. But in one of his first acts as chief executive, Jefferson had dispensed with the rather elegant carriage John Adams had donated to the use of his successors, and insisted on going about town on his horse, or in a small cart, or even walking if weather permitted.

And then there was the much-touted business with Anthony Merry, minister to the United States from Great Britain. Jonathan doubted that there was a citizen who did not know of it.

When Merry had arrived to present his credentials to Jefferson, the aristocratic Britisher had worn his most dazzling diplomatic uniform. Jefferson had greeted him clad in threadbare clothes and house slippers. Merry had taken this informality as a deliberate slap in the face. It was common knowledge that Thomas Jefferson had precious little nice to say about the English. Unacquainted with Jefferson beyond that, Merry had been unaware that Jefferson, like so many brilliant men, scarcely wasted a thought on his appearance. And it had not improved Merry's disposition to learn that Jefferson had recently greeted the less thin-skinned Danish minister in a similar condition. In that instance, no offense had been intended or taken.

Even worse, from Merry's perspective, was the dinner at the President's House to which Jefferson invited him and his wife. The Envoy Extraordinary and Minister Plenipotentiary of His Britannic Majesty was shocked to find that the French minister had also received an invitation. This was singularly poor form, since France and England were at war. The Merrys had expected a formal dinner and the place of honor at the table, as befitted their station as representatives of the ranking world power. The table, though, was round, with no head or foot to it, as had been Jefferson's intention. And the President had instituted what he called the rule of *pele mele* which, in plain English, meant that everyone sat where they pleased. Jefferson intended that no individual, regardless of rank, have precedence over another in *his* dining room.

An outraged Merry had furiously protested such incivility to his government. He refused to listen to an amused Jefferson, who tried to enlighten him on a fundamental fact of life in a democracy: Everyone was equal.

Jonathan thought the Merry affair amusing. Others did not. Wars between nations had been instigated by less. Merry was still in Washington, and still fuming. He was not, they said, the kind of man who would forget a slight. No doubt he was plotting revenge.

Reaching the President's House required the ascent of a carriage drive up a rather steep incline to the south entrance. The drive passed beneath a new gate—one of Jefferson's improvements—a triple-arched structure of brick trimmed in stone, with iron pickets in the two smaller side arches. Then the drive made a sharp turn around a row of scraggly trees. There seemed to be some work being done to erect a stone wall around the perimeter, but no one was working yet today. Jonathan wondered if it was because of the furor some Congressmen were stirring up about Jefferson's grandiose—and expensive— plans to improve the mansion. One evening in Conrad and McMunn's common room provided a visitor like Jonathan with all the scuttlebutt.

The president had designed east and west wings to the mansion, the "arch of triumph" gate, and a greenhouse, not to mention numerous interior enhancements. He had contracted Benjamin Henry Latrobe, the famous architect, to oversee the projects. If public economy was so important to Jefferson that he had wanted to do away with the army and navy altogether, asked his detractors, why was he intent on building a palace for the chief executive?

Jonathan held a lieutenant's commission in the navy. He had seen action against the Barbary pirates. So he knew all about Jefferson's scheme to mothball the handful of frigates that flew the American flag and to replace them with a fleet of coastal gunboats. Jefferson, of course, was an isolationist who saw no purpose in financing a powerful navy to patrol the open seas. But it had always seemed to Jonathan to be rather impractical, not to mention naive, to suppose that the United Sates, with its thousand miles of Atlantic coastline, would never need a navy.

Fortunately, the Barbary pirates had forced Jefferson to reconsider dispensing with the navy, and Jonathan was proud to say that the navy had acquitted itself quite well in the war.

Jonathan walked right up to the mansion. A wooden staircase provided access to a narrow balcony, also wooden, that circled the outer wall of the oval saloon. Jefferson had made a habit of opening the doors to the general public, who were invited to tour the state rooms at their leisure. This was a frank expression of republican principles. Jonathan understood that. The president was the servant of the people, and his house was their house.

Still, it didn't seem . . . *proper*, in the young lieutenant's view, that all manner of people could traipse through the President's House at their whim. It struck Jonathan as odd that Jefferson, a wealthy planter aristocrat from Virginia, was a man who often went to extremes to demonstrate those ardently held republican principles of his.

This perspective was colored by Groves's own background. Born into a Wilmington family that had for generations engaged in naval commerce, Jonathan had sailed the high seas as a cabin boy on one of his father's merchant brigs, before acquiring a midshipman's commission in the U.S. Navy. He was accustomed to the strict protocol of life on a seagoing vessel, where the captain was God, and discipline was strict, and every manjack knew his place or suffered for his ignorance.

But as to politics, Jonathan was *blissfully* ignorant. He had grown up during the fierce factionalism between Republican and Federalist, Jeffersonian and Hamiltonian, which had threatened to tear the fledgling republic apart. Spending most of his time on the open seas, the political squabbles of the landlocked held no allure for him. Nowadays, the Republicans held sway. The Federalists' last bastion was the judiciary; John Marshall, the Supreme Court's chief justice was, they said, a thorn in Jefferson's side.

Entering the oval saloon, Jonathan paused to take his first awed look at the interior of the executive mansion. It was, on the whole, an unprepossessing sight. The thirty-by-forty foot chamber was virtually empty. The windows were uncurtained. The carpet underfoot was distinctly ordinary. The eighteen-foot high ceiling only accentuated the emptiness of the room.

Expecting to be greeted by a house servant, Jonathan was quite surprised when the president himself arrived to meet him. Jefferson's long stride brought him swiftly across the room. Confronted by the commander-in-chief, Jonathan saluted reflexively. Jefferson shook his head, smiling, and extended a hand.

"You must be Jonathan Groves," said Jefferson. "It is precisely six o clock, and I was informed of your habitual punctuality."

"Yes, sir."

Jonathan couldn't help himself—he took note of the president's attire while trying not to appear as though he were doing so. Jefferson wore a plain black coat and trousers and an apricot-colored waist-coat, and his cravat was slightly awry. His black shoes wanted polishing, as did their brass buckles. His hair, a sandy red turning gray, was brushed straight back, bunching thickly over the ears and at the collar. His face was strong and severe. His blue-gray eyes alert and friendly.

"I saw you coming from the window of my office," said Jefferson. "I want you to know how grateful I am that you responded so promptly to my summons."

"Well, I . . ." Jonathan was caught off guard. Why was Jefferson *thanking* him? It was his duty to put aside all else and jump when the president sent for him.

"And thank you, as well, for coming in ordinary clothes. I suspect you are curious as to why I asked you not to see me in the uniform which you have, I am told, honored by your exemplary service."

"Well, yes, sir. I am a bit curious about that."

Jefferson's smile tightened a little. The lines at the corners of his eyes deepened.

"All will be made clear to you in time, Lieutenant. Trust me when I say that I have a very good reason. So, tell me, then. Is this your first visit to this house?"

"Yes, sir."

Jefferson looked about him at the room, hands on hips. "It is in my mind to make of this chamber a sitting room. I think the curtains and upholstery and carpet should be blue. Every room should have a character, an identity distinctly its own, don't you agree?" Much to Jonathan's relief, Jefferson did not wait for an answer. "I confess, I love houses and their planning. There are so many things I would like to do to improve this one. It is the grandest house in the country, yet it is an unlikely house for living in, and the changes come slowly. I have recalled Mr. George Andrews from Baltimore to add some decoration to the architraves and cornices of the door. Garlands and wreaths and the like, pleasing to the eye. And I have planned indoor privies—"

"Indoor privies, sir?"

Jefferson laughed softly. "Why, yes. You realize how undignified it would be to force the chief executive to traipse outside in all manner of weather, and in full view of the public, to the presidential outhouse. Come along. I will give you a full tour of the house."

Leaving the oval saloon, they entered the transverse hall. This, noted Jonathan, was plenty large enough to drive a wagon and team through. He was introduced to every room on the principal floor—the formal dining room, the formal sitting room, the private dining room. The vast East Room had been given over to storage. The furnishings were an eclectic mix of French, English, and American pieces, and most of it was approaching shabbiness, with worn upholstery, peeling gilt, and scarred wood. The only art of any consequence was Stuart's portrait of Washington. The major rooms were wallpapered. Some of this, Jefferson pointed out, was a very fine French product, much better than that made in England. The bluish windowpanes were of English crown glass, which had been purchased in large disks from the Baltimore mercantile house of Harrison & Maynadier, which had also provided the brass knobs and hinges on the doors, of which Jefferson approved.

They concluded the tour in Jefferson's office, the West Room. Jonathan was immediately struck by the excellence of the view, down the Potomac River to Alexandria. Daylight entered through towering windows in the west and south walls. Two fireplaces, east and west, hosted blazing log fires, and yet the huge room, twenty by thirty-eight feet, with the usual eighteen-foot ceiling, was still clammy cold.

The office was by far the best-furnished room in

the house, and the one with the most personality. In the center of the room was a long table, with drawers on two sides. There were bookcases and writing tables, chairs painted black and gold. Green baize covered the tabletops. The mahogany floor was bare. Maps and charts and globes were everywhere. The deep window seats were covered with potted plants—roses and geraniums in abundance. In a cage suspended in one of the windows was a mockingbird that, said Jefferson, he had succeeded in taming. He sometimes let the bird fly about the room. Jonathan was glad he did not do so now.

"Such an early appointment may have left you without an opportunity for breakfast," said Jefferson. "If you wish, I will have my cook prepare something for you."

"No, thank you, Mr. President."

"Well, then." Jefferson's smile was gone now. He looked deeply troubled. Jonathan realized he had been putting off unpleasant business with the leisurely tour. "I understand you only recently returned from the Barbary Coast."

"Yes, sir."

"You took an active part in the burning of the *Philadelphia*?"

"Yes, sir."

The USS *Philadelphia*, Captain William Bainbridge commanding, had been captured by the enemy after venturing too close to shore and running aground while participating in the blockade of the Tripoli harbor. The Tripolitans had thrown her crew of three hundred into a dungeon and proceeded to refloat the forty-four-gun frigate. Jonathan had been among the party of eighty sailors, led by the daring Stephen Decatur, that had slipped into the harbor in the dark of night aboard the ketch *Intrepid*, boarded the *Philadelphia*, subdued the Tripolitan crew, and set the frigate afire.

"A remarkable feat," said Jefferson. "I commend you."

"Stephen Decatur deserves the credit, sir. It was his plan. Without his courage and leadership, we could not have succeeded."

"Yet we had to ransom the *Philadelphia*'s crew. Was there no way to rescue them?"

"They would have all been put to death had we attempted a landing, sir."

"Ironic, that we had to pay ransom in a war that was started because we refused to pay tribute to those corsairs to insure safe passage of our merchant ships in the Mediterranean." Jefferson shrugged. "You have served your country well against the Barbary pirates, Lieutenant. I have it on good authority. The secretary of the navy, Robert Smith, has spoken highly of you."

"He is a friend of the family."

"Yes, but I have found his judgment sound on every occasion. I told him I required a man of proven courage. A man whose patriotism is beyond question. Most of all, a man who can keep a secret. He spoke your name."

"I am at your service, Mr. President."

Jefferson sighed. "I want to tell you a story, Lieutenant. It is the story of an extremely intelligent, ambitious, and daring individual. His name is Aaron Burr."

"The vice president?"

"He used to be. Now, I fear, he is a traitor, whose grandiose scheme threatens the very existence of the republic."

Chapter 17

"They wept in the Senate chamber," said Jefferson, without a hint of emotion in his voice, so determined was he to present the narrative to his guest with complete objectivity. "His farewell speech was dignified and deeply affecting, they said. As a measure of their respect for him, the senators afforded him the franking privilege for life—a privilege, I might add, that only George Washington and John Adams have enjoyed."

Jonathan knew something about Aaron Burr. Groves' father had insisted that he put the sea behind him for a few years and attend to his education. Jonathan had reluctantly complied. But he was well read for it, and well versed in the history of his country.

Aaron Burr had been born to a distinguished family. His father had been the esteemed president of the College of New Jersey. His maternal grandfather had been Jonathan Edwards, the famous minister and one of the chief architects of the Great Awakening. Superbly educated, Burr had served in the Revolution with distinction, at Quebec, Monmouth, West Point, and Westchester.

He had gone on to excel as a young attorney at the New York bar. He and Alexander Hamilton were considered the two finest lawyers in the state. Some said the rivalry had begun there, before the New York bar in the 1790s—the rivalry that had led ultimately to that tragic day at Weehawken . . .

At thirty-five years of age, Burr was elected to the United States Senate, defeating Philip Schuyler, Hamilton's father-in-law. A year later, he was in the running for the vice presidency, a rising star in the Republican firmament, the leader of a powerful faction opposed to the aristocratic New York Federalists headed by Schuyler, the de Lanceys, the Van Rennselaers—and Hamilton himself.

Burr had become a political factor to be reckoned with. He was a career politician whose goal, they said, was the highest office in the land. He was politically adroit, urbane, reserved—on the surface, at least, the perfect gentleman. But his foes, Alexander Hamilton principal among them, saw him as man without principle or integrity, a cunning manipulator who had no loyalty but to his own advancement. A man with dangerous ambitions.

In 1792, with Washington persuaded to serve a second term, the contest for the vice presidency was a heated one, since it was supposed that the man who held that office would be the favorite to succeed Washington when he retired to Mount Vernon, as he had sworn he would do in '96. The Federalists wanted John Adams for the job. Jefferson and his Virginian contingent of Republicans bypassed Burr and threw their support behind New York governor George Clinton. Burr had no chance then, and Adams won.

While in the Senate, Burr had been recommended for the post of minister to France. It was said that Hamilton, then Washington's secretary of the treasury, had used all his influence with the president to thwart the nomination. And when Burr sought reelection to the Senate, Hamilton again mustered all the forces at his command in New York to orchestrate Burr's defeat at the hands of none other than Philip Schuyler.

During the presidency of John Adams, when French corsairs plundered over three hundred American ships engaged in trade with Great Britain, Hamilton and other "High" Federalists clamored for war. Adams was dedicated to peace, but he reluctantly authorized the raising of a 10,000-man army. George Washington was lured out of retirement to lead the army. Aaron Burr actively sought a commission as brigadier-general, hoping to become Washington's second-in-command. Instead, Washington chose Hamilton. The result: more bad blood between Alexander Hamilton and Aaron Burr.

So virulent were the Hamiltonians in their thirst for war that they attempted to block peace negotiations between the president's envoys and the French diplomats. To stymie them, Adams threatened to resign. The Hamiltonians had no choice then but to step aside and allow the negotiations to proceed. To do otherwise would result in Vice President Thomas Jefferson's ascension to the post of chief executive, for Adams, determined to avoid a full-scale conflict with France, had every intention of making good his threat. Jefferson as president was Hamilton's worst nightmare; Hamilton was a spokesman for the Federalists, who believed in a strong central government run by the upper class, while Jefferson and his fellow Republicans desired a limited government that would be a servant to the people.

In 1800, Hamilton continued to snipe at Adams, who was seeking reelection. Hamilton penned a pamphlet questioning the president's fitness to hold that office. The pamphlet was designed for private distribution among Federalist leaders. But Aaron Burr acquired one and arranged to have it published in the newspapers. The revelation of such bitter discord in the Federalist ranks served the Republicans well. They wanted Thomas Jefferson to be president, and arranged to have Aaron Burr elected as vice president.

The election of 1800 proved to be a dirty one, as the Federalists depicted Jefferson as an anarchist and an atheist, whose election would result in anarchy, a bloody reign of terror to rival the one that France had suffered a few years before. The election also proved that the method of selecting a president as established in the Constitution was fatally flawed.

The president was selected by electors, who were allowed to cast two votes each, ostensibly one for president and one for vice president. The seventy-three Republican electors split their votes evenly between Jefferson and Burr. Adams, with only sixty-five electoral votes—cast by Federalist electors—was out of the race. The choice of president was thrown into the House of Representatives.

The Republicans expected Burr to announce that he wanted only the vice presidency, and that he would not serve if chosen president. But Burr, so close to the ultimate political prize, refused to settle for second best.

The Federalists perceived Burr to be the lesser of two evils, and a plan was put into action to give the presidency to Burr. But then Hamilton intervened. As much as he disapproved of Jefferson's politics, Hamilton's personal enmity toward Burr ruled him. The Federalist plot to elect Burr was derailed, and when Jefferson promised to refrain from a wholesale removal of Federalists from appointment positions, the Virginian was chosen to occupy the President's House.

Though he was vice president, Burr had alienated the Jeffersonians by his attempt to wrest the presidency from Thomas Jefferson. It was common knowledge from the beginning of his term that the Republicans would replace him in 1804.

Meanwhile, diehard Federalists in New England formed a group called the Essex Junto, and plotted secession from the Union. Better that, they declared, than to live in a republic dominated by Jeffersonians and their principles. The Junto's success depended on taking the powerful state of New York with them. In time they had established clandestine contact with Vice President Burr, who was always ready to lend any scheme his ear if it appeared he might profit from it.

"The plot orchestrated by Thomas Pickering and the Essex Junto," Jefferson told Jonathan Groves, "depended on Burr winning the 1804 election for governor of New York. But again, Hamilton was Burr's undoing. Hamilton exerted all his considerable influence in New York's political circles to insure Burr's defeat. Hamilton called him a dangerous man who could not be trusted with the reins of government.

"I must confess, Hamilton and I seldom agreed on anything. The man's grand design for the republic was a monarchy, and I have no doubt he envisioned himself its king. He once told me that in his opinion Julius Caesar was the greatest man who had ever lived, and he admired Napoleon Bonaparte, in spite of the fact that Bonaparte is emperor of the French. But in this case, I found myself in complete agreement with Hamilton. Burr *is* a dangerous man. His ambition makes him so."

"It is little wonder that they fought a duel," said Jonathan. "It seems almost . . . preordained."

"A foolish, tragic way to settle differences," lamented Jefferson.

Following his defeat in the New York gubernatorial contest, Aaron Burr had challenged Alexander Hamilton to a duel. While he disapproved of dueling in principle, Hamilton accepted the challenge. On July 11, 1804, the two met at Weehawken. Each man fired once. Hamilton's friends claimed he discharged his pistol into the air, having no intention of killing Burr. Burr's aim was true, and his intent was murder. Mortally wounded, Hamilton died the next day.

Alexander Hamilton lost his life at Weehawken, yet Aaron Burr lost everything *but* his life. Indicted in New York and New Jersey, his political career was ruined.

"At least," said Jonathan, "the scheme of the Essex Junto came to naught. The Union is secure."

"Secure? Lieutenant, it is not at all secure. You may not know this, but the Junto was in communication with none other than Andrew Merry."

"The British minister?"

"The same. I have it on good authority that Merry promised to aid the secession. Great Britain has long entertained the notion of dividing our republic. The Spanish, too, have intrigued to acquire the region west of the Alleghenies."

"The settlers in the west would never willingly accede to Spanish rule," exclaimed Jonathan, shocked. "Or British rule, either, for that matter. Would they, sir?"

"Perhaps not. But they are an independent sort. In 1796, Kentucky had her own secession movement. The purchase of Louisiana Territory put an end to that."

"A magnificent achievement, Mr. President."

Jefferson chuckled. "I wish I could take credit for

it. When I sent Livingston and Monroe to Paris to negotiate with Bonaparte I had no idea that Talleyrand would ask them how much we would pay for the entire Territory. It was New Orleans we had to have. The commerce of our western states depended on that port, which the Spaniards had closed to our use out of sheer spite.

"Truth be known, I feared that Bonaparte would attempt to establish his dominion over Louisiana. Had he done so, we would have been forced to ally ourselves with the British, and I would rather make a pact with the devil himself. Fortunately for us, Bonaparte was having a difficult time holding onto his sugar islands in the Caribbean, thanks to Toussant L'Ouverture and his rebels. So he gave up the idea of a New France in North America, and sold the entire Territory to us. He needed funds to wage his war against Great Britain. Livingston sealed the bargain without wasting time communicating the offer to me. As he should have. The credit belongs to him."

"Fifteen million for a continent! A bargain at the price, I would say, sir."

"Well, almost four million went to pay American claims against France for the losses incurred to the French privateers. As to what we purchased, we know so little! My first thought upon hearing from Livingston was that we had bought a wilderness to acquire a port." Jefferson gazed pensively out the west windows of the office. "I have sent my personal secretary, Meriwether Lewis, to explore the western lands. He is ably assisted by William Clark, younger brother of General George Rogers Clark. They have been gone the better part of two years. What a splendid adventure! Had I been twenty years younger, I would have gone with them."

He turned his attention back to Jonathan. "But the westerners are exasperated to the point of violence with the Spaniards, Lieutenant. The Spaniards have incited the Indians in the south to attack our isolated settlements. In fact, they have been engaged in this heinous activity for better than fifty years now.

"And there is more to it. A spirit runs deep in our people—a spirit of expansion. The Floridas and Mexico, they say, should belong to us. Indeed, the whole continent should be 'revolutionized.' Yes, I am certain that there are some who even cast their covetous eyes upon British Canada. The republic should stretch from sea to sea, in their opinion. It is the American destiny. I sense a conviction among our people that war with Spain is inevitable."

"But can one nation contain a land so vast?" wondered Jonathan.

"Indeed, there's the question," said Jefferson, nodding. "I sometimes have my doubts on that score."

"Did not Aaron Burr propose an invasion of the Floridas and Louisiana many years ago?"

"Yes, and the idea, I'll wager, is still with him. After the duel at Weehawken, Burr traveled west. There remains out there a strong sentiment for him—a sentiment made stronger by his killing Alexander Hamilton. You see, the westerners are of the opinion that their best interests come second to those of the eastern states. I fear that perception is rooted in the events of the Revolution. I know that when I served as governor of Virginia the Kentuckians pleaded for military aid which I could not provide them. They were beset by hostile Indians, who were being manipulated by the British. Now the westerners speak often, and bitterly, of eastern domination in affairs both political and economic."

"As I understand it," said Jonathan, "the British are still supplying the Indians with guns and ammunition. Were they not supposed to evacuate their forts in the Northwest?"

"So much for the Treaty of 1783. And much has been made of the sale of public lands. Our government depends on those sales for revenue. Yet the settlers cry 'squatter's rights.' But again, I stray from the point of it all. Burr has toured the west. He recently returned and, if rumors are right, contacted the British minister."

"Andrew Merry again!"

Jefferson nodded. "Through Merry's aide, a man named Peter McLeod. Do you know the name?"

"No, sir."

"He was born in England, but once owned a plantation in the Carolinas. He was Loyalist during the war, and served with the Tory Legion."

"Tarleton's butchers!"

"He commanded the squadron which almost captured me at Monticello in 1781. After the war he fled to England. Now he's back."

"It strikes me as an intended insult that he has been assigned to Merry."

"I have no doubt that it is. Yet to protest would be useless."

"But why has Burr contacted the British minister?"

"For funds."

"Funds? To what purpose, Mr. President?"

"I believe in order to effect the severence from the Union of those states beyond the Allegheny Mountains, and an invasion of Mexico in the bargain."

Jonathan was aghast.

"I have evidence," said Jefferson.

Chapter 18

"I have three documents in particular," continued Jefferson. "I will show them to you in the strictest confidence. You must be apprised of every aspect of this situation if you are to serve as my agent, and I believe that I can trust you. After all, you have demonstrated a willingness to give your life for your country."

As the president went to his desk, Jonathan Groves shifted uncomfortably in his chair. He had the feeling he was in over his head. He had the urge to respectfully inform Mr. Jefferson that he had no desire to involve himself in such a desperate affair. It wasn't the danger—though it sounded dangerous enough. Rather, it was the sheer scope and impact that overwhelmed the young naval officer.

He watched apprehensively as Jefferson frisked himself for a small key lodged in one of the pockets of his coat. With this key the president unlocked one of the desk drawers and brought forth some papers.

"You may be acquainted with William Eaton, Lieutenant."

"Yes, sir."

William Eaton had been appointed consul to Algiers by President John Adams. In 1804, Jefferson had made him the United States Naval Agent to the Barbary States. Eaton had plotted to overthrow the pasha of Tripoli and replace him with his brother who, in exchange for American aid, had promised better relations between the United States and Tripoli, at a time when relations between the two countries could hardly have been worse. The coup failed, however, and Eaton had blamed the American fleet, with which Jonathan had been serving, for the failure, for it had not supported the land-based expedition. Eaton then petitioned the government for reimbursement of his out-of-pocket expenses in the venture.

"I refused to sanction payment to Eaton for his expenses," said Jefferson. "The affair was of his own design."

"There was talk," added Jonathan, "that had he succeeded in replacing the old pasha with a new one, he would have resigned his position with this government and become the commander-in-chief of the Tripolitan army. Not to mention the pasha's most trusted counselor."

Jefferson grimaced. "The man behind the throne? It seems Burr has been communicating with a number of gentlemen who, for one reason or another, harbor hard feelings towards me or my administration. One of them is Eaton. It is a complicated scheme. If war were to break out with Spain, Burr would be ready with an army of invasion to seize Mexico. And, apparently, General Wilkinson, whom I recently appointed to the command of our forces in Louisiana, is in the pot, too. Burr has been in secret correspondence with Wilkinson for some time, devising means by which Wilkinson might surreptitiously instigate such a war.

"As to Eaton, he was assured by Burr that this plan was under the authority of my administration. Burr offered him command of a division in the invasion army. If the invasion were to succeed, Burr would establish an empire in Mexico and divide the Union. He assured Eaton that within a year's time he could incite an insurrection in the valley of the Mississippi."

"Mr. Eaton told you this, sir?"

"Yes. At first, verbally. I later persuaded him to make a deposition to that effect. Here is it."

Jefferson handed the document to Jonathan and moved to the window where the caged mockingbird was singing. The president was silent for a while, enjoying the bird's sweet symphony, and giving Jonathan time to read what William Eaton had written.

"This is . . . unbelievable," said Jonathan when he had finished reading.

"Wilkinson's duplicity comes as no surprise to me," said Jefferson. "He was one of the leaders of the Kentucky secession movement in '96, remember."

"I have heard that he is also a paid agent of the Spanish."

"Have you? So have I. I daresay this affair is the subject of conversations in every common room from Boston to Savannah."

"There seem to be a lot of rumors floating around," mused Jonathan. "And a lot of men involved whom one would be a fool to trust. How can you be sure that what Eaton has written here is true? How do you decide who to believe, Mr. President?"

"There's the rub," agreed Jefferson, and handed Jonathan a letter. This one was from General Wilkinson, and was recently dated.

Jonathan read:

A numerous and powerful Association, extending from New York to the Mississippi, has been formed to levy and rendezvous Eight or Ten Thousand Men in New Orleans & from thence to carry an expedition against Vera Cruz.

It is unknown under what Authority this Enterprize has been projected, from whence the means of its support are derived, or what may be the intentions of its leaders in relation to the territory of New Orleans.

The Magnitude of the Enterprize, the desperation of the Place, and the stupendous consequences with which it seems pregnant, stagger my belief & execute doubts of the reality, against the conviction of my Senses, & it is for this reason I shall forbear to commit Names. I have never in my whole Life found myself in such circumstances of perplexity and Embarrassment as at present; for I am not only uninformed of the prime mover and Ultimate Objects of this daring Enterprize, but am ignorant of the foundation on which it rests.

I have been assured that you connive at the combination and that our country will justify it. If this be not true, then I have no doubt the revolt of this Territory will be made an auxiliary step to the main design of attacking Mexico.

"I am surprised," said Jonathan, having finished Wilkinson's letter, "that you have not replaced the general."

"At present he is of more value to me at his post."

"May I speak freely, Mr. President?"

"Please."

"I would not be surprised if General Wilkinson *was* in the pay of the Spanish. Doubtless he foresaw the unlikelihood of an expedition into Mexico succeeding. His best interests lay in foiling such a scheme. That way, he could continue to receive his Spanish stipend, and then portray himself to you and his country as a patriot and a hero. He had everything to lose by joining Burr, and everything to gain by betraying him."

Jefferson nodded approvingly. "Secretary Smith was right to recommend you. You have the knack for clear logic, and for reading between the lines."

"The general's letter is as valuable for what it doesn't say—"

"Precisely. He takes me for a fool. Burr concluded

his tour of the west with a visit to New Orleans. Have you ever heard of the Mexican Association?"

"No, sir."

"A group of wealthy businessmen in New Orleans, some three hundred in number, who are devoted to 'liberating' Mexico. Which means, of course, acquiring the region so that they could profit through exploiting its abundant natural resources."

"There are very rich gold and silver mines in Mexico, aren't there?"

"Indeed. Among the association members are Mayor John Watkins and Judge James Workman. They are eager to befriend Burr, and no doubt promised him the full measure of their assistance."

"And the third document, sir?"

Jefferson handed it over.

"A letter from Colonel George Morgan. The veracity of which is attested to, as you can see by the signature at the bottom, by the chief justice of Pennsylvania. Colonel Morgan and his sons reside in a settlement on the Monongahela. Burr visited the colonel, who has been outspoken in his condemnation of our public-lands policy. In the letter, Morgan testifies that Burr spoke of me and my administration with contempt. Morgan may be critical of my policies, but he is loyal to the republic. And Burr's contempt for me is understandable, considering the circumstances. I could readily forgive him for such harsh judgment. But, according to Morgan, Burr went on to say . . . well, you can read it for yourself."

"My God!" breathed Jonathan, leaning forward in

his chair. " 'Burr stated to me that two hundred men could drive the Government into the Potomac, and that with five hundred New York could be taken. At the very least, the Western States could be detached from the Union, and would be the better for it.' "

Aghast, Jonathan looked up at Jefferson. He suddenly felt the utmost sympathy for the president. Thomas Jefferson was a man of peace. A philosopher, not a fighter. Ambitious, ruthless men were apparently scheming to destroy the republic that Jefferson had labored so diligently and brilliantly to create—and he was ill equipped to deal with them.

"This *is* treason!" exclaimed Jonathan. "You must have Aaron Burr arrested."

Jefferson nodded gravely—and, thought Jonathan, a little sadly, too.

"I suppose I must. But I need more evidence."

"More?" Jonathan held up the letters. "Here is your evidence."

"At best, hearsay, and dubious sources in the case of Wilkinson, and perhaps Eaton. Do not be deceived, Lieutenant. There are many men who hold Aaron Burr in high esteem. He has pulled the wool over the eyes of our western citizens, with his talk of driving the Spaniards into the sea, and hinting that his plan is sanctioned by this government. If I have him arrested and charged with treason and brought before the court I must have irrefutable proof. There must be no doubt as to his guilt. Because a Federalist—perhaps even Chief Justice Marshall himself—will most surely preside over those proceedings. And any Federalist judge would do all in his power to embarrass me by setting Burr free."

"I see," said Jonathan, subdued.

"Yes. Marshall seeks vengeance for my attempt to impeach Judge Chase."

Jonathan nodded. During the Adams presidency, Federalist judges like Samuel Chase had used the Alien and Sedition Acts to jail Republican newspapermen who dared criticize the administration. Assuming the presidency, Jefferson had tried to impeach Chase, hoping to drive the Federalists from their judicial stronghold. He had failed in the impeachment, but succeeded in exacerbating bitter warfare between the executive and judicial branches of government.

"What can I do?" asked Jonathan.

Jefferson moved to a long table covered with charts. He motioned Jonathan over. Spreading out a map, he pointed to a spot on the Ohio River, near its confluence with the Little Kanawha.

"Here there is an island. It is owned by a man named Blennerhasset. I know little about him, except that he is Irish, has money, and is said to be rather eccentric. He resides there on the island in a mansion which I am told is quite extraordinary."

"But that's in the middle of the wilderness," said Jonathan.

"As I said, he is an eccentric. He has fallen in with Burr. It is possible that Burr has stockpiled arms on Blennerhasset's island. He is also collecting a fleet of flatboats there, if my information is correct."

"You want to confirm those rumors."

"I do. If necessary, offer your services to Burr. Gain his confidence."

"Mr. President, you are asking me to present myself as a traitor to my country!"

Jefferson smiled. "The men who rally round Burr consider themselves patriots. I am convinced that most of them sincerely believe they are volunteering for an expedition against the Spaniards in Mexico—an expedition sanctioned by my administration. Only a handful of Burr's most trusted associates are acquainted with his true motives."

"I see," said Jonathan, dubious.

"Confirm that Burr is amassing weapons and provisions at Blennerhasset's estate. That is all I need to know."

"Then you will have him arrested?"

Jefferson crossed the room to his desk. He returned with a sealed envelope, which he presented to Jonathan.

"I will have *you* arrest him, Lieutenant."

"Me?"

"Here is your authorization to do so, by my hand. This letter renders unto you the fullest cooperation of all military and civilian officials who by their circumstances must answer to me. The letter also requests that every true patriot give you all the assistance it is within their power to give."

Jonathan realized that while the letter had its

worth, it could also be his death warrant, were it found on his person by Burr or one of his fellow conspirators.

"May I rely on you, Lieutenant?" asked Jefferson solemnly.

His throat quite dry, Jonathan said, "Of course, Mr. President."

"I knew I could from the moment I saw you. This is a dangerous task which I have given you, sir. But bear it always in mind that your country is depending on you."

"I will, sir."

"I have but one more thing to give you. It is the name of a man, a Virginian by birth, a Kentuckian now. He is a man I met but once. Yet I know you may depend on him. His name is Nathaniel Jones, though he is better known by some these days as Flintlock Jones."

Jefferson returned to the window where the caged mockingbird was still singing. "Once you leave this house, Lieutenant, you will step into a world of intrigue and betrayal. You will not know who to trust. But I believe Jones is one man you *can* trust."

"Begging your pardon, sir, but how can you be sure of that if you've met him only once? Have you corresponded with him?"

"I have kept track of him. He has earned quite a reputation as an Indian fighter. But I wrote him one time, a few months ago. Admittedly, I have yet to receive a reply."

That left Jonathan completely unconvinced that

this Flintlock Jones merited his trust, but he made no comment.

"I am sure of him," Jefferson said. "You see, many years ago, he was engaged in an heroic undertaking much like yours. Everything hung in the balance then, as it does now."

Jefferson turned to face Jonathan. "He resides near Boonesboro. If you need help, Nathaniel Jones is the man to turn to."

Jonathan stepped forward and saluted briskly. As he brought his hand down, Jefferson grasped it and shook it.

"Good luck, Lieutenant."

"I won't fail you, sir, or my country. I will bring you Aaron Burr, in irons."

Chapter 19

The house where the British minister to the United States resided was not far from the President's House. It was a two-story structure, part brick, part frame, and it had obviously been erected in a hurry. The lumber used had been green, with the result that now the house leaked like a sieve. It was impossible to keep the house warm in winter, even with all the roaring fires in all the hearths.

The house had been built by a High Federalist who, upon leaving Washington on the heels of John Adams, fleeing the onslaught of the Jeffersonians, had deeded the house to the British government for precisely the purpose it now served. Minister Merry had contracted for a stables and carriage house to be built behind the main house, adjacent to the kitchen. The outbuildings had then been encompassed by a wall that, for the most part, was made of freestone from the Aquia Creek quarry forty miles downriver from the federal city. Stone from that same quarry had been used in the construction of the executive mansion. The stone wall had not been completed; Merry and the contractor had quarreled about its quality. A rather crude stockade of upright poles had finished the enclosure.

Merry and his wife resided in the upstairs rooms of the main house. The downstairs, a hallway and four spacious parlors, were given over to the conduct of ministerial affairs.

On the morning that Lieutenant Jonathan Groves visited Thomas Jefferson, a nondescript individual in seedy, mud-splattered clothes came calling at the Merry residence. He was a man of slight build and indeterminate age. His features—pointed chin, pouchy cheeks, beady eyes—had a sly cast to them. Major Peter McLeod thought he bore resemblance to a ferret. All in all, he was the kind of man one would be unlikely to pick out of a crowd; one would be equally hard pressed to remember much about the man an hour after meeting him on the street. Which, McLeod supposed, was an advantage for him, considering the kind of work he did under the auspices of His Majesty's government.

His name was Dabney Brown, an ordinary name for an ordinary-looking fellow who performed quite an extraordinary job. A thief by trade, he had of late served the British as a spy.

McLeod arrived at Merry's house shortly after Brown. He had ridden from his quarters in a boardinghouse on Massachusetts Avenue. The doorman, one of Merry's personal retainers, informed him that

Brown was waiting in the front parlor. When McLeod limped into the room, he found Brown at the sideboard, helping himself to the Madeira in one of the crystal decanters located there.

"Hope you don't mind, Major," drawled the spy. "Thought I'd just help myself. I been standing out in that cold wind since before dawn."

"Help yourself." McLeod unfastened his greatcoat and draped it over the back of a wing chair, placing his shako atop it. He inspected his uniform for mud. Every street in this godforsaken place was a disgraceful quagmire. It was damned difficult keeping one's clothes from being soiled in this filthy town.

McLeod was proud of his uniform, that of an officer in the 7th Royal Fusiliers. He liked the looks he got from these rebels—he still thought of United States citizens as such—when they caught a glimpse of his red single-breasted surtout with its blue facings and gold lace. With the Federalists out of power, Britishers received a rather cool reception in most quarters of the federal city. McLeod figured he would get even uglier looks had the people known of his service with Tarleton's Tory Legion during the war.

He sat heavily in one of the chairs in the well-appointed room. Merry had brought some very fine furnishings over with him. McLeod noticed that Brown had tracked mud across the Wilton Carpet. And the spy was about to deposit himself in one of the brocaded chairs.

"Don't sit down," rasped McLeod. "The minister would have your head."

Brown shrugged, knocked back the Madeira, and grinned at McLeod. It wasn't a pretty sight, that grin. What teeth Brown had left were crooked and yellowed.

"Noticed you were limping pretty bad there, Major. Wouldn't be on account of John Raymond's wife, now would it?"

McLeod was grinning now—a wolfish grin. "My God, Brown, you're a cheeky sort."

"So are you, Major, if you don't mind my saying so."

"Oh, I do mind. But it wouldn't make any difference to an obnoxious, loose-tongued rogue like you."

"I am all of that," agreed Brown, pleased. "Which is why you like me."

"I don't like you. I think you are useful."

"Well, you're plenty cheeky, too. Having an affair with a married woman. And not just any married woman, mind you. Oh, no. This one is the wife of an official of the United States government. John Raymond works in the War Department, I believe."

"Indeed." McLeod affected an air of bored indifference.

"You see," said Brown, with a sly wink, "there isn't much goes on around here that escapes my attention."

"I limp," said Mcleod, with cool disdain, "because

a piece of shrapnel is lodged very near the bone in my hip. It is a wound I received seven years ago, to the month, at Bergen. It pains me particularly on cold, damp days such as this one."

"Bergen? Where's that?"

"The Netherlands. It was during one of the wars against Bonaparte. They're calling it the War of the Second Coalition these days, to distinguish from the others, I suppose. In fact, it's really just one big war. The purpose of which is to remove that bloody Corsican from the palace at Versailles. It's still going on—the war, I mean—and I would much prefer being in it than sitting here."

"You like war, don't you, Major?"

"I'm good at it. We all have our talents, don't we? You are adept at prying into the private affairs of others."

"Yes, I am. Very good. Did you win?"

"Eh?"

"At Bergen. You strike me a a man who very much hates to lose."

"We won the second battle. Not the first. The Duke of York lost that one for us. Since the first one did not go so well, we thought we'd try it again. We were up against Brune and his Frenchmen. We had some Russians with us. Very brave, those Russians, but not very bright. Good cannon fodder, though. Yes, we won the second battle of Bergen, but it was all for naught. Brune checked us again at Castricum four days later. Twelve days after that the diplomats signed the Convention of

Alkmaar. A month later, Bonaparte staged his coup and made himself First Consul of France, and we had another war. I missed most of that one, being laid up in hospital. It really wasn't much of a war. Bonaparte annihilated the Austrians at Marengo. The Austrians sued for peace, which left us on our own, since the Russian Tsar had decided he didn't like the British, and was fashioning his bloody League of Armed Neutrality."

"Why are you here, Major? We have no war here."

"Not at the moment. I'm here because I was ordered here."

Brown was leering at him. "Could it be because you were a Tory?"

"Adam and Eve were cast out of the Garden of Eden because they knew too much."

Brown chuckled. "I didn't know you were a religious person, Major McLeod."

"Why don't you get on with telling me what you have learned?"

"Mind if I get another drink first?"

McLeod gestured toward the sideboard. As Brown poured himself another generous dollop, McLeod stretched out his left leg, wincing at the gnawing ache in his hip.

"I'm getting old," he muttered.

"You look in fighting trim to me," said Brown.

"Getting old. I should have died a long time ago, on some bloody battlefield-turned-boneyard."

"That syphilis will kill you before too much longer, I suspect."

"You bastard."

Brown shrugged, knocked back the Madeira. Watching him, McLeod had a sudden thought: Dabney Brown, in spite of his down-at-heels appearance and crudity, was a very erudite man. Not just cunning. Intelligent. A keen mind, extremely observant, with excellent nerves. Cunning, yes— Brown had lured him into talking about himself, something he rarely did, and he was just now realizing it.

He wondered, too, if there was anything about anyone in this city that Brown didn't know.

"A man paid a call on the president at dawn," said Brown. "He was in the President's House for almost two hours. Then he returned to his boardinghouse. Conrad and McMunn's tavern."

"Who is he?"

"Jonathan Groves. Lieutenant, United States Navy. Been serving with the Mediterranean fleet, fighting those Barbary pirates. Robert Smith, the Secretary of the Navy, is well acquainted with his father, a prosperous merchant of naval stores in Wilmington."

"I see. Is that all?"

"Certainly not. I earn my money. Groves called on the president dressed in civilian clothes."

"Indeed. How interesting."

"I thought so.'"

"He still holds a commission?"

"I believe he does. I can find out for certain."

"Anything else?"

"He arrived by coach yesterday. He is looking for a horse to buy."

"So he came for the express purpose of seeing Jefferson."

"Yes. As though he were summoned."

"Where do you suppose the lieutenant is off to, Brown?"

"West. I don't suppose it. As I say, Groves wanted to buy a horse. So naturally he went to see James Rooney. He mentioned to Rooney that he needed a sturdy mount, as he was going overmountain. But Rooney would not sell one of his horses. Not at first. He makes too much renting them out. That's when Lieutenant Groves made his mistake."

"Mistake?"

"He read from a letter he carried on his person."

"Were you standing right there?"

"I was close enough to hear everything that was said. Of course, they did not see me."

"Of course not."

"The letter was by Jefferson's hand. In it, Jefferson requests all citizens to give the lieutenant any assistance he might ask for."

McLeod leaned forward. "Did this man Rooney actually read the letter?"

"The lieutenant showed him only the signature. As I said, he read from the letter. Rooney was persuaded. He sold Groves a horse."

McLeod got to his feet. "There is no time to lose."

"What's it all mean, Major?"

"I'm surprised you don't know."

"Might it have something to do with Aaron Burr?"

"You're entirely too clever for your own good."

"I know you don't mean that as a threat."

"Are you certain?"

"I'm certain that Burr has been communicating with Mr. Merry, through you. I know that Burr is west of the mountains even as we speak, planning some kind of mischief. But then, that's common knowledge, isn't it? Tavern talk centers on little else these days. And I know Lieutenant Groves clearly possesses an important and confidential commission from the president himself, and that he is heading west to carry out that commission."

McLeod went to the chair over which he had draped the greatcoat. Returning to Brown, he tossed the spy a small pouch. Brown caught it handily, and smiled at the sound of coins clinking together.

"Gold sovereigns?"

"Of course," said McLeod.

"You are extremely generous, Major."

"You don't get to keep it all. I want you to find me three men. Cutthroats, who don't mind getting their hands bloody. I am confident that you know such men."

"Sure, I do. What do I tell them?"

"Tell them to come see me. You need know nothing else. Pay them out of what you have there. Strike a hard bargain, as you'll keep what's left."

"Is there killing involved? I must know, as it will affect the price."

"Yes."

Brown shrugged. "Killers come cheap."

"They must be capable."

"Of course. I know men who would cut their own mother's throat for a single crown."

"Find them quickly. I want to see them in an hour's time."

"Here?"

"No. At the corner of this street and Massachusetts Avenue should do."

"Dealing in murder on a street corner, Major?"

"Where better? Walls have ears—don't they, Brown?"

Brown nodded. He glanced longingly at the decanter of Madeira, but thought better of asking the major if he could have one drink for the road. He consoled himself with the knowledge that he could buy all the Madeira he could drink in a month's time with what McLeod had paid him. So he put down the empty glass and, giving the major a jaunty salute, started for the door.

There he paused, and looked back.

"It's the young lieutenant you're going to have them kill, isn't it, Major?"

"Do you really want to know?"

Something in the way McLeod said that made Brown purse his lips and shake his head.

"No, I guess not. It's been a pleasure doing business with you."

"In the end," muttered McLeod, after Dabney Brown had left the parlor, "you will not think so."

Chapter 20

The house servant who answered the door at the Raymond house took one look at Major McLeod, and a fierce scowl crossed her ebony features.

"What you want here?" she demanded, blocking the doorway, fists planted on wide hips, chin jutting defiantly, and her eyes shooting daggers.

McLeod's smile was as cold as the wind tugging at his greatcoat.

"Is Mrs. Raymond in?"

"No, she ain't home."

"Celia, who is it?"

This query came from somewhere inside the two-story brick house. The sultry female voice with its honey-sweet southern accent stirred the blood in McLeod's veins.

"Lies and discourtesy both," murmured McLeod, piercing Celia with a glare that was filled with both disdain and reproach. "Nothing a little discipline wouldn't cure."

She was afraid of him, and tried to hide it, but there was something about this man, with his scarred face—a dark and violent something coiled just beneath the debonair surface. Celia was a superstitious woman, and she believed that evil walked the land, and McLeod was proof of that. She stepped aside, and he crossed the threshold, handing her his shako, shedding his greatcoat and giving her that, too.

Jane Raymond was coming into the hall from the front parlor. Recognizing McLeod, she beamed with a breathtaking radiance. McLeod decided she was the prettiest woman he had ever seen—and he had seen a great many—with her lustrous chestnut hair in ringlets on alabaster shoulders, her captivating hazel eyes in a pert round face with perfect features and perfect peaches-and-cream complexion. Her voluptuous figure was encased in a dress of purple organdy, its low-cut neckline accentuated with lace ruffles, and the high waistline displaying to seductive effect her full breasts and long legs.

Being a man ruled by his passions and unfettered by any concern for decorum, McLeod moved to take her in his arms, but at the last minute Jane remembered herself and gave him a look that spoke volumes about discretion. By turning to Celia she foiled his rough embrace—or at least postponed it.

"Thank you, Celia. That will be all."

"Yessum," muttered the house servant, and headed down the hall, throwing a single hostile glance over her shoulder at McLeod.

"Spare the rod, spoil the slave," said McLeod, loud enough for her to hear.

"Now, Peter," said Jane Raymond. "Celia's been with me all my life. Heavens, she's raised me from the cradle."

"A good lashing would cure her insolence."

Jane made a face. "Oh, I never could."

She took him by the hand and pulled him into the well-appointed parlor. Shutting the pocket doors, she turned—right into his arms. He crushed her lips with a hard and passionate kiss. His hands roamed boldly, his body pressing insistently against hers. She pushed him away, squirmed out of his grasp, and escaped, laughing breathlessly, her cheeks flushed.

"You're a bold man, Major."

"That's one of the things that attracts you to me, isn't it?"

"You really shouldn't have come here," she said, pretending to scold him. "People will talk."

"Let them."

"It is evident that you care nothing for my reputation."

"I haven't exactly forced you into my bed against your will."

"Perhaps you should leave."

He moved to her with quick strides. "Don't put on airs with me. You like the adventure. You enjoy taking risks. You're no lady, so don't pretend to be one."

She slapped him—or tried to. He was quicker, grabbing her wrist before her hand had reached his face. He twisted the wrist and she fell onto a camel-back sofa. Before she could catch her breath he was on top of her. She fought him at first, but it was really just a token resistance. He was rough, but that excited her. Their lovemaking was fast and furious, and she buried her face in his chest to stifle her scream of ecstasy—it simply wouldn't do to have Celia come running in to find them this way. Not that she labored under delusions about what Celia knew or didn't know. But still . . .

When they were done McLeod stood up and quickly adjusted his clothes. He limped to the cabinet where Raymond kept his liquor, and poured himself a glass of whiskey. He didn't ask for her permission to avail himself of these stores, or if she wanted a spot of sherry. It was still morning, and he assumed she did not indulge at such an early hour.

"Why do you stay with him?" he asked, his back to her.

Sitting primly on the edge of the sofa, patting at her hair, she said, "He is my husband."

"But you don't love him."

"No, I never have. I didn't love him when we were wed."

"So why did you marry him?"

"Because he loved me."

"Is that all there was to it?"

"Not all. It was . . . an arrangement. I was with child. Not his. He offered to marry me, to save me from disgrace. I accepted, to save my family from embarrassment."

He turned. "I didn't know."

"Very few people do." She lifted her shoulders, an

indolent shrug. "I lost the child. But by then the marriage was a *fait accompli*."

"And you won't leave him?"

"Certainly not."

"Not for me?"

"Not for anyone. Especially not for you, Peter. Oh, does that hurt your feelings?"

"Don't flatter yourself."

She laughed. "Besides, you really don't love me. You desire me. You want me because I belong to someone else. But were I free to be yours, you would no longer want me."

McLeod thought it over. "You are probably right."

"I know I am."

"I want you to do something for me."

"What is it?"

"Can you get away? I mean by that, can you tell your husband that you are going to visit friends in the country, or something to that effect, and be gone for a day or two?"

"I suppose. What did you have in mind?"

"Not what you think, my dear. This is business."

"Business? What is its nature?"

"Your father was a Tory, wasn't he?"

"You know that he was."

"What is your opinion of President Jefferson?"

"I despise him, as you well know." She was on her feet now, walking restlessly, aimlessly, about the room. "As governor of Virginia, Jefferson ordered the confiscation of all property belonging to Loyalists. They took virtually everything my father had worked so hard all of his life to acquire, and then sold it to finance their rebellion. But my father never surrendered to fate. He refused to be run out of the country. It was his country, he would say, as much as the rebels'. He stood fast, and survived the abuse and contempt that they heaped upon him, and he started all over again after the war. Still, he died an untimely death, and I am convinced that it is the result of the hardship he endured at the hands of the rebels—Jefferson being chief among them."

"Then I suppose you would jump at the chance to strike back at Jefferson."

"What do you think?"

"There is a young man, a naval lieutenant named Groves, who is bound for Kentucky on a mission of vital important to Jefferson. I want him stopped."

"Why?"

"Take my word for it, Jane—he must be stopped."

"So what would you have me do?"

He limped across the room to her, stroked her cheek. "Play the damsel in distress. And such a comely damsel you are, too. Lieutenant Groves could not fail to stop and render you aid."

"I'm not sure I understand . . ."

"A trap, darling. An ambuscade, if you will. And you will be the bait."

"What are you going to do to this lieutenant, Peter?"

"I? Nothing. I will be here in Washington. But I have just come from meeting with three rather rough characters. While you distract Groves, they will close in and . . . dispense with him."

"Murder?" she whispered.

He smiled at her. Her eyes were bright with fear and, yes, excitement. Her lips were parted, a breathless look.

"This is no trivial matter, my love," he said. "The future of the United States hinges on whether Groves accomplishes the mission Jefferson has given him. This land belonged to His Majesty once, and it will again. The war isn't over. What we have today is an armistice at best.

"You know that Jefferson is fond of the bloody French. In time, this country will be aligned with Bonaparte. Mark my words, it will happen. There will be war again between Great Britain and this nation of traitors. It is inevitable. Nothing was settled at Yorktown. If Groves fails, Jefferson will never see the Louisiana Territory become a part of this Confederation. Will you do this for me, Jane? If not for me, then for your father?"

"Yes."

Leaving the Raymond house, McLeod mounted his horse and rode to the end of the street, where three men were waiting. A gentle rain was falling now. The men looked uncomfortable, but McLeod didn't think it was on account of the cold drizzle. They looked out of place on this street, where the upper crust of Washington lived, and they knew it. The docks and dives of the riverfront were the environment to which they were accustomed. Here they were singularly conspicuous, and it put them ill at ease.

One of the men stepped forward as McLeod checked his horse. This one was a lanky character wearing a slouch hat and blanket coat. There was a belligerent cast to his features.

"Well, what's it to be?" he asked, his tone curt. "Are we on, or not?"

"Didn't realize you were in a rush," said McLeod, sarcastic. "Am I keeping you from a pressing engagement?"

"We just don't like waiting around here."

"You never know when a constable might come along," said another, his tone more conciliatory.

"Yes, and I imagine the constables are on the lookout for the three of you, aren't they?"

There was no response to that.

"Have you been paid?" asked McLeod.

"Brown paid us," said the first man. "You know that."

"Then you are working for me, and you will wait anywhere I tell you to wait, for as long as I tell you to wait there," barked McLeod.

The first man lowered his gaze, and nodded.

"Fortunately, your wait is over," said McLeod, more amicable now that the test of wills was won. "What are your names again?"

"I'm Jackson. That's McGready. And that's Cochran."

"Cochran, how many men have you killed?"

"Oh, a dozen, at least," bragged Cochran.

"And you, McGready?"

"I've cut my share of throats."

"Jackson?"

Jackson, the man in the blanket coat, shrugged and said nothing.

McLeod smiled and nodded. "Excellent. There is a woman who lives four houses down the street on the left. McGready and Cochran, you will present yourself to her. She is expecting you, and she is acquainted with the plan. You will do precisely what she tells you to do. She will point out to you the man I want you to kill. No harm is to come to her. Be clear on that last point, gentlemen."

"We won't let nothing happen to her," promised Cochran.

"Touch a hair on her head and you will have to answer to me. That is something you do not want to have to do. Now go. When you have accomplished your mission, let me know immediately. You know how to find me. If I do not hear from you in, say, forty-eight hours, I will assume you have failed. That you are no longer among the living."

"We won't fail," said the gruff McGready.

He and Cochran headed up the street.

"What about me?" asked Jackson.

"Are you a friend of Dabney Brown's, Mr. Jackson?"

"I wouldn't say a friend."

"Know where he can be found?"

"I know where he lives."

McLeod leaned forward in the saddle. "Then pay him a call—and kill him."

Jackson was startled. He began to speak, thought better of it.

"I gave Mr. Brown fifty crowns today," remarked McLeod.

"Fifty crowns!" breathed Jackson. "I've never seen that much hard money all in one place."

"It's yours if you kill Brown."

Jackson let out a rough laugh. "He's as good as dead, Major."

Chapter 21

Jonathan Groves crossed the Potomac by the ferry above George Town and proceeded down the road to Falls Church. From there he would go to Fairfax, and then make due west for the Appalachian Mountains. He had a compass, and had purchased a map, which had been represented to him as a very accurate piece of work.

He hoped that this was so, as he was heading into country that he had never seen before—a country of rugged mountains and wild rivers, wild Indians and, no doubt, highwaymen. This road, according to the map, would take him to a passage through the mountains into the valley of the Shenandoah. Beyond the valley lay the Alleghenies, and then, if he could strike the Little Kanawha, that river would take him to the Ohio, and Blennerhasset's Island. As the crow flies, from the gap in the Appalachians to the Ohio, was a journey of two hundred miles, most of it rough terrain.

Jonathan paid little attention to the gently rolling hills, the soggy fields, the dripping forests past which he rode. He spent much of the first day lost in thought—second thoughts, not so much regarding the mission as his ability to carry it through to a successful conclusion.

Why had the president burdened him with this task? He was a naval officer, and knew next to nothing about the frontier. Quite an accomplished seaman was he, but as a backwoodsman he was destined to fail miserably. Surely there were men better qualified for the job than he.

But what choice did he have? The president of these United States had asked it of him, and one could not refuse the president.

His uniform and a few personal belongings were crammed into a small carpetbag tied to the cantle of his saddle. Tomorrow he would put on the uniform. He didn't know if that was a wise thing to do or not, but he would do it nonetheless. The uniform gave him confidence—something he sorely needed. His cutlass, taken from a Tripolitan pirate who had tried to separate his head from his shoulders with it, rode, encased in its leathern scabbard, on the saddle beneath his right leg, tied securely.

He saw few people on the road that day. A lone horseman, just outside Falls Church, heading the other way. Jonathan rode through the hamlet without stopping. Falls Church consisted of a scattering of houses, and, of course, a white-steepled church. No one was stirring out of doors in this weather. Warm golden lamplight gleamed in a few windows. Cold and wet, feeling sorry for himself and very much alone, Jonathan rode on.

A few miles west of Falls Church a carriage came up behind him, careening wildly on the muddy road, the four horses in the traces running flat out, the cloaked man in the box whipping them up. In jeopardy of being run down, Jonathan pulled his horse off the road and shouted crossly at the driver as a viscous brown spray of mud splattered him.

The coach sped by, and he caught the merest glimpse of a woman's face in one of the carriage windows. The woman's beauty took his breath way. Had she smiled at him? He couldn't be sure—the vision had been so fleeting. Yet that vision stayed with him long after the coach was out of sight down the road toward Fairfax.

His thoughts turned to women, a subject about which he knew precious little, and that sad state of affairs gave him another golden opportunity to indulge in melancholy self-pity. Having gone to sea at a very tender age, and spent all but a few years before the mast, his lack of experience in that regard was understandable.

There had been one young lady—Rebecca. He had made her acquaintance while attending college. Falling head over heels in love, he had managed, after many wasted months spent getting up the nerve, to ask if she would consent to marry him. It was quickly and painfully apparent to him that he had overestimated her affection for him. She had respectfully declined his offer, and a short while later, married another. Jonathan couldn't really blame her. Who would want to marry someone whose mistress, the sea, constantly beckoned him?

Now, it seemed, he would never learn about women, since there were strong odds against his surviving such a perilous mission as the one upon which he had so foolishly embarked.

He had not gone much further when he saw the carriage, half on the road, tilted precariously on the rim of a flooded ditch. The horses were still in the traces, but by the way they were disposed, Jonathan could safely surmise that they were tangled in their harness.

Kicking his horse into a quicker gait, Jonathan hurried on, alarmed by the fact that he could see no one around the coach. Could the driver—and the woman inside—be injured? As he drew closer he could see that one of the wheels—or what was left of it—was wedged at a peculiar angle. Either the axle had broken or the wheel had come off the spoke.

Reaching the coach, Jonathan jumped off his horse and rushed to the carriage door, throwing it open.

The woman lay crumpled on the floorboards between the seats. her brown serge traveling dress and lacy petticoats were in such disarray that a shapely leg was bared from the knee down.

Even in such a moment of crisis the young lieutenant was struck by her beauty. And, while it shamed him, he was aroused by the sight of so much feminine flesh.

"Miss?"

She stirred, moaning, and her eyes flickered open.

"Are you hurt?"

"I . . . I don't think so."

She sat up, rubbing the back of her neck. Then she noticed that her dress was raised to immodest heights, and, without haste, corrected the situation.

"What happened?" she asked, her voice a little shaky.

"It appears you have lost a wheel. Or perhaps an axle."

"My driver . . ."

"I will see."

Jonathan walked around the coach, steering clear of the horses, which were straining and prancing in the hitch. Indeed, on closer inspection, it was clear that the team was hopelessly entangled in the leathers, and they were none too happy about it.

He expected to find the driver on the ground, thrown violently from the coach, perhaps with his neck broken. But he found no sign of the man, and returned, perplexed, to the carriage. He could only assume that the driver had run off; having caused the wreck and injury to his passenger by his careless driving, he had left the scene in haste.

The young woman was balanced precariously on the iron steps hinged to the gracefully cambered flank of the coach beneath the door. She was holding onto the door with one hand. The back of her other hand was pressed against her forehead, as she looked with dizzy dismay at the brown quagmire that passed for a Virginia road. On the stage, the pose she struck could only mean that a fainting spell was imminent, and Jonathan rushed to her.

"Ma'am, you had better sit down."

"Oh . . . I don't feel at all well."

"You must have struck your head. Please . . ."

Too late! She swooned, toppling forward. Jonathan caught her in his arms. Staggering, he fought to keep his balance, the ugly vision of the two of them sprawled in the muck motivating him to extra effort in his endeavor to stay upright. This he managed somehow to do. She wasn't really all that heavy, hanging limply in his arms. Momentarily nonplussed, he stood there, staring at her beautiful face.

"Don't move."

The gruff voice, filled with menace, came from behind him.

Jonathan started to turn.

"Don't turn around, neither."

The movement was off to his right—he fired a glance that way. Another man, who had been concealed in the roadside trees, leaped the ditch and rushed forward. He was armed with a pistol and a very large knife. Jonathan didn't like the look on his face, either.

"May I put the lady down?" asked Jonathan, suddenly quite calm.

It happened to him that way. On several occasions during the war with the Barbary pirates he had learned that when he came into harm's way this impenetrable calm overtook him. His mind was crystal clear and racing.

"Do it nice and easy," said the man directly behind him.

Jonathan set her on the floorboards of the carriage. As soon as he had done so, she opened her eyes and smiled at him in a sleepy sort of way.

"Get away from her," growled the man.

For a confused moment Jonathan wondered if these men were the woman's companions, and had mistaken him for someone who meant to do her harm.

"I'm here to render assistance," he said. "I just happened by and—"

"Shuddup."

But that didn't seem quite right, thought Jonathan. The man he could see looked like riffraff, and the woman was obviously upper class. The coach was an expensive, custom-made affair, with its shiny brass appurtenances, velveteen curtains, plush upholstery on the benches . . .

He looked at her again, and something in her expression steered him to a new and sobering line of thought.

You will step into a world of intrigue and betrayal, Jefferson had warned him. *You will not know who to trust.*

He wasn't even armed, and called himself for a fool for carrying his pistol in his carpetbag.

She looked beyond him, and addressed the man he could not see, the one directly behind him.

"What are you waiting for?" she asked, irritated. "An invitation? Shoot him."

Jonathan turned then, raising his hands away from his sides, to see the burly, bearded McGready not five paces away, and aiming a pistol at him.

"I'm unarmed," said Jonathan.

McGready's grin wasn't pretty. "That's of no consequence to me." He took two more steps, raised the pistol slightly, wanting to shoot at point-blank range.

The second man was closing in from the side. This brought him close to Jonathan's horse, which stood behind the carriage, reins dragging, and cropping the rank marsh grass on the road's verge. But the approach of the man spooked the horse. Its head came up sharply, and it whickered, and then it shied away, bolting right between Jonathan and McGready.

Thinking fast, Jonathan grabbed for the cutlass tied to the saddle. He got a grip on the guard. The horse rushed past. The blade slipped out of the scabbard.

"Look out, McGready!" yelped the second man.

As soon as the horse was out of the way Jonathan lunged forward. A downward stroke of the cutlass—and McGready's hand, the one with the pistol in it, was severed cleanly from the arm.

The hand plopped into the mud, the finger spasmed on the trigger, and the pistol went off. The report was drowned by McGready's guttural howl as he spun away and fell, blood spurting from the stump where his hand had been.

The second man fired his pistol even as Jonathan whirled to face him. But seeing the fate that had befallen McGready shook the cutthroat named Cochran to the core, and he fired wildly. The bullet missed Jonathan by inches, even though Cochran was no more than spitting distance from his intended target.

Jonathan couldn't believe Cochran had missed at that range. In fact, for an instant, he figured he had been hit and just didn't know it. Cochran was so close he could smell the powdersmoke, and imagined he felt the heat from the muzzle flash.

But Cochran knew immediately that he had missed. He took one look at Jonathan's exotic, blood-smeared cutlass, judged it against his own knife, and, hurling the empty pistol away, turned and ran like a man who has the devil breathing down his neck.

It was reflex that prompted Jonathan to take two steps in pursuit of Cochran. Then he thought better of it. The man was fleeing down the road like he wasn't going to stop until he reached the Potomac. He was completely unnerved. He fell twice while Jonathan watched, bouncing up each time and running on, casting fearful looks over his shoulder.

Jonathan glanced at the woman. She was very pale, staring in horror and fascination at the severed hand lying in the mud of the road.

Moving to McGready, who was writhing in the muck and making strange noises, Jonathan tore the neckerchief from his throat and, sticking the cutlass in the ground, knelt to help the wounded man. He tied the neckerchief around McGready's wrist and pulled it as tight as he could, trying to make of it a tourniquet adequate to the task of stanching the flow of blood. McGready gave him no trouble—he was in no condition to, and he could tell that Jonathan was trying to save his life. All thoughts of fulfilling his contract with Major McLeod had left him the instant his hand left his arm.

"We must get you to a doctor," said Jonathan. "That wound must be cauterized, or you'll not see tomorrow."

He felt little animosity toward the cutthroat. That was just the way he was. When the fight was over, there was no residual anger left in him, and no desire for vengeance. Helping McGready to his feet, he turned to the carriage. It was in his mind to put the wounded man in the conveyance, untangle the team, and proceed with all haste to nearby Fairfax.

But when he saw the woman pointing the pistol at him, he froze in his tracks.

It was a small flintlock, the kind designed specifically for women to carry, or for men to hide on their persons—a very fancy weapon with silver inlays, but very deadly, too.

He could tell she was going to shoot. He could see it in her eyes. He reached for the cutlass, plucking it from the ground, moving forward, swinging McGready around in front of him, all at once. She fired. The bullet struck McGready in the head. Jonathan felt the warm spray of blood on his face. McGready died instantly. As he fell, Jonathan lunged forward. The cutlass pierced Jane Raymond between the breasts an instant after she fired the pistol, piercing her heart and killing her outright.

Jonathan stepped back, aghast. He had struck instinctively. Now that he had time to consider his actions, he realized what he had done. A wave of nausea overcame him. He reeled, doubled over, and dry heaved, leaning heavily on the cutlass.

With one last remorseful look at the dead woman, he stumbled toward his horse, which, having run only a short distance, was standing at the side of the road, a stone's throw from the coach.

Chapter 22

Admitted into Andrew Merry's office, McLeod found the minister seated behind his desk, glowering at a newspaper spread out before him. Merry was a slight, almost frail man, impeccably dressed and groomed. Today he was attired in a plum-colored coat with velvet lapel and cuffs, silk stockings, and an apricot cravat. McLeod thought of him as somewhat of a fop. But Merry despised the Americans, Jefferson in particular, and that, in the major's opinion, was Merry's real strong point. That, and his utter ruthlessness. McLeod could appreciate ruthlessness.

"Ah, Major," said Merry. He spared McLeod the merest glance before returning to his reading.

McLeod stepped up to the desk, expecting Merry to ask him to be seated. The minister had always shown him the utmost courtesy. They spent a lot of time discussing war and politics, which were really two peas in the same pod. Merry seemed always to value McLeod's perspective on issues of the day. As a diplomat, he would say, it behooved him to be acquainted with a warrior's perspective. And he had systematically harvested McLeod's considerable knowledge of American society and personages.

But today he left McLeod standing while he finished reading what the major could see was today's edition of the *National Intelligencer*.

When he was done, Merry removed his pince nez and squeezed the bridge of his nose, very hard. Then he sat back with a grim sigh and looked at McLeod.

"You will have to leave Washington immediately, Major."

"I beg your pardon?"

"I gather, then, that you haven't heard."

"Heard what, sir?"

Merry tapped the newspaper. "A woman named Jane Raymond was found dead on the road to Fairfax."

McLeod worked to keep his expression as impassive as stone. He'd sensed that something had gone wrong. Day before yesterday he had dispatched Jane, with the cutthroats McGready and Cochran, to catch and kill Lieutenant Groves. Since then he had heard absolutely nothing. He had told the two men he would give them forty-eight hours, after which he would presume they had failed in their mission. Now he did not have to wait the few remaining hours to know the truth.

"I'm sorry to hear that," he said. "But what does it have to do with me?"

Merry cocked his head slightly and scrutinized McLeod like a man who is looking at something he has never seen before and cannot identify.

"My God, but you're a cold-blooded bastard, Major."

"I take that as a compliment, Your Excellency."

Merry snorted—a rather unexpected response from a man who prided himself on being the perfect gentlemen. But this, realized McLeod, was far too grave a situation to worry about keeping up appearances. You always knew the truth about a man in moments of crisis.

"I have no doubt that you do," said Merry wryly. He brandished a gilded snuff box from a coat pocket and indulged in a pinch. A snow-white handkerchief, monogrammed, was tugged from beneath a cuff. Merry dabbed at his upper lip with the handkerchief, before tucking it back into place under his sleeve, with just a discreet corner sticking out. McLeod decided he was stalling, giving himself time to think. Merry was positively Machiavellian in his thought processes. He was a man who looked at a situation from every conceivable angle, seeking the means by which he could turn it to his advantage.

"Major McLeod," he said, at length, "your amorous exploits are deservedly notorious. You seem to be attracted exclusively to married women these days. There was, I believe, the case of the general's wife . . ."

McLeod stiffened. "Sir, my personal affairs—"

"Are my affair, as long as you are seconded to me, sir."

"I don't see what that has to do with—"

Merry held up a hand. "Please, Major. Indulge me. I trust you will not deem it necessary to challenge me to a duel of honor because I speak so bluntly on the subject. Being a diplomat, I rarely have an opportunity to be candid, and when I do, I seize it with relish. I exhume the . . . uhm, affair with the Lady Hughes only to point out that history has a habit of repeating itself. After all, that little peccadillo is the reason you missed a great deal of action in the latest war waged against that Corsican ogre."

"No, sir. I was recuperating from the wound I received at Bergen."

"Now, with Mrs. Raymond murdered, you are in a bit of a spot again. You see, the journalists have been talking to her servants and her neighbors. It was a rather sensational demise, and their interest is piqued. They smell a scandal. And apparently you were less than discreet."

"What happened to her?"

"She died badly."

Trying to keep a tight rein on his anger, McLeod leaned forward on the desk. "If you are cognizant of any more details, Your Excellency," he said, with just a trace of sarcasm, "I would be most grateful were you to share them with me."

"She was run through with a sword, or a very large knife. A ruffian whose identity is not yet known was found dead on the scene. He had been shot. There was a discharged pistol in her hand. And another in his hand. Oddly, though, his hand was no longer connected to his arm."

McLeod straightened and clasped his hands behind his back.

"It sounds like a robbery to me," he said, looking out the window behind Merry's chair.

"That is the early consensus." Merry abruptly slammed a fist down on the desk. "Damn it all, McLeod! It's quite bad enough, your . . ." —Merry made an exasperated gesture as he sought the proper if elusive word—". . . liaison with the wife of an official of the United States government. But you sent her and that . . . that rogue after Groves, didn't you?"

"When I imparted to you the intelligence I had received concerning Groves, you expressed the opinion that he had to be stopped, or Burr warned. You also expressly ordered me not to tell you how I went about carrying out your wishes in that regard."

Merry was trying very diligently to regain his composure. "I fear this will reflect poorly on us."

"They cannot connect me to this incident."

Merry was skeptical. "Jefferson's people will most assuredly try. If only to embarrass His Majesty's government. It's a damned messy business, Major. Worst of all, it seems Lieutenant Groves got the better of us."

"One battle doesn't win a war."

"You feel no remorse, Major?"

"I've seen many friends die by the sword."

"This was a woman, for God's sake."

"She was fighting for a good cause."

"The cause. Are you sure that is what *you* are fighting for, McLeod? Or is it vengeance you seek? The rebels killed your wife, did they not? Burned your estate?"

"Which is why you requested that I be seconded to you, Your Excellency."

"Well, you were *persona non grata* in the 7th Fusiliers as long as Hughes commanded that regiment."

McLeod shook his head. "You brought me to Washington as an insult to Jefferson. And because you thought I might be able to make trouble for him. Are you not motivated by revenge, Your Excellency?"

"Hmmm." Merry was up and pacing now in front of the window, staring at the floor, then the ceiling, then the floor again. "Quite so. I am the one who bears the responsibility for this disgrace. I did, after all, cry havoc and let slip . . . you, Major."

"You said I was leaving Washington?"

"Yes. You must go."

"In what direction? East? Or west?"

Merry stopped and gazed out the window at the street, turning his back on McLeod. "West. You will locate Burr. You will inform him that we are no longer in a position to render him assistance in his scheme."

"May I have a letter to that effect?"

"You certainly may not."

"He may not take my word for it, without proof."

"I could not care less what he believes and doesn't believe. I wash my hands of this whole affair. At least we can take some consolation in knowing that the seeds of discord have already been planted. Burr has gone entirely too far to turn back now. We will see what develops and hope for the best—that is to say, we will hope that the worst befalls Jefferson and this upstart republic of his."

"Is that all, sir?"

"There is one more small matter. I will not provide you with a letter for the simple fact that if you fall into the wrong hands I will disavow you completely. I will declare you a renegade, for whom Great Britain shoulders no responsibility. Is that clear?"

"Perfectly."

"After you have communicated with Burr, I suggest you proceed to Detroit, or some other one of our frontier outposts. If and when this all blows over . . . well, we shall see then what is to be done with you."

"Yes, sir."

"Naturally, you will under no circumstances return here to Washington."

"Naturally."

"You may go."

McLeod left the room without another word.

He waited in the hallway while the valet fetched his shako and greatcoat. Staring bleakly at the wall, he thought about Jane Raymond. Poor Jane. What a bloody waste.

As for Merry's orders, he really didn't mind being cut loose. Serving as the minister's aide had been entirely too restrictive a role for him. He had no real allegiance to His Majesty anyway. Merry was right. His allegiance was to himself, and to vengeance. His target was grand enough: the United States of bloody America. He would do what Merry had ordered him to do. After that . . . he would just have to wait and see. He had one clear objective, at last. Lieutenant Jonathan Groves.

He had never met the man, but, quite possibly, upon his shoulders rested the future of this damned republic of traitors. It had nothing really to do with Jane Raymond—at least McLeod didn't think it did—but he was going to kill the young lieutenant.

The valet arrived with his things. McLeod donned the shako and shrugged into the greatcoat. The valet held the door for him. His horse was tethered to an iron hitching pole in front of the Merry residence. The rains had finally ceased. The overcast sky was breaking up—there were promising patches of blue sky above. The wind, though, was still cold and damp, and it cut right through McLeod, making his old war wound ache.

"Have a pleasant evening sir," said the valet.

That brought a wolfish grin to McLeod's rakish features. He climbed into the saddle, reined the horse so sharply that it reared on its hind legs. Mc-

Leod swept the shako off his head in a cavalier salute to Andrew Merry, who was still standing at the office window. Then, as the horse came down on all fours, McLeod raked his spurs and galloped away, leaving ringing laughter in his wake.

Chapter 23

In Scarlet Town where I was born
There was a fair maid dwellin',
And every youth cried well away,
Her name was Barbara Allen.

Buckskin-clad Stephen Cooper sang at the top of his lungs as he traipsed through the Kentucky woods. He had a good voice, a lusty baritone shattering the peaceful solitude of the forest. A small doe was drinking delicately from a stream dancing over its rocky course up ahead. It raised its head, listening, tension in every fiber. Stephen saw the doe before it saw him, in time to watch it bound into the brush, disappearing in a flash.

Stephen laughed. He carried a flintlock rifle, tilted negligently over a shoulder, but he didn't try for a shot. Hunting was not what he was about today. The only reason he carried the gun was on account of Indians. Even this close to Boonesboro—why, they could probably almost hear him singing at the stockade—there was no security. The Shawnee could

strike at any time and anywhere. They were bold as
new brass, those Shawnee. But Stephen wasn't worried.

> *All in the merry month of May,*
> *When green buds they were swellin',*
> *Young Jemmie on his death bed lay*
> *For love of Barbara Allen.*

Stephen figured it was too splendid a day for
Shawnees. It was cool and clear, the birds were singing up a storm, the breeze rustling through the up-
permost boughs of the trees was redolent with the
fragrance of spring: new dew-sweetened bluegrass
and a profusion of wildflowers. Mother Nature was
decked out in her finest, and all was right with the
world. Best of all, he was in love. Life was grand indeed! There was no room for Shawnees and death.

> *So slowly, slowly she came up*
> *And slowly she came nigh him.*
> *And all she said when there she came,*
> *'Young man I think you're dying.'*

It was Sunday. His father, a devout Christian, did
not think one ought to work on the Lord's Day. That
suited Stephen just fine. He was right tired of plowing. Seemed like that was all they'd been doing since
forever. Of course, it hadn't been quite that long.
The last winter storm had come and gone, said the

old-timers, confident. They knew because the earth told them in a hundred little ways.

Stephen was a strapping young man, tall and strong, with a long stride and wide powerful shoulders made so by the wielding of the axe and the handling of the plow. He had an unruly mop of black hair that he constantly swept out of his eyes. His features were too chiseled to be handsome, but he had a quick and winning smile.

> *'If on your deathbed you do lie,*
> *What needs the tale you're tellin?*
> *I cannot help you from your death,*
> *Farewell!' said Barbara Allen.*

Hard work usually didn't bother Stephen Cooper, but for the last few months he'd been strangely ambivalent toward his chores. His disgusted father knew the signs, and declared his son "love-struck."

Stephen reckoned that was true. Reckoned, too, that it had happened during the dance a couple months back in Drayton's tobacco barn. That was when he had danced a reel with Rebecca Jones and gotten up the nerve to ask her if she thought that just maybe there might be a chance somewhere down the road that she would marry him.

And she had replied, in that perky, playful way of hers, that yes, there was a slim chance she might consider it.

Stephen's whole world had changed then.

Breaking free of the woods, he saw the cabin in

the clearing. It was a pretty scene. The bluegrass hill beyond the cabin had been enclosed with a split-rail fence, and the fine thoroughbred horses belonging to Flintlock Jones were grazing there. A plume of smoke rose from the cabin chimney. A redbone hound, sprawled in front of the cabin door, lifted its head and looked his way, sniffing the air.

Stephen paused. He found himself suddenly afflicted with a severe case of weak knees and lump in the throat. Part of it was the prospect of seeing Rebecca again. Lord, but she was prettier than a hundred sunsets. He would have to remember to tell her so. Of course, he spent a lot of time thinking up all kinds of nice compliments, but in her presence his wits always abandoned him, and about the best he could manage to do was stare and stammer. He wondered how it came to happen that way.

Another reason for his sudden affliction of cold feet was Flintlock Jones. Stephen was in awe of the man. Why, he was an out-and-out legend. Every bit as much as Dan'l Boone and Simon Kenton. He had never menaced Stephen in any way; in fact, he had always been courteous. But Stephen knew, as did everyone else in Boonesboro, that Rebecca was the apple of Flintlock's eye. His daughter, and his wife Amanda, were more important to him than life itself.

But the thing about Rebecca was that Flintlock Jones had lost one son to the pox and another to the Shawnees, and Rebecca was his only surviving child. Well, they had never found the mortal remains of young Simon, the one the Indians had snatched, but

Flintlock had searched deep into Shawnee country, and killed a heap of warriors without finding hide nor hair of his son. So everybody figured Simon was dead, since he'd been missing now for the better part of two years.

So it seemed to Stephen that Flintlock, being mighty attached to Rebecca, would not be pleased were he to learn that Tom Cooper's son was bound and determined to take Flintlock's daughter away.

The redbone hound was on its feet now, and barking, a long mournful baying that set invisible fingers to tickling Stephen's spine. It was because he had come crashing out of the woods and then stopped dead in his tracks, and hadn't moved for a spell. The hound, Ranger, couldn't pick up his scent and distinguish him from an Indian, so it was calling the alarm. Flintlock had trained the hound to hate Indians, by hiring the Delaware, the one they called Quashquame, to sneak up on the pup and pound it with a willow stick at every opportunity. The hound purely despised Indians now. One couldn't come within an arrow's flight of the cabin if the wind was right without setting Ranger off.

Now that he had been found out, Stephen squared his shoulders, grit his teeth, and approached the cabin.

Ranger's noisy warning drew Amanda Jones to the window. She wiped dough from her fingers on the apron tied around her slender waist, then brushed an errant strand of cornsilk-golden hair out of her bright blue eyes.

"It's young Stephen Cooper," she announced.

Her daughter, who had been helping her make bread, rushed to the window with what to Amanda was unseemly haste. She watched Rebecca's face as Rebecca saw Stephen. A strange light danced in her daughter's eyes, and a smile graced her lips.

"I wonder," said Amanda, being disingenuous, "what he could have come all the way here for."

"Oh, Mother."

Amanda smiled. "You are a beautiful young woman."

"Am I?" The compliment delighted Rebecca. "So are you, mother. Everyone says I look just like you."

It was true, thought Amanda, and no denying it. The same fine, straight yellow hair and lively blue eyes. The same slender figure. Even after three children, Amanda had somehow managed to retain her willowy form. And though the hardships of twenty-five years of frontier life, compounded by the tragedies with which God in his ineffable wisdom had seen fit to test her, she had kept her beauty, too—the lines at the corners of her mouth and eyes were scarcely visible.

Stephen was almost to the door. Ranger's tail was wagging now, and Stephen petted the hound as he halloed the house.

"May I let him in, Mother?"

Amanda was pleased that Rebecca used "may" instead of "can." She had tried to educate her daughter, as her mother had done her, and for the past three years had been ably assisted in that task by the schoolteacher, Mr. Gregg, a truly learned man.

"It would not be too neighborly if we didn't," she replied. "But I will open the door."

Which she did, ushering Stephen into the cabin.

"Hello, Mrs. Jones. I've come to . . ."

And then he saw Rebecca, standing in a shaft of sunlight by the window, looking positively angelic.

"Oh, hullo Rebecca."

"Hello, Stephen."

Amanda was amused to see her daughter, usually so outspoken and outgoing, become suddenly, painfully shy.

"You . . . uh . . . you look as pretty as . . . uh . . . pretty as a sundered huns . . ."

"What?" asked Amanda and Rebecca in perfect, startled unison.

"I mean . . ." Stephen blushed furiously. "A hundred sunsets." He was miserable now. It always happened—inevitably he would become tongue twisted and make a complete fool of himself.

Rebecca managed, somehow, to repress a giggle. Sundered huns? She would have to remember that, to torment Stephen with at some later date. Not now, though. It wouldn't do. He looked positively skittish. One little thing and he might take off running.

"Would you like something to eat, Stephen?" asked Amanda.

"Oh, no, ma'am. I just came to . . . well, I . . . is Flintlock . . . I mean, Mr. Jones, here?"

"No, he isn't," said Amanda. "He should be back tomorrow, or perhaps the next day. He and that Delaware are out trying to track down the panther which has been killing livestock hereabouts."

"Don't tell me you came all this way to see my father, Stephen Cooper," warned Rebecca.

"Oh, no, Becky. I came to see you."

"That's better."

Stephen turned to Amanda. "Would it be all right if Becky was to take a walk with me?"

Amanda's first inclination was to say no. If they strayed out of sight of the cabin she would begin to worry. The cabin was almost within hollering distance of Boonesboro, but still it was in an isolated spot. Many times in the past twenty-five years they had found Indian sign in the vicinity, and a half-dozen times Indians had attacked the cabin.

But she could look at Rebecca and tell that her daughter desperately wanted her to say yes. Young people in love needed their privacy. Amanda liked Stephen Cooper, and told herself that Rebecca would be safe with him. So, against her better judgment, she consented.

"Now don't go far," she warned. "And take Ranger with you."

They were out the door before she could even finish with the caveats. Wearing a pensive smile, she stood at the threshold and watched them angle across the bluegrass slope toward the woods. Ranger trailed along behind them, barking at one of the horses that ran up to the fence, tossing its head, as the two young people drew near. Rebecca cast an over-the-shoulder glance at the cabin but didn't see her in the doorway shadows, and, not seeing her, allowed Stephen to hold her hand.

It must be nice to be young, thought Amanda—a bittersweet thought. Stephen and Rebecca were so full of life and hope for the future. The horse that trotted along the fence parallel with them was young and full of life, too. The whole world, wrapped in the splendor of springtime, was young. Seeing all of this, Amanda felt old. Lonely, too. She always felt empty inside when Nathaniel was away. Only when he was with her did she feel youthful.

Nathaniel wasn't often gone. He did his best to keep the promise he had made her twenty-five years ago, when first they had come to Kentucky with nothing but a horse and a rifle—and the horse had been stolen by that peddler. What was his name? "Lord, I hope I'm not getting absentminded," she murmured.

Yes, Nathaniel had vowed never to leave her alone. But as the years went by, the folks hereabouts had turned more and more to him for leadership in times of crisis, especially now that Boone had moved on. He didn't like leaving her and Rebecca, but sometimes he simply had no choice. This business with the panther was a case in point. There was no braver and better tracker than her husband in all of Kentucky, unless it was Quashquame, the Delaware.

Amanda gazed longingly a moment at the surrounding hills and wondered where Nathaniel was and if he was thinking about her. She smiled again. Yes, he probably was. Their love had deepened with each passing year. It was as strong as life itself, and as vibrant as this young country.

Her heart aching, she turned back inside. Idle hands led to idle thoughts. She would busy herself with the task of making bread, and a hundred other tasks that needed doing around the place, keeping herself busy until Nathaniel returned.

Chapter 24

No sooner had Stephen and Rebecca reached the woods than Ranger picked up a scent and took off into the brush, leaving Stephen and Rebecca to fend for themselves. They made for the spring, which came trickling out of an outcropping of rock, filling a shallow rock pool, and then spilling over into a rivulet dancing down a slope to the rambling creek below.

Few words passed between them until they had settled on a big log beside the spring. Stephen was so happy just to be alone with Rebecca that he was for a while rendered speechless. Her dainty hand resting in his callused one sent electric jolts through his entire body. Every nerve ending in his body was atingle, and he was light headed to boot.

"Becky, did you mean what you said at the dance?" he asked, when finally he had worked up enough gumption.

"What did I say?" she asked, just playing with him. The look on his face at this response—chagrin mixed with sheer terror—made her laugh. "Stephen, I was only joking."

"Don't play a prank like that on me!" gasped Stephen. "I swear, my heart stopped beating."

"Are you saying you would die without me?"

"Reckon I would."

She leaned against him and put her head on his shoulder. He breathed deep the fragrance of her golden hair. *This is as close to heaven as I can get,* thought Stephen, *without crossing over the River Jordan.*

"Of course I meant what I said," she replied. "My folks brought me up never to say anything unless I meant it."

"I knew it all along."

"Knew what?"

"That we would marry, you and I. Ever since we were children I knew it somehow."

"Stephen Cooper! You thought about marrying me when we were children?"

"Well, I . . ."

She laughed again. The sound was music to his ears. He knew she was laughing at him, but he didn't mind, because there was nothing malicious about it. She was just so full of life and happiness, and he made her laugh, and he was glad to be able to do so.

"I know I haven't got much to offer a wife," he said. "But we'll get a section of land, the prettiest section of land in all of Kaintuck. And then I'll build you the best cabin in the whole country. You're sure you won't mind being a farmer's wife?"

"Of course I wouldn't mind. Don't be silly."

"Well, it's just your pa has those fine thoroughbred horses and all—"

"And he never has been much for farming."

"We won't have much at first—"

"Neither did my folks, when they came here," said Rebecca. "Fact is, they didn't have anything at all, except each other. But, Stephen, that's everything."

"And we'll have children of our own."

For once in her life Rebecca felt some heat in her cheeks. The idea of making love to Stephen left her all weak and warm inside. She tried to cover her discomfiture by making light of the subject.

"Why certainly, Mr. Cooper. At least nine or ten."

"Nine or ten?"

"Oh, at least. Don't you think we can?"

"I reckon we can sure try," he said, grinning, and reached for her.

She pushed him away. "We don't try until we're married."

"Come on, Becky. Just a kiss?"

She pretended to resist. The more he leaned forward the more she leaned back. And then they toppled off the log and rolled, laughing, entangled, down the slope, and came to rest with him on top of her. They both abruptly stopped laughing. Rebecca langorously snaked her arms around his neck. She closed her eyes. He kissed her.

When their lips parted, Stephen raised himself up a little and gazed at her face. Her eyes were still closed, her full ruby-red lips parted slightly. She was the most beautiful girl in the whole world, decided Stephen. And he was the luckiest feller . . .

She opened her eyes.

And screamed.

Shocked, Stephen jerked away from her. That sudden movement saved him from being killed instantly. The tomahawk struck him a glancing blow, instead of cleaving his skull in two. Still, the impact knocked him sideways. He rolled downslope, sprawling, and tried to get up. His rifle, he realized, with a sick feeling, was leaning against the log, ten yards upslope. His vision was blurred—it was as though the blow from the tomahawk had knocked his eyes out of alignment. Someone kicked him viciously in the ribs, driving all the air from his lungs. Wheezing, he fell— and as he tried to get up he felt a pain in his back unlike any pain he had ever felt. Unbelievable pain that washed over him in inky black waves and carried him away into nothingness.

Still screaming, Rebecca tried to run. But the Indians were everywhere. They were Shawnees. One grabbed her, tried to cover her mouth with his hand. She bit him, to the bone. With a snarl, the Shawnee hurled her to the ground, cursing her, and raised his tomahawk. Rebecca raised an arm in feeble defense.

Another warrior stayed the hand of the one about to slay her. This one barked a curt command, and the murderous rage drained from the first Indian's face. The second warrior turned and grabbed Rebecca's upraised arm, hauling her to her feet.

"You scream," said the warrior, in English, "you die."

Rebecca almost screamed anyway. She almost couldn't stop herself. And it would be better, she thought, to die here with poor Stephen than suffer the fate she would assuredly meet at the hands of these savages. In the end, she could not opt for death. *I am too cowardly,* she thought bitterly. *I will wish before long that I had been just brave enough to die.*

There were seven warriors. One of them was bending over Stephen. His knife flashed in the sunlight as he scalped the man he had felled with his tomahawk. He lifted his bloody trophy aloft and yelped in triumph. The warrior who had spoken to Rebecca snapped at him, and the scalp-taker uttered no further loud exultations.

Witness to the scalping, Rebecca was horrified, and she buried her face in her hands and sobbed. The English-speaking Shawnee cuffed her hard enough to knock her off her feet.

"No cry," he rasped. "Make no sound."

A sudden commotion drew his attention away from her.

Ranger had burst out of the underbrush and, growling, launched himself at the nearest Shawnee. His massive jaws clamped on the Shawnee's throat and jawbone. With a muffled scream the Indian went down. Ranger tore his throat out. There was one massive convulsion, then the Indian lay still in death. Bloody flesh hanging from his bared fangs,

Ranger turned away to find a new victim. In sheer terror, the nearest Shawnee raised his rifle and fired. The bullet knocked the hound off its feet. But somehow Ranger got up and lunged again. Two more bullets crashed into him. He was dead before he hit the ground.

The English-speaking warrior was furious. Fists clenched, his whole body trembled, so extreme was his cold fury. With chill disdain he rebuked the warriors who had fired, then gestured angrily at Rebecca.

One of the Indians jerked Rebecca to her feet. Numb with shock and despair, she stared blankly at the bodies of Stephen and Ranger. She stood there and allowed the Indian to bind her wrists in front of her body with a rawhide thong.

With the English-speaking warrior in the lead, the Shawnees left the spring with Rebecca amongst them. She kept her eyes on Stephen as long as she could see him, praying he would move. He couldn't be dead. This couldn't be happening.

Then she thought about her father—and it gave her strength, and she glowered at the Shawnee who had a painful grip on her arm, and was hurrying her along.

"My father is going to hunt all of you down and kill you," she said, matter of factly.

He shook her roughly and hurried her along.

When Amanda heard the three shots in quick succession, her blood ran cold.

She grabbed the rifle that always stood, primed and loaded, beside the door. There, on a wooden peg, hung powderhorn and shot pouch. These, too, she collected, and rushed outside.

She ran in the direction Stephen and Rebecca had taken, into the woods, making instinctively for the spring, guessing that that was where her daughter and the Cooper boy had gone. It was a romantic spot. She and Nathaniel had spent hours there, with him sitting with his back to the log, and her leaning back against him, with his strong arms wrapped around her.

There was trouble—of that she was certain, and she suspected the worst. The worst being Indian trouble. Three shots, close together, and that meant more than one rifle, since no man could reload that swiftly.

Nearing the spring, she paused long enough to pour powder into the rifle's flashpan and check the flint. All in order. She had become an accomplished shot; Nathaniel had seen to that. Her heart was hammering against her ribcage, for she expected an Indian to jump out of the bushes at her.

But the Shawnees were long gone.

When she reached the spring all she found was Ranger and Stephen and the dead Shawnee whose throat had been ripped out. A small cry escaped her lips. The hound was dead. For an instant she thought Stephen was, too. But then he moaned, very faintly, and one of his hands twitched slightly. He was alive! It was truly a miracle. One side of his face was covered with blood. The back of his buckskin tunic was soaked with blood . . . and he had been scalped.

Amanda looked frantically around for Rebecca. Her daughter was nowhere to be found. In a way, Amanda was relieved. She called out her name, time and time again. The forest was a mute witness to her frantic search of the brush around the spring. When finally she came upon some clear tracks she could see that they were made by six men, and a woman with small bare feet. It had to be Rebecca. The Indians had taken her. Amanda broke down, sobbing uncontrollably.

Her first thought was to go after them. They couldn't have gone far. But what would happen if she caught up with them? Then what? The answer was clear enough. They would kill her. And maybe Rebecca, too.

No, it made more sense to hurry to Boonesboro with the news. That way, a party of frontiersmen could be in hot pursuit of the Indians within an hour's time. If she didn't carry the news of this ambush to Boonesboro—if she surrendered to her maternal instincts and went after Becky and the Indians alone—no one would know about the attack until it was too late to help her daughter.

Turning back toward the cabin was the hardest thing she had ever done.

To ride one of the horses bareback to Boonesboro was the quickest way to get there, yet she toyed with the idea of hitching up the wagon and trying to take

Stephen along with her. In the end she decided against this course of action, realizing that she couldn't get the wagon very close to the spring where Stephen lay; knowing, too, that if she attempted to drag him through the woods—she certainly could not carry him—it might well kill him. And even if she could get him to the wagon, how would she lift him up into it? No, she had to hope he could hang onto life long enough for her to fetch help.

She had no trouble catching up a horse. Her favorite, the mare she had named Daphne, was waiting for her by the fence. Daphne's sire was Jumper. Like Jumper, she was a blood bay. And she could run like the wind. She would not let anyone but Amanda ride her.

Amanda abandoned the rifle. Climbing up onto the split-rail fence, she jumped astride Daphne and grabbed handfuls of mane. She kicked the horse into motion, circled her, and jumped the fence, galloping down the bluegrass slope away from the cabin and toward the road that led to Boonesboro.

Halfway there, her prayers were answered.

Nathaniel and Quashquame were walking down the road from the settlement.

When he saw Amanda, Nathaniel could tell immediately that something was wrong, and said as much to the slender young Delaware. Quashquame's bronze features remained impassive, but he grunted his agreement with Nathaniel's assessment, and his dark eyes—Rebecca said he had the soulful eyes of the doe—were clouded with concern.

The buckskin-clad hunters broke into a run so as to close the distance between them and the still-distant rider that much quicker. They both had legs like steel springs and lungs like bellows, and both were fleet of foot, with the stamina to run all day—though Quashquame, twenty years younger than Nathaniel, was perhaps a little faster.

Amanda was calling out to them, but Nathaniel could not make out her words above the thunder of the blood bay's hooves and the pounding of his racing pulse, loud in his ears. As they came together, Amanda leaped off the horse and threw herself into her husband's waiting arms. Quick thinking as always, Quashquame jumped to snare Daphne as the horse raced by, latching onto the blood bay's mane. Daphne didn't take to that kind of handling from anyone save Amanda, and balked. But the Delaware hung on tenaciously and murmured horse-talk, soft and low. The horse-talk worked its magic on the bay—Daphne was soon as docile as a lamb.

"Rebecca!" gasped Amanda. "Dear God, Nathaniel, they took her! They took our daughter! And Stephen—Stephen's hurt bad . . ."

"Slow down," said Nathaniel, feeling sick to his stomach. "Who took Rebecca?"

"Indians."

The news was a knife thrust into his heart.

"It's all my fault," cried Amanda. "I let her and Stephen go down by the spring. Ranger went with them . . . but, but they killed poor Ranger. And they scalped Stephen . . ."

"The Cooper boy?"

She nodded, gulping air. "He's still alive, but just barely. Rebecca . . . *they took our little girl!*"

"It isn't your fault," said Nathaniel. "If anything, the blame rests with me. I would have been home, except that we took the panther's pelt to Boonesboro. Naturally, we had to tell the story several times of how we tracked it down and killed it."

"You've got to get Rebecca back," said Amanda. "I won't lose the last of my children to those bloodthirsty savages!"

She glanced at Quashquame, dimly aware through her grief and torment that the Delaware might be offended by her words. But his eyes reflected compassion and understanding.

"Don't worry," said Nathaniel, in deadly earnest. "You go on to Boonesboro. Send some men out to fetch Stephen. Quashquame and I will find Rebecca."

She held him tight, suddenly afraid to let him go, for if Rebecca was lost for good, as she feared, Nathaniel was all that she had left. She could not survive losing them both.

Nathaniel gently pried himself loose, kissed her on the cheek, and lifted her effortlessly aboard the blood bay.

"Stay at Boonesboro until I return," he said, and slapped the horse soundly on the rump, sending it down the road at a gallop. He stood there a moment, watching her go, feeling profoundly sad, as he always did when forced to part with her, hating to leave her in such despair.

Then he glanced at Quashquame and uttered a single word—a word that spoke volumes.

"Shawnee."

The Delaware nodded grimly.

They ran up the road in the direction of the cabin and the spring in the woods, where they would pick up the trail. Nathaniel knew he could not—would not—return without Rebecca. He had failed to find his son, Simon, and had returned empty handed, and ever since had wondered if he had looked long enough. The guilt had plagued him. This time he would not return at all if he did not have his daughter.

Chapter 25

Even with a map Jonathan Groves got lost deep in the mountains.

He had lost the compass on the Fairfax road, no doubt during the fight, and had only discovered that it was missing hours later. He wasn't about to go back and look for it.

As for the map, he concluded that there was nothing really wrong with it—he supposed that it was, as advertised, a very splendid and accurate example of cartography. The problem lay with him. Ironic, that a man who could find his way across uncharted seas, was readily confused in constantly changing terrain where dozens of odd-shaped hills and rock outcroppings and branching streams and waterfalls afforded the traveler with countless landmarks. Problem was, it all looked the same to him.

Jonathan resorted to the simple expedient of putting his back directly to the sun when it rose in the morning, and thereafter did his utmost to steer a true course due west for the remainder of the day. Of course, the terrain did not lend itself to this endeavor, and he often found himself going south or north by the end of the day. Often, too, the days were overcast. At night he could get his bearings easily, thanks to a familiarity with the stars in the heavens, but he could not travel at night. He realized that without map or compass his progress would be quite slow, as there were several days when he got completely turned around and traveled miles in the wrong direction. But this scarcely fazed him. In fact, very little could for days following the incident on the road. He accepted every setback with almost whimsical detachment.

For some time he puzzled over this apparent indifference to his fate. In time, he came to the conclusion that two reasons lay behind this uncharacteristic ambivalence.

For one, he had killed a woman. Admittedly in the heat of battle, but that did not assuage his conscience. He had killed her unnecessarily, as she had fired the pistol, missing him cleanly. The memory of that terrible moment was one he was sure he would never succeed in extracting from his troubled dreams.

For another thing, the weight of the burden that President Jefferson had laid upon his reluctant shoulders was just too great. He was willing to wander, lost in the wilderness like the tribes of Israel. Or rather, like the outcast from society that he deserved to be for killing a woman. He wasn't really sure he wanted to find his way, because when he did he would be obliged to do his best to accomplish his mission—and of course he would fail.

The soul searching required to arrive at this conclusion also, belatedly, triggered his dormant sense of duty and obligation to his country and stirred the embers of his pride. He could not pander to fear of failure. If he did, the republic would be lost. He had to do his best.

The mountains, it seemed, would never end. When on the occasions that he could pause on some high point to gaze hopefully westward, all he saw was row after row of forested heights, stretching into a mist-bound infinity. The sheer vastness of this land left him in awe.

For ten days Jonathan saw not a living soul, nor any sign that a human being had ever passed this way. He had been given to understand that there were a few isolated settlements in these mountains, but he crossed nary a trail, nor saw a telltale wisp of chimney smoke.

Yet he did not feel alone. There was abundant wildlife—deer, beaver, fox, wolf, raccoon, possum, otter, as well as an astonishing variety of birds. The creeks were teeming with fish. Preferring the latter to the prospect of having to stalk, kill, and clean game, he used to good advantage a hook and a stout piece of twine that, with customary foresight, he carried in his valise. At night, if he wasn't so bone-weary that he fell into exhausted sleep as soon as he stretched his aching frame upon the ground, he would try to read a little from a small book of En-

glish poems. There was Dryden and Marvell, Herrick
and Herbert. Jonathan's favorite was Thomas Gray.
One night, as his heavy eyelids drooped, he read . . .

> *The boast of heraldry, the pomp of pow'r,*
> *And all that beauty, all that wealth e'er gave,*
> *Await alike the inevitable hour:*
> *The paths of glory lead but to the grave.*

Jonathan thought about Aaron Burr when he read
that verse.

He came to appreciate the fact that he had struck
an excellent bargain with that man Rooney for the
sorrel horse, which he named Rosinante. He thought
the name amusingly appropriate, since he felt very
much like Cervante's Don Quixote. The sorrel was a
sturdy, sure-footed creature that never vexed him,
and never seemed to tire. In no time at all Jonathan
had developed an attachment to the horse, his true
and faithful companion—a fondness all the more remarkable since he had never had much use for
horses, feeling much more at home on the quarter-
deck of a sailing ship than in a saddle.

A fortnight out of Washington, Jonathan nearly
lost his sorrel companion, and his life.

He had paused at a creek, in the middle of an un-
seasonably warm and humid day. Dismounting, he
tied the reins to a willow sapling and ventured down
the stream a ways, to a pool where the cold, clear
waters beckoned to him. Shedding his uniform tunic, he sat on his heels in the shallows and washed

his upper body. Then, upon contemplating the grimy, sweat-stained condition of the tunic, he proceeded to douse the garment in the water, rubbing it virgorously between his fists.

At that moment a brown bear burst from the underbrush.

Rosinante went berserk. Roaring, the bear stood up on its hind legs and advanced on the sorrel. Leaping to his feet, Jonathan's blood ran cold. Ever since the incident on the Fairfax road, when he had been caught without his pistol, he had carried the weapon in his belt. Now, with his heart threatening to jump right out of his chest, he grabbed the pistol.

The pistol felt suddenly very small and powerless in his hand, and Jonathan was assailed by grave doubts. There was no guarantee he could even hit the bear at this distance, about twenty paces; though the target was large, his hand was trembling badly. And he wondered if a one-ounce lead ball could kill such a creature.

But he had to do something. He couldn't just stand by and watch the sorrel perish.

With a wild cry, Jonathan raced forward, straight at the bear. At that moment Rosinante reared back, snapping the reins that attached it to the sapling. As the horse galloped away, crowhopping, the bear dropped down onto all fours and whirled to face Jonathan. Jonathan fired at a distance of less than ten feet.

The ball struck the bear in the shoulder. Its roar of pain and rage seemed to shake the earth to its very foundations. Still yelling like a banshee, Jonathan hurled the empty pistol at his adversary and drew the Tripolitan cutlass from its sheath.

The bear reared up again. Jonathan slashed at the exposed belly, drawing blood, and ducked under a massive paw with yellow claws the size of whale teeth as the bear took a swipe at him. Jonathan's thrust carried him past the creature, and the cutlass drew blood again as he laid open the bear's back. The lumbering animal dropped to all fours again and turned to confront him. Jonathan considered running then, but quickly thought better of it. He seemed to remember hearing that bears were exceeding swift of foot and could not be outrun on level ground. If he ran, the bear would surely give chase. For better or worse he had to stand and fight.

A third time the bear raised up on its hind legs. Face to face with the creature, Jonathan judged it to stand at least seven feet high, and he had no doubt it outweighed him by several hundred pounds. All he had going for him was quickness and agility. If the bear got hold of him with those claws, he could be torn limb from limb.

The bear moved toward him, roaring. Jonathan backed up, trying to maintain a safe distance, and began to circle, but the bear turned with him, and he could find no opening. So he let the bear lumber closer, and when it took a swipe at him, as he knew it would, he struck with the cutlass. The blade cut deep. The bear howled, lashing out at him with its other paw, quicker than Jonathan expected, and catching him with a glancing blow. The claws opened up great bloody gashes in his shoulder, and the impact sent him sprawling, gasping at the incredible pain. He lost his grip on the cutlass, scrambled desperately for it, as the bear was down on all fours now and closing in on him. He could almost smell its rancid breath.

Faintly, above the bear's roar, he heard two shots in quick succession, and the ground beneath him shuddered as the bear collapsed, inches from his feet. Though it looked dead, Jonathan was in no mood to take chances. He scrambled to his feet and quickly put some space between himself and the fallen animal.

But it was dead, and Jonathan looked around for the man—or men—who had saved his life.

At first he saw no one. Mystified, too scared by his brush with death to even think, he just stood there.

A moment later a man emerged from the woods across the creek. A white man, buckskin clad, carrying a flintlock rifle. The man did not call out. Wading across the stream, he spared Jonathan a brief, unreadable glance, then approached the bear with caution, to prod the carcass with the rifle. Satisfied that no life remained in the creature, he turned to Jonathan and nodded soberly.

"Are you bad hurt?"

"No. I don't think so."

The man stepped closer for a better look at the gashes in Jonathan's shoulder.

"You'll heal up. You were lucky. That was the

durndest thing I've ever seen—you taking on that bear with a sword." The hunter looked around, spotted the cutlass on the ground, went to fetch it. "What kind of long knife is this? I've never seen the like."

"Tripolitan. Who are you?"

"Name's Nathaniel Jones."

Jonathan was stunned. He couldn't believe he had heard right. "Jones? Nathaniel Jones?"

"That's my name."

"*Flintlock* Jones?"

Nathaniel grimaced. "I've been stuck with that for a spell, but I can't say I cotton to it much."

"President Jefferson told me about you."

"The president?"

Jonathan proffered a hand. "I'm Jonathan Groves, Lieutenant, United States Navy. You know, I never put much stock in coincidence—until today."

"What's a naval officer doing out here in the wilderness?"

Jonathan smiled. "I've been asking myself the same thing. It's a long story."

"Tell me later. We'd best get moving."

"Why? Is something the matter?"

"There's a party of Shawnee, not too far."

"Shawnee?"

"Indians."

"Oh, yes, of course." Jonathan reddened. "It's just I've been traveling for weeks, and haven't seen a soul, and then all of a sudden you show up . . ."

"You and that bear were making a commotion."

". . . and now you say there are Shawnee . . ."

Nathaniel handed him the cutlass. "Let's go."

"My horse."

"Quashquame is bringing it in." Nathaniel pointed with his chin.

Jonathan turned to see an Indian coming up along the creek, with the sorrel in tow.

"Look here," said Jonathan. "The president told me about you, Mr. Jones. He assured me that I could rely on you if I needed help . . ."

"I can't help you."

"But . . . I don't understand . . . I . . ."

"I'm after those Shawnee," said Nathaniel, his eyes ablaze. "I've been tracking them for days. They have my daughter."

"I see," said Jonathan. "Then it is I who will help you, sir."

Nathaniel looked him over with, thought Jonathan, some ill-disguised skepticism.

"Bear's one thing," said the hunter, laconic. "A Shawnee warrior is something else."

Chapter 26

All that day Jonathan was afforded no opportunity to discuss his mission with Flintlock Jones. Nathaniel and Quashquame were on the run until sundown. As far as Jonathan could tell, they did not stop once. He was amazed by their stamina. How could they maintain such a killing pace? Jonathan could scarcely keep up with them on horseback.

The going was rough. The trail the frontiersman and his Delaware friend followed took them through thick brush, across swift streams, and up steep grades. Quite often Jonathan was compelled to dismount and lead his horse through a seemingly impenetrable thicket or over a ridge.

Several times Jonathan lost sight of the hunter and the Indian altogether. Always, though, as he was beginning to think himself truly lost, Jonathan would see Quashquame off in the distance, Nathaniel having sent the Delaware back to find him and bring him on. As soon as Quashquame was sure that Jonathan had seen him, he would commence to run again, with Jonathan hurrying along in his wake as best as he was able.

Just after sunset, as thick blue shadows gathered in the forest, Nathaniel Jones appeared so suddenly in Jonathan's path that the young lieutenant gave a start.

"Get down," said Nathaniel curtly.

Dismounting, Jonathan winced at the pain in his shoulder and the ache in his bones.

"The Shawnee are camped just up ahead," announced the frontiersman.

"How far?"

"I don't know. But not far."

"You don't know? Then how can you be so certain?"

"I'm sure. They are close."

It made no sense to Jonathan. "Really, sir," he said, tired and irritated. "If you haven't actually seen them you can't very well tell me that you are certain they are near."

"The sign tells me that they are close. It tells me that for the last mile or so they've been looking for a good campsite. They are tired. And my daughter . . ." Nathaniel looked away, and Jonathan saw that savage gleam in the hunter's eye again. "My daughter is exhausted. Her feet are bleeding. She can't go much further without rest."

"There is no time to lose. We must go in and rescue her."

"Very gallant." There was a trace of sarcasm in Nathaniel's voice. "But I want to go in and save her, not get her killed. So you're not going anywhere, Lieutenant. You're staying here until it's done."

"But, I can't just stand by and—"

"You could get us all killed."

"How many Indians are there?" asked Jonathan, trying another tack.

"Six."

"Then you need me. I can fight."

Nathaniel relented some, and the ghost of a smile danced across his lips.

"Yes, you are a brave man. You fight bears with a big knife."

"I've fought my share of Barbary pirates, too," said Jonathan, defensive, thinking that Nathaniel was mocking him still. "These Indians cannot be any worse than Barbary pirates."

Nathaniel shrugged. "I wouldn't know about that. I've never tangled with a Barbary pirate. But I do know this. The Shawnee would hear you coming. You make too much noise. That's why you'll stay here."

"I will not," said Jonathan stubbornly.

Nathaniel lashed out and grabbed a handful of the lieutenant's tunic.

"Yes, you will," he replied in a fierce whisper.

Jonathan said nothing. But he met the hunter's piercing green gaze without flinching.

Nathaniel let him go. "You'll stay. Quashquame and I will deal with the Shawnee."

"The odds are too great," protested Jonathan.

"We have surprise on our side. I know you want to

help, and I thank you for that. But I can't risk it. This is Becky's only chance. If we fail, she is doomed."

Jonathan was silent a moment. Then, reluctantly, he nodded.

"She's your daughter, Mr. Jones. So it must be as you say."

Nathaniel searched Jonathan's face in the dying light, and saw the sincerity there. Satisfied, he turned and vanished into the deepening shadows.

Jonathan secured the sorrel to a tree and sat on his heels, disconsolate. Watching the night fall, he strained his ears to hear the first shots. It bothered him that Flintlock Jones did not think he had the wherewithal to sneak soundlessly through the woods. But on further reflection he decided that the frontiersman was probably correct, and that conclusion served only to reinforce his feelings of inadequacy of performing the monumental task Thomas Jefferson had set for him. He—and the republic—would no doubt fare better if he left the commission to track down and arrest Aaron Burr to Flintlock Jones.

Try as he might, he couldn't sit still. To think that action was imminent and close at hand was almost too much to bear. He could remember the fear that had mortified him on the eve of his first fight with the Barbary corsairs. Yet he had acquitted himself surprisingly well in that engagement, and in all subsequent ones. Now, for the first time, he was able to sit back and reflect and reach the startling conclusion that he thrived on battle. And he knew it would be impossible for him to sit here in the dark while others fought—especially when they were fighting for such a cause as the rescue of a young woman from the clutches of savage Indians.

Jonathan checked the pistol in his belt and, drawing the Tripolitan cutlass from its sheath, advanced with grim resolve through the trees, in the direction in which Nathaniel had gone.

He hadn't gone far when he heard the first shot.

The sound fetched him up short. He listened with bated breath.

Then—a flurry of shots, and the blood-curdling scream of an Indian.

Jonathan broke into a run.

He fell once, tripping over a root, and nearly ran himself through with the cutlass. He gathered himself up and pressed on. Straight ahead he could see the orange-red glow of a campfire. Onward he rushed, with wild abandon. A shape loomed suddenly in front of him. Was it Flintlock, or his Delaware friend? Jonathan hesitated—a hesitation that almost proved fatal.

With a cry reminiscent of a panther's scream, the Shawnee hurled his tomahawk. Jonathan was already throwing himself to the ground, yanking the pistol from his belt. He felt the passage of the tomahawk on his cheek, so close did the weapon come. On the ground, he fired. For an instant the muzzle-flash illuminated his adversary's face, a snarling rictus of hate. The Shawnee was charging straight at him. With a grunt he pitched forward, and Jonathan knew he had hit his mark. But it wasn't a killing shot, as the Indian was up immediately, and coming on, knife drawn, screaming at the top of his lungs.

Jonathan rose up from the ground and into the charge, catching the Indian in the midsection with a shoulder and straightening to flip the Shawnee head over heels. Whirling, Jonathan drove the cutlass through the warrior's chest before he could rise.

Jonathan jerked the cutlass free, turned, and ran for the Shawnee camp.

He burst onto a scene of pandemonium.

Quashquame was locked in desperate hand-to-hand combat with a Shawnee brave. They rolled across the ground, their knives flashing in the firelight, each trying to pin the other to the ground and strike the fatal blow by overpowering his foe. They rolled right over the fire in a shower of sparks.

As for Nathaniel Jones, he was standing with flintlock to shoulder, and as Jonathan watched, exchanged fire with a Shawnee warrior on the other side of the clearing. The rifles spoke simultaneously. The Indian crumpled. With unshakable aplomb, Nathaniel began to reload, moving across the clearing. Another Shawnee launched himself at the frontiersman from the cover of underbrush, tomahawk raised. Nathaniel turned and drove the stock of his rifle into the warrior's midsection. The Shawnee doubled over. Nathaniel slammed a knee into the Indian's face. The warrior jackknifed and fell.

The frontiersman had not quite finished with reloading—the ramrod was still in the rifle's barrel. Nathaniel calmly poured a dollop of powder in the flintlock's flashpan as the Shawnee was picking himself up off the ground. He fired at point-blank range. When the smoke cleared Jonathan could see the ramrod had pierced the falling Shawnee just below the ribcage, one end of the rod protruding from his sternum, and other from his back.

A woman's scream captured Jonathan's attention. The last warrior still standing had torn a blanket from the naked body of a young woman cowering at the base of a tree across the camp from where Nathaniel stood. The Indian raised his tomahawk. Nathaniel roared something unintelligible and charged forward. He did not have time to reload the flintlock. Jonathan realized he was closer. He hurled himself at the Shawnee, swinging the cutlass. The Shawnee turned away from the girl, ducked under Jonathan's wild swing, and struck with the tomahawk.

The weapon gashed the lieutenant's forearm and broke the bone. The cutlass slipped from the lieutenant's useless fingers. Jonathan lowered his shoulder and bulled right into the Shawnee, yelling like a madman. The warrior, off-balance, stumbled and fell, but pounced quickly to his feet. Jonathan threw himself across the young woman's body, shielding her. The warrior moved in for the kill. Jonathan knew, with a peculiar detachment, that he was going to die.

But even as the tomahawk came sweeping down, Nathaniel arrived, swinging the flintlock like a club. The rifle's stock smashed the Indian's face, dropping him. With a snarl as savage as a wild animal's, Nathaniel drove the stock into the Shawnee's face again, and again, and yet again—until the warrior's skull was a bloody pulp, and he lay still in death.

Feeling weak and dizzy, Jonathan rolled off the young woman, clutching his arm, and watched the blood stream through his fingers.

Nathaniel fell to his knees beside Rebecca, draping the blanket around her shoulders and holding her close. She was crying softly, and her tears fell onto his buckskin hunting shirt.

"I knew you would come for me," she whispered.

Nathaniel could not speak. Tears brimming in his eyes, he looked up at Quashquame. The Delaware had slain his foe. He was bloodied and charred from the fire.

"Take care of the lieutenant," said Nathaniel. "He saved Becky's life."

Quashquame nodded impassively and knelt beside Jonathan, tried to gently pry the lieutenant's hand from his wound.

"I'm fine," mumbled Jonathan. "Just fine . . ."

Quashquame grasped his arm at wrist and elbow and with a deft twist snapped the fractured bone back into place.

Jonathan fainted dead away.

Chapter 27

When Jonathan came to it was daylight. The sun, slanting through the trees, nearly blinded him. Then Nathaniel loomed over him, blocking out the sun.

"How do you fare?" asked the frontiersman.

Jonathan took a moment to answer. His arm hurt like hell, done up in a sling tightly against his chest. There was a smelly poultice on the wound, but he decided it would be better not to ask what the poultice was made of. The wounds he had gotten from the bear's claws stung like a thousand ants biting into his raw flesh. Apart from that, every bone and muscle in his body ached.

"I've had better days," he admitted, and managed to sit up. He looked around, expecting to see dead Indians. But they were in another clearing, deep in the forest. "Where are we?"

"Not far from the Shawnee camp. But far enough."

"Did we . . . Are they all dead?"

"All done for."

The image of the Shawnee warrior bending over him, tomahawk raised, made Jonathan shudder involuntarily.

"They are worse than Barbary pirates, I think," he said.

Nathaniel sat on his heels. "I owe you thanks. Reckon you saved Becky's life."

"How is she?"

Nathaniel glanced over his shoulder. Jonathan looked that way. Quashquame was hunkered down by a small crackling smokeless fire. He was heating the blade of a knife. Beyond him, wrapped in a blanket and sound asleep, was Rebecca.

When Nathaniel turned back to him, Jonathan saw some dark and fierce emotion cloud the hunter's features.

"They . . . mistreated her."

"My God," breathed Jonathan, comprehending.

"But she's alive. And she's strong, in mind and body. She'll be fine."

"I'm glad of that."

"I was wrong about you, Lieutenant. I apologize for that.

"No need. I just couldn't miss a fight, I guess."

"I see why Jefferson chose you."

The compliment stunned Jonathan. He had been so unsure of himself, so assailed by self-doubt—and now this man, this frontier legend, was praising his bravery. Jonathan suddenly felt markedly better.

"Thank you," he mumbled, embarrassed.

"You said you needed my help."

"I'm looking for Aaron Burr."

"What for?"

Jonathan looked around. "My horse . . . ?"

"Yonder."

"There is a letter, in my bag. It will explain . . ."

"I'll fetch it."

When Nathaniel returned with the letter Jonathan let him read it.

"Jefferson sent you to *arrest* Burr?"

Jonathan nodded.

"That's a tall order."

"Which is why I need your help, Mr. Jones."

Nathaniel looked dubious.

"He's not a friend of yours, is he?"

"A friend? No. But I've met him. He's been in Kaintuck a few times the last year or two. Trying to enlist men in an army. Says he's been commissioned by the government to prepare an expedition to invade Spanish Mexico, or Florida. There's no love lost in Kaintuck for the Spaniards. They closed down the river and put the hurt on a lot of people. And they rile up the southern Indians to raid our settlements."

"He is not sanctioned by the United States government," Groves said. "In fact, the president has evidence that he plans to create a separate state, with him at the top of it, out of this region."

"I don't think that will happen."

"But it doesn't mean he won't try."

"You're saying he's a traitor."

"It appears so."

Nathaniel thought about that for a minute. "Jefferson gave you my name?"

"He did. He said I could rely on you. That many years ago you were engaged in—he called it an heroic undertaking, I believe. When everything hung in the balance."

Nathaniel remembered. Those hours—when the Tory dragoons rode into Louisa, killed his father and Amanda's mother, and rode on for Charlottesville, with the intention of capturing Governor Jefferson and the entire Virginia assembly—yes, he remembered. Those events were indelibly etched in his memory. That midnight ride he had undertaken, on the farmer's blood stallion, Jumper, with the Tories hot on his heels . . .

"Don't recollect feeling much like a hero," he said. "I do recollect being scared to death. I was just a boy then. There was this Tory soldier . . . He had orders to kill me, and I reckon he could have, easy enough. But he didn't, for some reason. I never have figured that out."

"The president said he wrote you once . . ."

"Yes. I recollect that, too."

"You did not reply?"

Nathaniel shrugged. "I'm not much for letter writing."

Jonathan wondered if Flintlock Jones was as committed to Jefferson—and the republic—as the president had made him out to be.

Nathaniel seemed to be able to read his mind on that score.

"I think Jefferson's a good man," said the frontiersman. "A good president. If what he says about Burr is true, then Burr must be stopped."

"Then you'll help me?"

"I wouldn't be wasting all this breath if I didn't aim to."

"I am told Burr might be gathering men, arms, and flatboats at Blennerhassett's island. Do you know . . . ?"

"I know of it. It's less than two days from here."

"That close!"

Nathaniel smiled faintly. "You weren't lost, were you, Lieutenant?"

"Well . . . I wouldn't say lost . . ."

"No. Just turned around some. We'll leave first thing in the morning."

"What about your daughter? Is she able to travel?"

"Quashquame will stay with her. When she's able, he'll take her home."

"You would trust her with him?"

Nathaniel's expression informed Jonathan that he had spoken carelessly.

"I . . . I didn't mean to imply . . ."

"I'd trust Quashquame with my life. Truth is, I have already, and on more than one occasion."

"He doesn't talk much, does he?"

"He can't. His tongue's been cut out. Been so ever since I met him."

"Cut out! Why, in God's name?"

"He has yet to tell me how or why it happened, Lieutenant."

Jonathan reddened. "I wish I could learn to think before I speak."

"It's a good habit to have," agreed Nathaniel.

"What is he doing with that knife?"

Quashquame had finished heating the blade, and even as Jonathan posed the question the Delaware glanced across the camp at him.

"Those wounds in your back have festered," said Nathaniel. "I'm to blame for that. I should have tended to them right away. But I was in a hurry to save Becky. Anyway, those wounds must be bled, and then cauterized."

Every trace of color drained from Jonathan's face. Quashquame was up now, and walking toward him.

"Now wait . . ." he said. He needed time to prepare himself.

"No time to waste," said Nathaniel. He knew what Jonathan was trying to do. Knew, also, that delay served only to give the imagination free rein to work its evil on a man's courage. You could not prepare yourself to endure pain. It didn't work that way. In fact, it made the pain worse. No, you had to get it over with, quick as possible. "Poisoned wound like that can kill a man." He held out his hand, palm turned up. A strip of leather lay in his palm. It looked to Jonathan like the tip of a cinch strap. "Bite down hard on this. Or, if you want, I'll knock you out."

"Absolutely not," said Jonathan, offended.

"Meant nothing by the offer."

"No."

Jonathan took the strip of leather, put it between his teeth, and bit down hard. Looking up at the impassive Delaware standing over him, he nodded. He was sweating all of a sudden. It ran down into his eyes, stinging them. As he closed his eyes the last thing he saw was Quashquame bending over him . . .

A couple of hours later Jonathan was feeling much better. The pain he had suffered while Quashquame cut open his wounds to let the infection drain, and then cauterized them with the blade heated in the fire, was but a dim memory now. At first Jonathan had laid curled up on the ground, too weak from the ordeal to sit up. When finally he did rise, he noticed that Quashquame was gone. Nathaniel told him that the Delaware had gone out hunting supper. A short while later, they heard a shot, off in the distance, and Quashquame was soon back, with a doe slung over his shoulder.

He had already bled the carcass. Now, a short distance from the camp, he and Nathaniel set to butchering it. Before long they had venison steaks sizzling over the fire. The smell of the roasting meat awakened Jonathan's appetite, and that appetite proved to be monstrous.

While they were cooking the meat Rebecca woke up. The day was coming to a close. The shadows of evening reached across the valley, and the temperature was dropping. She was cold, and sat huddled in her blanket, close to the fire. When Nathaniel asked her how she was feeling, she only smiled, wanly, and nodded. He did not press the issue. He could see that her composure was a very fragile thing indeed. She had endured a horrible ordeal, and there were many words of comfort that as her father he wanted to say, but he was wise enough to realize that it would just make matters worse at this juncture.

Little was said between them as they sat around the fire in the deepening gloom and ate their fill. Nathaniel and Quashquame broke open the bones and scooped the marrow out with their fingers. Jonathan tried it, and didn't like it at all, but the frontiersman encouraged him to eat the marrow anyway "It'll give you strength," he said.

Jonathan couldn't help but notice that Rebecca was watching him. When he looked up to meet her gaze, she would quickly avert her eyes. After a while he stopped looking directly at her. That was not easy to do. Though her face was smudged with dirt, and swollen some, and her yellow hair was tangled and matted, she looked pretty as a picture, as far as he was concerned.

When they had finished eating, Nathaniel informed Rebecca that Quashquame would see her safely home when she felt strong enough to travel. Jonathan expected her to react poorly to this news. After such an experience as she had suffered at the hands of the Shawnee, she would naturally be dismayed by the prospect of parting company so soon with her father. He felt bad about taking Flintlock from her. But she accepted the news bravely. Nathaniel explained to her that he was obliged to help Jonathan in a matter of some importance. He did not elaborate, and she did not ask him to.

The next morning Jonathan felt almost as good as new. He courteously offered his horse to Rebecca, through Nathaniel.

"She is in no condition to walk all the way home," he said.

Nathaniel was grateful. He took his leave of Rebecca with great reluctance, holding her in his arms for a long time. To Quashquame he merely nodded, and said nothing. Between such true friends, mused Jonathan, no words were necessary. It was understood that Quashquame and Rebecca would remain at the camp at least one more day. There was plenty of venison left, and Nathaniel urged his daughter to eat as much as she could, to regain her strength.

With that he and Jonathan departed the camp, heading almost due west, in the direction of the island estate of Harman Blennerhassett. Only two days away, Flintlock had said. Jonathan wondered if that would be the end of his trail. With any luck, Aaron Burr would be there.

But the young lieutenant couldn't help wondering if he was due some luck or if he had run out of luck altogether.

Chapter 28

After almost three weeks in the wilderness, and not
having seen so much as a ramshackle hut in all that
time, Jonathan was awestruck by the sight of the
mansion on Blennerhassett's Island.

Even in the cities he had visited—Charleston,
Richmond, and Washington—he could not recollect
having laid eyes upon so splendid a structure, with
the possible exception of the President's House. Nor
could any of the dozens of plantation manors he was
familiar with measure up.

The Blennerhassett mansion was a stately white
monument to the architectural discipline. It was
fronted by a row of elegant columns. Numerous outbuildings could be seen behind it. In front of the
house, a grassy lawn sloped down to the water's
edge, where two piers jutted out into the swiftly
flowing waters of the Ohio.

From where he and Nathaniel stood, concealed
in the brush across the river, Jonathan could see
nary a soul stirring. His heart sank. He had
expected—nay, hoped—to see dozens of burly

frontiersmen encamped on that lawn, and flatboats, laden with supplies, moored to those piers. And perhaps even Aaron Burr himself, strolling among his men.

But there was no activity. None. The island appeared deserted.

"I think we are too late," said Jonathan.

Nathaniel nodded. "Looks that way."

"Where could he be now?"

The frontiersman shrugged. "If he was here collecting men and boats, he's probably already downriver. But you never know about Burr. He's a crafty devil. He might never have been here."

"What do we do now?"

"I reckon we ought to go knock on that door. See if anybody's home."

With some trepidation, Jonathan eyed the broad river that lay between them and the island. Blennerhassett's moat.

Nathaniel noticed the expression on the young lieutenant's face.

"You can swim, can't you?"

"Well . . . I can manage."

"I just figured a sailor could swim."

"If you're a sailor and in the water, Mr. Jones, it usually means your ship has sunk, or some other disaster has struck."

"I see."

With that Nathaniel led the way upriver. He stopped about a half-mile up from the island.

"If we enter the river here," he explained, "and swim hard, the current'll get us to the island."

"My arm . . ." reminded Jonathan.

"You could wait here for me."

Jonathan studied the river. As peaceful as the island seemed, he had learned that appearances could be deceiving. He couldn't let Flintlock Jones go in alone.

He shook his head.

"Shuck your clothes."

They stripped down to the bare skin. Nathaniel placed his shot pouch in one of Jonathan's boots, and his powderhorn in the other. Then he packed the boots tightly with other articles of clothing. Lastly, he wrapped the boots in the rest of their clothes, making a bundle that also contained his pistol, and Jonathan's.

Once he was shed of his clothes, Jonathan gingerly placed his broken arm in the sling. He felt a little foolish, standing there buck-naked wearing just the sling, with the Tripolitan cutlass in his good hand.

"How's the arm feel?" queried Nathaniel as he ran the barrel of his flintlock rifle through the knot he had made to tie up the bundle.

"I have no feeling in my hand," said Jonathan flatly. "I can't move my fingers. Haven't been able to since it happened."

Nathaniel looked at him, startled, and for a moment was grimly silent as he digested this news. Then he glanced at the river, and said, in an off-handed way, "I reckon that tomahawk did plenty of damage."

"I suppose I shall have to learn to write left-handed."

Nathaniel made no reply. Jonathan realized the backwoodsman was feeling some guilt about the condition of his hand, since he had lost the use of it in saving Rebecca's life.

"I would have gladly given my entire arm, even my life, Mr. Jones, to save your daughter."

Nathaniel nodded curtly. "I'll do most of the swimming," he said. "You just hang on to one end of this rifle and float."

Jonathan wondered what to do with the cutlass. He wound up putting it between his bad arm and his ribcage—pressing down with the arm he could hold it in place.

They slipped into the water. It was cold—so cold that it took Jonathan's breath away. It was running swiftly, too, sweeping them downstream. Nathaniel swam with a long, powerful sidestroke aided by strong scissor kicks. He held onto the stock of the rifle while Jonathan clung to the barrel. Between them floated the bundle of clothes.

Being only a mediocre swimmer, Jonathan knew that if he got into trouble he would be hard pressed to get to shore, hampered by his bad arm. The devilish current seemed intent on prying him loose from his precarious hold on the slippery wet barrel. He fought down panic, tried to relax the upper part of his body, and float on his side. There was nothing wrong with his legs, so he kicked, trying to help Nathaniel as best he could. When his leg cramped he almost panicked again, but through sheer willpower maintained his composure.

It seemed like forever before his leg brushed bottom mud. He looked up, blinking river water out of his eyes, and was amazed to find that they had made it across.

Apparently they had made their landfall on the northern tip of the island, for he could see both broad blue channels rushing away. The woods were thick along here, the house out of sight.

As he stood there, shivering uncontrollably, reveling in the heat from the sun on his back and shoulders, Nathaniel unwrapped the bundle of clothes. The outer layer had been his buckskin hunting shirt, and Jonathan was amazed to see that the rest of their clothing was only slightly damp. He dressed quickly. Before donning his own garb, Nathaniel took the precaution of cleaning out and reloading the flintlock rifle. His powder and shot were bone dry. That done, he dressed, then reloaded and primed the pistols.

"Ready?" he asked.

"If we meet someone, what will we tell them?"

"That we've come looking for Burr—to join up."

"But this uniform . . ."

Nathaniel shook his head. "Means nothing. If what you say about Burr and his band is true, they're all traitors. What's two more?"

Jonathan grimaced. "The president made the same suggestion."

"Jefferson's a smart feller, I hear. Sending you to do this job is proof enough of that."

It was the second such compliment the frontiersman had paid Jonathan, and it meant every bit as much to the lieutenant as the first.

"Tell them you were cashiered," suggested Nathaniel. "You're looking for adventure."

Jonathan laughed.

"What's funny?"

"I've had my fill of adventure, I think."

"When you meet Burr, you can make it plain you harbor ill will towards the government. I reckon he does, too, and he'll be glad to make your acquaintance."

"You mean *if* we meet Burr."

"I meant it the way I said it."

"It will be a difficult role to play."

"If Burr's not here, we'll catch up with him sooner or later. When we do, we've got to get close to him. We won't get close if he knows you're carrying the president's warrant for his arrest. In fact, we could get killed."

Jonathan nodded. "I'll do what I must."

"Let's go."

They marched through the woods, breaking out into a tobacco field. A big tobacco barn stood at one end of the field. The river was on the other. Straight ahead was the mansion, so incongruous in this wild country that Jonathan had difficulty accepting that it was real, and not some frontier mirage.

Crossing the field, then the grounds, passing beneath stately ash and hickory trees, they arrived at the front door unchallenged. Nathaniel pounded on the door with his fist. They listened with bated breath for any sound from within.

Nothing.

There was something very peculiar about it all, mused Jonathan, ill at ease.

"There have been plenty of men here recently," remarked Nathaniel.

"How can you tell?"

"Sign all over." Nathaniel smiled. "You'll learn to read it, if you live long enough."

"I . . ." Jonathan was set to inform the frontiersman that he had every intention of returning to the life of a seafarer when this mission was over, but the door opening cut him short.

A wizened black man stood there. He wore a black swallowtail coat and snow-white shirt and gloves. He said nothing. Just stared dolefully at them.

"We're looking for Aaron Burr," said Nathaniel.

"Ain't here."

"Blennerhassett?"

The man looked him up and down, then gave Jonathan an impassive once-over. Finally he nodded.

"Follow me."

They entered a long hallway. There were polished marble tiles underfoot, and crystal chandeliers dangling from the ceiling. Ornately framed painting graced brocaded walls, elaborate molding and architrives were above the doors. It was all quite opulent, and again Jonathan was overwhelmed by the incongruity of it all, here, so removed from civilization.

The valet led them to pocket doors that, when slipped open, revealed a parlor. The maroon velveteen curtains on the windows barred the sunlight. The room would have been quite dark but for an oil lamp fluttering low on a taboret near one of the richly upholstered wing chairs that obliquely faced a cold hearth.

"Massuh, two gennelmun . . ."

A man rose from the wing chair like quail bursting from cover. He was short, paunchy, moon faced, with hair in wild disarray and thick side whiskers that nearly met at a weak, slightly quivering chin. He wore a green brocade smoking jacket with satin cuffs and lapels. His eyes were brimming with apprehension. He gaped at Jonathan's uniform.

"They have come for me at last!" he exclaimed.

Jonathan was nonplussed. This had to be Blennerhassett. He certainly looked eccentric. But what was he talking about? *Who* was he talking to?

Nathaniel was quick to grasp the situation. He realized that Blennerhassett believed that Jonathan was here as an officer in the service of the United States to arrest him for his participation in Aaron Burr's treasonous plot.

"Not what you think," said the frontiersman.

"We've come to join up with Aaron Burr. We heard he'd be here."

Blennerhassett's eyes widened. "You mean . . . you're not . . ."

"No, I'm not," said Jonathan. "I . . . they cashiered me. I was false accused of cowardice in the face of the enemy. I gave years of my life—my sweat and my blood—in the service of my country, and that's the thanks I get. I—"

Nathaniel shot him a sidelong look. Jonathan wondered if he was laying it on a little thick, overplaying his new role as a traitor to the republic.

"Oh, thank heavens," heaved Blennerhassett, wringing his hands. "I thought for a terrible moment that you had come to carry me off in chains." He laughed nervously. "May I offer you some food or drink?"

"We just want to find Burr," said Nathaniel.

"I am afraid you missed him by two days."

Jonathan could not mask his disappointment. Burr *had* been here. So close, and now God only knew how far away.

"But don't despair," said Blennerhassett cheerily. "With luck you can catch up with him."

"He went downriver by boat?" asked Nathaniel.

Blennerhassett nodded. "He and sixty men, in three flatboats."

"Bound for New Orleans, I reckon."

"I believe that is the case, yes."

Nathaniel turned to Jonathan. "The sooner we go, the sooner we'll catch up with him."

"Must you go so soon?" asked Blennerhassett. "It gets rather lonely out here, you know. Oh, there's my wife, of course, but . . ." He shrugged, smiling sheepishly.

"Let's go," said Nathaniel.

"If you have need of a boat—".

But they were gone.

Once outside the house, Jonathan said, "A strange bird, Blennerhassett. I wonder what he's doing out here?"

"Who knows?"

"Where are his slaves?"

"Want to go back and ask him?"

"No, thanks."

"Well, we won't catch Butt on the river. He'll have to portage around the falls of the Ohio, but that won't slow him down enough. He'll make good time. The river's running strong."

"So what do we do?"

"Go overland. We can make my cabin in three or four days if we press hard."

Jonathan had visions of trying to keep up with Flintlock Jones as he raced through the forest from sunrise to sunset without respite. It was doubly discouraging that the frontiersman was at least a dozen years older than he.

"We'll get horses there," continued Nathaniel, "and go on to Natchez. With luck we'll be there waiting for Burr."

Jonathan couldn't help but speculate on what they would do about the sixty men accompanying Burr.

He told himself not to worry about it. Tried, in fact, to look on the bright side. At least he would get the chance to see Rebecca Jones again.

The prospect was a pleasing one.

Chapter 29

Flintlock Jones had calculated correctly—in four days they reached his cabin near Boonesboro.

Jonathan remembered little about those four days except that they were long, and filled with the exhausting drudgery of traipsing through the forest. The best that he could say about it was that it had been a damnably long walk, and he was very glad to be done with it. The tedious days were all blended together into one long tribulation.

But he perked up some as they drew near the cabin, happy to be afforded the opportunity to see Rebecca Jones again.

As they ascended the long slope of bluegrass from the road into the settlement, Nathaniel called out to the cabin. An instant later Rebecca and Amanda were bursting out of the door, running toward them. Nathaniel couldn't restrain himself. He broke into a lope. Jonathan watched the three embrace. A bittersweet smile touched his lips. He suddenly felt homesick. Not for the house of his parents in North Carolina. No, he hadn't felt comfortably at home there for quite some time now. His father was a severe man, not given to any overt demonstration of affection. And his mother was quiet, reserved. Jonathan remembered her as a broken-spirited woman, and he had come to the conclusion that his father was responsible.

Still, he was homesick, longing for the home and hearth he did not have. And he envied Flintlock Jones. The frontiersman possessed that which was worth more than all the gold in the world.

Jonathan marveled at how much Rebecca and her mother resembled one another. But he did not spare Amanda too many glances. Rebecca was the focus of his attention. When Nathaniel and his wife started for the cabin, arm in arm, Rebecca turned and came toward him. Jonathan's heart began doing funny things. She was smiling, and her golden hair was radiant in the sunshine. He noticed how small and delicate her feet were as she walked through the windswept bluegrass, and just for one brief, ecstatic moment he could imagine that she was his, coming to greet him with a hug and a kiss as he returned from a long absence. A wonderful, if short-lived, dream.

She stopped face to face with him. Her smile turned shy. Jonathan groped for something to say. Why didn't she say something? Was she as bashful as he? Try as he might, he could find no words, though there were many things he would have liked to say.

Then she reached out and took his hand, and they walked on up to the cabin at the top of the hill.

"How is Stephen Cooper?" asked Nathaniel, after they had settled down to dinner.

"Tom insisted on taking him home," replied Amanda. "I didn't think it wise to move him so soon. He was welcome here, but Tom wouldn't hear of it. The poor man. He broke down at the sight of his son lying there so near death."

"Stephen's all he's got left."

"I was planning to go see him today," said Rebecca. "Will you come along?"

"Gladly," said Nathaniel.

Rebecca turned to Jonathan. "Will you come, too, Lieutenant Groves?"

"Mm!" Jonathan was caught with his mouth full of stew. All he could do was nod.

"Stephen was with me down by the spring when the Shawnees came," explained Rebecca. "He was badly wounded and . . . and they took his scalp."

Jonathan was instantly sorry he had agreed to go along. It sounded suspiciously like this Stephen Cooper was Rebecca's beau. Down by the spring? And what had they been doing down by the spring? As his imagination went to work, Jonathan's heart sank.

"Rebecca," murmured Amanda, shaking her head.

Rebecca's temper flared. "Well, it happened, didn't it? There is no point in not talking about it—pretending it never happened."

No one said anything for a moment. Jonathan

gaped, spoon poised between his bowl and his mouth.

"Sorry," said Rebecca, penitently.

They were finishing up the meal when Quashquame arrived. In his arms was a squirming ball of fur.

"A puppy!" exclaimed Rebecca, delighted.

"I was told you were out hunting," laughed Nathaniel.

Quashquame's shrug professed innocence as loudly as any words could have done. He put the puppy on the floor. Rebecca got down on her hands and knees to play with it. The puppy rolled over on its back, legs akimbo. When she scratched its belly, the puppy writhed with delight. When she stopped scratching, it scrambled to its feet, jumped up, and licked her in the face.

"Thank you, Quashquame," said Amanda, from the bottom of her heart.

The Delaware nodded.

"Yes! Thank you!" gasped Rebecca. She leaped to her feet and gave Quashquame a hug.

Nathaniel laughed again. "By gum, Quashquame. I've never seen you blush before."

Jonathan pretended to have an abiding interest in the dollop of stew left in the bottom of his bowl. He felt a sharp twinge of jealousy, directed at the Delaware, and reproached himself for it. He had no right to be jealous.

Quashquame and the puppy—promptly named Ranger by common consent—stayed with Amanda while Nathaniel and Jonathan accompanied Rebecca to the Cooper cabin. They cut through the woods. Jonathan straggled, bringing up the rear, the reluctant companion. This was just what he needed, he thought—another long walk through the woods.

Reaching their destination, they found Tom Cooper sprawled in a rocking chair on the cabin's porch. A big, square-cut man, his arms hung limply, his knuckles brushed the plank flooring of the porch as he creaked slowly back and forth. His chin rested on a burly chest. His hair was awry and deep shadows surrounded his eyes.

"He's let his place go," murmured Nathaniel, as they approached the cabin.

Tom Cooper didn't seem to notice them until they were on the porch. He looked up with fevered eyes. Recognizing Rebecca, he thumbed in the direction of the cabin door.

"He's inside," he said hoarsely.

"Thank you." Rebecca went into the cabin.

"How do you fare, Tom?" asked Nathaniel.

"I'm alive." Cooper didn't sound too happy about it.

"You could use some sleep and some food, looks to me."

"Don't worry about me, Flintlock."

Jonathan detected a note of hostility in Cooper's voice. He glanced at Nathaniel, but the frontiersman, if he had noticed, did not show it.

"How is your son?"

"Knockin' on death's door there for a spell. Sometimes he comes to, and he acts plumb crazy."

"He's a strong lad. He'll pull through, and be right as rain."

"Oh, he might pull through, but he won't be right. Ever. Something's done snapped inside of him."

"I'm sorry."

Tom Cooper just glowered.

"I could be wrong," said Nathaniel, leaning on his long rifle in a deceptively casual stance, and peering out across Cooper's field, "but I get the feeling you blame me and mine, somehow, for what happened to Stephen."

"Let's just say I'druther you and yourn stay away from my son."

Nathaniel looked him straight in the eye for a long half-minute, and Jonathan tensed, scarcely breathing, expecting violence to erupt between these two men. But then the frontiersman gave a curt nod, and looked at him, and said, "I'd be obliged if you would go inside and fetch Becky."

Jonathan reluctantly complied. He did not want to see Rebecca Jones mourning at the bedside of her lover.

He found her in a small room in the back of the cabin, and indeed she was standing beside a bed. He couldn't see much of the man lying in the bed; a coverlet was pulled up to his chin and his head was swathed in bandages. He didn't appear to be conscious. Rebecca was holding his hand in both of her own. The look on her face as she gazed sadly at the pallid features of Stephen Cooper was not something Jonathan had wanted to see. His worst fears were now confirmed. Rebecca Jones was in love.

Standing in the doorway, Jonathan cleared his throat to get her attention.

"Your father told me to come get you," he said. "Mr. Cooper doesn't want us here."

"Why not?"

Jonathan shook his head. "I'd better let your father explain. We'd better be going."

Rebecca leaned over and kissed Stephen Cooper on the cheek.

Jonathan turned away. He couldn't bear to watch.

On the way back to their cabin, Nathaniel explained the situation to Rebecca. She absorbed the news without comment. Deeply disturbed, she didn't say a word all the way home.

That evening, over supper, Nathaniel informed his wife and daughter that he would be leaving on the morrow with Jonathan. He explained that the lieutenant had a commission from the president himself to arrest Aaron Burr. They would take the Natchez Trace and hope to intercept Burr and his party before they reached New Orleans by the river route. Quashquame would stay at the cabin until they had returned.

Amanda made no protest, though it was obvious that the news saddened her.

"I reckon it seems of late like I'm always breaking my promise," said Nathaniel gently.

She reached out and covered his hand with hers.

"We will just have to make the most of what time we have together."

Once again Jonathan felt like the villain. What right had he to take Flintlock Jones from his home and family?

"Why don't you stay, Mr. Jones?" he suggested. "I can find my way from here."

"I told you that I would help."

"I don't hold you to it."

"I hold myself to it. I owe you."

"I forsake any debt you may think is due me," said Jonathan, with an impatient wave of his hand.

Nathaniel peered at him, speculatively.

"What's bothering you, Lieutenant?"

"This is my affair," said Jonathan stiffly.

He realized that one of the reasons he wanted to go on alone was because he knew that every time he looked at Nathaniel from now on he would think about this cabin, or, more precisely, about the frontiersman's daughter, and Jonathan couldn't wait to put this place, and her memory, behind him. Of course he could not admit as much.

"No, I don't reckon," was Nathaniel's softspoken reply. "If Aaron Burr has plans for this country that go counter to its best welfare, then it's my business, too—and the business of every man who has a stake in this republic."

Jonathan just stared, at a loss as to how to argue with such patriotic sentiments.

"So we'll be leaving at daybreak," concluded Nathaniel. "Now, we don't have to stick together, but since we're both headed down the Trace, the only way to travel to Natchez, it makes sense that we travel together. That's a robber-festered road if ever there was one."

Jonathan merely nodded. There was nothing more he could do. And he felt as though he had made a complete fool of himself—again.

Nathaniel and Amanda retired to their bedroom immediately after dinner, with the intention of making their last night together for who knew how long a memorable one.

Quashquame went outside to sleep beneath the stars. Rebecca explained that the Delaware could not bear to sleep indoors.

As for Rebecca herself, she made sure Jonathan had a comfortable pallet of blankets on the floor in the common room near the hearth, and piled another log on the fire, as a cold northerly wind had swept down that evening, a reminder that winter was imminent. Utterly miserable, Jonathan watched her do these things for his benefit and thanked her as she prepared to retire to her own room. Scooping up the puppy, which had followed her everywhere all evening, she bestowed a sweet smile on Jonathan—a smile that wrenched at his poor heart. And then she was gone, and he sat there on his pallet for quite a long time, listening to the howling wind, staring morosely into the fire.

He did not think sleep would ever come, but it finally did.

Hours later he woke with a start, and found Rebecca sitting in front of the dying fire. Her golden hair was tousled. She wore a long white cotton gown, and he could tell she was cold. She sat with her knees drawn up tightly.

"Rebecca?"

"I'm sorry if I woke you."

"What is it? What's wrong?"

She was reluctant to tell him. A shudder coursed through her slender body. Jonathan draped one of his blankets around her. For one brief moment he was endowed with the courage to bare his soul to her, to share his true feelings. This would be his only chance.

"Rebecca, I—"

"I find it hard to sleep," she whispered. "I keep . . . every time I start to drift off I wake up in great fear, my heart pounding, and I think . . . I think there are Shawnee warriors out in the night . . . and they can see me . . . they are watching through the window . . . and they've come to steal me away . . ."

A single tear escaped her eyes.

Jonathan knelt beside her, placed a comforting arm around her shoulders.

"There, now. Don't cry. You're perfectly safe here. I . . . your father wouldn't let anything happen to you. And remember, Quashquame is out there somewhere. I don't think there's Shawnee living who could slip up on him."

"They did . . . terrible things to me, Lieutenant," she whispered.

"It's all in the past now, and it doesn't matter, anyway."

"It doesn't?"

"Of course not."

"I'm . . . I'm . . ."

"The most wonderful person I have ever met," he blurted out.

She stared at him, surprised—but no more surprised than he.

Then Ranger arrived, galloping across the floor and sliding to a stop. Laughing, Rebecca picked him up and held him close. The puppy squirmed in pure ecstasy, licking her arms and hands and chin.

"Do you mind if I sit here for a spell?" she asked Jonathan. "I have been sleeping with my mother until tonight and . . . I know I'm being silly."

"I don't mind at all. Do you mind if I sit with you?"

"You can go back to sleep if you want. I know you must be tired. And you have a long day ahead of you."

"I would rather stay awake and look at you."

Rebecca blushed.

They sat side by side, in silence for quite some time.

Then, out of the blue, she asked, "Will you be coming back this way?"

The question caught him completely off his guard. "Well, I . . . I don't know . . ."

"I guess you want to get home as soon as possible. Where is home?"

"North Carolina. But no, on the contrary, there is nothing in North Carolina for me."

Then you *will* come back?"

"Why, yes."

Later, with the puppy asleep in her arms, she dozed off, Jonathan's arm around her, and her head resting against his chest.

Chapter 30

It had started out an Indian trail, used by the Choctaws and Chickasaws, although their legends hinted at an even older culture than theirs—a people who had vanished into the mists of time hundreds of years before. These people had built temple mounds that yet remained as mute and mysterious monuments to a lost civilization.

These ancient, extinct people had constructed sprawling villages, too; created flint and pottery objects of beguiling beauty; and established a trade network linking all their villages together. The Trace, then, could have been their creation.

The Choctaws and Chickasaws were related. They spoke the same Muskhogean language, as did the Creeks and the Seminoles. But the Choctaws and Chickasaws had been enemies forever. According to their tradition, they had come to the Mississippi Valley region as one people from somewhere to the west. At a place called *Nanih Waiya* there was a quarrel between the two sons of a dying chief. The sons could not reconcile their differences, and went their separate ways, each accompanied by a sizeable number of loyal followers. There had been bad blood between the two tribes every since.

The Choctaws went south and developed into an agricultural people, inclined to peace, except where the Chickasaws were concerned. One of their more distinctive customs was the flattening of their infants' heads. The French explorers had taken to calling them Flatheads as a result. Another Choctaw peculiarity was the existence of a caste called the Bone Pickers. The Bone Pickers were identifiable by their unusually long fingernails. Their job was to ascend a burial platform and pick the rotting flesh from corpses. The flesh was burned, while the picked-clean skeleton was transferred to a coffin, its final resting place—a custom unique to the Choctaw.

The Chickasaws were hunters who scorned farming. They were inveterate warmakers, too. Hunters and fighters without peer, they were the exact opposites of their Choctaw cousins. Their nation was located in the northern region of the Mississippi Territory. Their fortress villages, about a dozen of them, straddled the Trace. Down the trace they would venture to make war against the Choctaws, whenever the urge moved them. Fortunately for the Choctaws, they outnumbered the aggressive Chickasaws almost two to one.

The Chickasaws had houses for summer and houses for winter. The summer houses, long rectan-

gles, open at the eaves, with peaked roofs, were constructed of pitch pine, sassafras, or cypress. They
were virtually bulletproof. The structures were cool
and airy and easily defensible, which was a good
thing, since the warlike Chickasaws had many enemies besides the Choctaws. Their winter houses, on
the other hand, were round, about twenty feet in di-
ameter. Passing through the narrow door of a Chickasaw winter house, one would have to wend his way
through a six-foot-long winding passage. This passage
kept the cold winter wind out. It also made the winter house very defensible.

Until the mid-1700s, the Mississippi region was
populated exclusively by the Indians. The French
had tried to establish some sort of control over the
area, but after the massacre of the Fort Rosalie gar-
rison and the defeat of a French force at the hands
of the fierce Chickasaws, only a handful of itinerant
French and Spanish traders could be found. These
intrepid souls often traveled the old Trace, visiting
the villages of the Choctaws and sometimes even the
Chickasaws.

But in the 1760s the pioneers came, the overmountain man was in the caravan. From the beginning the Chickasaws made it clear that these
interlopers would not be greeted with open arms.
Like the Cherokees and Shawnees to the north and
east of their hunting grounds, the Chickasaws challenged the frontiersman.

But the migration of the pioneers was inexorable.
They built sturdy "stations" for defense against In-

dian attacks, and proceeded stubbornly to put down roots. They wanted the land and they were going to have it. And the Indians' arrows and warclubs were no match for the frontiersman's long rifle.

The pioneers had to float their produce down the river by flatboat to the markets at New Orleans and Natchez. By 1800, dozens of boatloads of Tennessee and Kentucky goods were arriving every month at these two towns. Having brought their goods to market—tobacco, hemp, or hogs—farmers would sell their flatboats for lumber. It was far too difficult a task to pole a vessel back upstream. The backwoodsman would then walk home along the old Indian trail that came to be called the Natchez Trace.

Naturally, the existence of farmers hoofing it along an isolated, 400-mile woodland trail with their pockets full of hard money led to a proliferation of highwaymen along the Trace. The most notorious band of cutthroats in the early days of the Trace was the Harpe Brothers Gang. Big and Little Harpe, as they were called, were hardcase killers of the lowest sort. Many a hapless "Kaintuck" met his end with throat slashed and pockets turned out. Little Harpe, one of the frontier's most despicable creatures, was finally caught and hanged until, in the words of the judgment rendered against him, he was "dead, dead, dead."

In the early flatboat days, white settlers along the Trace were exceedingly few and far between. But gradually several inns sprang up, offering meals of boiled bacon and cornpone for the hungry traveler, or rotgut liquor for the thirst, not to mention a pallet indoors where one could sleep without fear of being an overnight victim of the highwaymen.

When the Mississippi Territory was organized, its first governor persuaded the federal government that the Trace ought to be improved, so that mail service could be established between the thriving river port of Natchez, and the Trace's northern terminus, Nashville.

It was to Nashville that Nathaniel and Jonathan rode after leaving the Jones cabin. Their first day out, a norther struck, dumping three feet of snow and icing the creeks. The journey to Nashville took almost a week under these conditions, and at the end of it Jonathan had concluded that it had been the most miserable week of his life. It made the previous ordeal of traveling afoot through the Kentucky hills from Blennerhassett's Island to Boonesboro seem like a garden party by comparison. Jonathan didn't think he would ever thaw out.

But of course he did, and quite nicely, too, in front of the big blazing fireplace in the log home built a few miles north of Nashville by Andrew Jackson, on a piece of land the lawyer-merchant had called The Hermitage.

The Jackson house was a square two-story block-house with three rooms—one big common room downstairs and two rooms above. Jackson had recently sold his Hunter's Hill plantation to pay off debts he had incurred from reckless land deals gone sour, and bought this 420-acre tract. With John Hutchings and John Coffee, he had established a thriving business at Clover Bottom, operating a store, boatyard, tavern, and racetrack there. He also supervised over a dozen slaves at The Hermitage, who raised cotton, corn, and wheat, and bred horses and mules. Once again prosperous as a merchant and farmer, Jackson was a man with a well-deserved reputation for being a hot-tempered duellist. He was charming but rough, a frontier aristocrat, brave to the point of foolhardiness, largely unschooled but with a keen mind and good instincts.

"I first met Aaron Burr back in ought-five," Jackson told them, as they settled into the warmth of the house. "I was honored to have such a distinguished guest under my roof. While it was true he was *persona non grata* back east, he was well received here. You know, he was instrumental in getting Tennessee admitted into the Union. Folks in these parts have long believed that here was a man, albeit an easterner, who had their best interests at heart. His killing of Hamilton didn't hurt his standing out here none, either. More buttered rums, boys?"

They were drinking hot toddies in the bitter winter chill. Once the pewter tankards were topped off, Jackson proceeded with his narrative.

"He did hint around at something about an expedition against the Spaniards. I admit, the notion appealed strongly to me. By God, those people have been nothing but trouble for us from the very beginning. This country just isn't big enough for the both of us. One must go—and it won't be us, I assure you."

"What did he tell you of his plans, exactly?" asked Jonathan.

"Damn little. He's a canny dog, that Burr. I arranged a ball at Talbot's, in Nashville, in his honor. He asked me that evening to draw up a list of men who were fit to be officers in volunteer regiments. I asked him if this scheme of his was sanctioned by the Government. He assured me that it was. I drew up the list he had requested. Then he asked me to build him five bateaux for descending the river, and gave me $3,500 in Kentucky banknotes to pay for the boats and enough provisions for an expedition to China."

He leaned forward, elbows planted on bony knees, his blue eyes ablaze with a fierce light.

"Boys, I love my country more than life itself, and I hate the Dons with a bloody passion. I would delight in seeing the Spaniards driven from our soil, but I would die in the last ditch before I saw the Union torn asunder."

"Looks like that's what Burr has in mind," said Nathaniel.

"It does, doesn't it?" Jackson wore a sour look on his face. "A damned shame, too. With two thousand volunteers I could march on Santa Fe and conquer

Mexico myself. Not to mention the Floridas. *Especially* the Floridas. The time will come, mark my words, gentlemen, when we must take Spanish Florida. The Spaniards are encouraging the Creeks and Seminoles against us, and we here on the frontier will not stand for it much longer. If the government does not take steps to solve the problem, we'll have to take matters into our own hands, as far as those hostilities are concerned."

"When did you learn the truth about Burr?" asked Jonathan.

"But six weeks ago. One of his agents, a Captain John Fort, arrived at my door. The man was loose lipped. He let slip that one of Burr's plans was the capture of New Orleans. I knew then that there was something amiss, as it occurred to me that New Orleans was already a part of the Union.

"I plied young Fort with whiskey. Some of my own, by the way. Used to have a distillery, you know. Damn fine distillery, if I do say so myself. Not a stone's throw from where we sit, over by that wonderful sweetwater spring. Alas, the distillery burned a couple years back. But I still have a stock of homegrown tongue oil, and it worked its wicked magic on Fort.

"I asked him for details, and he gave them gladly. He told me that the plan was to capture the bank, close the port, then conquer Mexico, and join the western part of the Union with the conquered territory to make a great empire for Burr to rule over. 'What of General Wilkinson?' I asked. 'He might have something to say about the seizure of New Orleans.' And that damnfool Fort just laughed, and informed me that Wilkinson was in the stew as deep as Burr."

"What did you do?"

"I wrote President Jefferson a letter, that's what I did. Offered my services, and that of the Tennessee militia, to stop Burr. I hope Jefferson has received that letter by now." Jackson scowled. "Burr tricked me. I'll not have his shadow darken my doorway again. Now there are those who wag their tongues and claim I conspired with him."

"I am confident the president has complete faith in your loyalty, sir," said Jonathan.

"Nice of you to say," said Jackson, skeptical. "But, as for your mission. Were you not aware that Burr was arraigned only a fortnight ago before a Kentucky grand jury?"

"What?" exclaimed Nathaniel. "Where?"

"Frankfort. The governor of Ohio ordered his militia to Great Falls, whereupon they seized all of Burr's boats. Then Jonathan Hamilton Daveiss, the Kentucky prosecutor, had Burr brought before the grand jury. Daveiss is a damned Federalist. Alexander Hamilton was his hero. Hell, he even assumed Hamilton's name for part of his own! So naturally, he dislikes Burr most adamantly."

Nathaniel and Jonathan stared at one another, stunned by this news.

"We were within two days' ride of Burr," said Nathaniel.

"Then it's over," breathed Jonathan. He wanted to shout for joy at the top of his lungs, and dance a jig around the room, so great was his relief. Now he could return to Rebecca, and . . .

"Over!" roared Jackson. "Not by a country mile, sir."

"But you said that Burr's been arrested, his expedition seized—"

"I said Burr was arraigned. He was also defended by a young lawyer, name of Henry Clay. They say that Clay has never lost a case. Must be true. Burr went free. The grand jury returned the bill of indictment not true, for lack of evidence. Daveiss bears part of the blame. He and his Federalist cronies were too busy alleging that almost all the Republican politicians in Kentucky were embroiled in Burr's audacious scheme. So when it came time to produce real evidence, they were at a loss. In fact, they had to admit that most of their allegations were insupportable. You must have two witnesses to prove a charge of treason, you know. And what man would put his own neck in a noose to see Burr hanged?"

"Where is Burr now?" asked Nathaniel.

"He took two of the boats I had built for him down at Clover Bottom, and headed down the Cumberland. I did not know of this until he had gone."

Nathaniel looked at Jonathan. "Then we must hurry to Natchez after all."

"If you catch him," said Jackson, "bring him to me. I'll hang him, with the utmost pleasure, and no damned silk-tongued lawyer will be able to get him off. More rum?"

Chapter 31

They stayed that night at Jackson's Hermitage. The next morning dawned bright and clear—and cold. The sky was a brilliant blue, the sun's glare on the snow enough to blind a person. They partook of a hot breakfast and stepped out of the blockhouse to find their horses ready and waiting, with a couple of extra blankets rolled up and tied behind their saddles. Jackson had also thoughtfully provided them with some beans, coffee, flour, and jerked venison.

"You have no time for hunting," said Jackson. "Or I should say, you are after much bigger game."

They thanked him.

"And I hope," added Jackson, "that when the time comes to take Spanish Florida, the two of you will consent to join me in the venture. I'll need good men."

"I'd be honored," said Jonathan. "As long as it has the blessing of the government."

Jackson laughed.

South of Nashville, the Trace crossed rolling hills
and fertile fields. The land was open, and dotted
with homesteads. They reached Gordon's Ferry that
afternoon. John Gordon was an old Indian fighter
who had served with distinction in the Coldwater
and Nickajack expeditions against renegade Cherokee some years back. He had been granted this tract
of fine bottomland in reward for "meritorious deeds
in many hazardous undertakings against the Indians."
His home was quite a handsome one, a two-story
brick structure on the banks of the Duck River. Gordon invited them to stay overnight, but they respectfully declined. There was still an hour or two of
daylight left.

The Duck River had iced up during the norther,
but the day's warm sun had broken up the ice, so
that now there were thick floes hurtling down the
fast-moving river. Gordon advised against a crossing
until at least the morrow. Jonathan showed him the
letter President Jefferson had written. Gordon spoke
no more of the perils of crossing the river. He
rounded up his two sons and they set out on the
ferry.

Gordon's sons did the poling, while Nathaniel and
Gordon used their own poles to fend off the ice
floes. With but one good arm, Jonathan was rele-
gated to holding the horses. Some of the floes were
as big as the ferry, and Jonathan figured that if one
of them hit them dead on, they would all be spilled
into the freezing waters. But Nathaniel and Gordon
managed to push the smaller floes around the ferry,

and at least slowed or deflected the larger ones, so that when they did strike it was not a severe collision.

They reached the southern bank of the Duck River without mishap. Jonathan thanked the Gordons profusely. The old Indian fighter and his two stalwart sons had risked their lives in the crossing. Gordon dismissed the gratitude with a wave of his hand. "It was our duty as patriots, sir, and we did it gladly."

The Trace plunged into thick woods. They pushed hard to make as many miles as possible before sundown, and spent the night at Grinder's Stand. The Grinders were a pleasant couple. Their cabin was a dogtrot, deep in the forest. The next morning, Nathaniel and Jonathan ate another hot breakfast, paid for their room and board, and rode off at a rapid gait on fully rested horses. It occurred to Jonathan that he could probably use Jefferson's letter in lieu of cash payment for meals and lodging on this trip, but he did not seriously consider doing so. Besides, he deemed it the wiser course to use the letter only as a last resort, as had been the case at Gordon's ferry. There was no assurance that every man to whom he might reveal the letter was as loyal to the republic as that old Indian fighter. Burr apparently had many friends in this country.

It was bitterly cold as they rode through dark woods all that day. Jonathan kept an eye peeled for cutthroats. Yet the only person they saw was a mail rider, galloping south.

They were forced to camp out under the stars that night, and Nathaniel rejected the idea of building a fire, which was not good news for Jonathan, who at that point would have given all he owned for a little warmth. But Nathaniel was concerned about highwaymen, too. The temperature plummeted after sunset, and the frontiersman finally changed his mind. He could tell that Jonathan was suffering, albeit in silence. Nathaniel dug a pit and built a fire in the bottom of it, laying sticks across the hole to keep the firelight to a minimum. Then he dug a second pit, and built a second fire.

Jonathan was mystified, but too cold to bother asking questions. His teeth were chattering so loudly that he didn't think he could make himself understood anyway. When the firewood had been reduced to red-hot embers, Nathaniel smothered the fires with a thin layer of dirt. He bade Jonathan sit cross-legged over one of the holes, and covered him with two blankets. Jonathan peered out of his woolen cocoon to see Nathaniel sit atop the second firepit and drape himself with a blanket. The young lieutenant doubted that he could sleep sitting up. But the blessed warmth rising up out of the firepit so relaxed him that he soon dozed off. He woke with a terrible crick in his back, but he was well rested after a long sleep.

They reached Colbert's Ferry across the Tennessee before midday. George Colbert was a Chickasaw chief. A number of Chickasaws and Choctaws had reached the conclusion that the "Long Rifles" were here to stay, and decided to profit in one way or another from their presence. George's brother Levi owned a stand called Buzzard's Roost, on the other side of the river. The brothers were shrewd businessmen. They owned farms, slaves, a salt spring, and a grist mill between them. George Colbert dressed and talked like a white man, but for his copper complexion and dark eyes and the lank black hair beneath his hat, he would have looked like just another backwoodsman.

He spotted Jonathan's uniform beneath the lieutenant's longcoat and, as a result, insisted on a fee for crossing that Jonathan thought so exorbitant it bordered on robbery. Before Nathaniel could stop him, he had produced Jefferson's letter. Colbert couldn't read, so Jonathan read it to him. The Chickasaw listened impassively, chewing on a quid of tobacco. When Jonathan had finished, Colbert spat a stream of yellow juice and repeated the price for the ferry service. Jonathan fumed. But there was no other way across the broad Tennessee short of building one's own raft or canoe, and Nathaniel paid up.

Once across the river, Jonathan made an unflattering comment concerning Colbert, and Nathaniel chuckled.

"Now what makes you think a Chickasaw Indian would give a hoot about the United States and whether the republic is in peril?"

"Well, I—"

"It's that uniform," said Nathaniel. "Maybe I should have decked you out in buckskins before we left Kaintuck."

"What about my uniform? I'm damned proud of wear it."

"That feller Colbert figured that since you were the White Father's soldier you had plenty of hard money."

"Why would he think that?"

"Maybe because the White Father seems to like to buy land and such for money. Doesn't make much sense to the Indians, the buying and selling of land, but when the money's offered they'll take it."

They rode on by Buzzard's Roost, Levi Colbert's stand, and made camp that night in the woods. Since crossing the Tennessee River, Nathaniel was particularly interested in their backtrail—so much so that Jonathan eventually reached the conclusion that something might be amiss. When he asked if this were so, Nathaniel simply shook his head.

That night, the frontiersman built a nice warm roaring fire. Jonathan was surprised but immensely grateful, and not at all inclined to look a gift horse in the mouth. He figured that Nathaniel had judged it safe enough to permit a fire, and that was good enough for the half-frozen young lieutenant.

Later that night, just as Jonathan was dozing off, Nathaniel quietly announced that he was going off to collect more wood for the dying fire. Jonathan was too tired to think anything of it. Nathaniel disappeared into the night. Just when Jonathan began to think his companion overdue, he heard the crunch of footsteps in the snow behind him.

"I was starting to wonder—"

Jonathan spoke as he turned. What he saw cut him short—and scared the living daylights out of him.

Three Indians were trying to sneak up on him.

They were dressed like white men, and he had sufficient wits about him to conclude that they were more likely Chickasaw than Shawnee, since the Shawnees he had seen wore breechclouts and leggins and warpaint.

But that didn't make Jonathan feel any better about the situation, because anyone with eyes could see by the expressions on their faces, and the way they were skulking around in the darkness, that these three Indians, whatever tribe they belonged to, were up to no good.

Discovered, the Indians froze. Jonathan leapt to his feet, casting aside his blanket and grabbing for the pistol wedged under his belt. The Indians charged him then, counting on closing the distance before he could draw and fire. One wielded an axe handle, and the other two brandished knives. Jonathan realized that they had calculated correctly—he would not even get off one shot. But the thought of running never entered into his mind.

A rifle spoke.

One of the Indians pitched forward. Howling, he

writhed in the blood-splattered snow, clutching his left leg. Stunned, his two companions stopped in their tracks and searched the darkness. Nathaniel appeared at the edge of the firelight, calmly reloading his flintlock rifle. He looked at them, and they stared back.

"Git," he said.

They took off running, leaving their wounded comrade behind. The latter forgot about his pain and went limping after the others as fast as he could go, casting frightened glances over his shoulder, fearful that Nathaniel would shoot him in the back.

His knees suddenly unreliable, Jonathan sat down by the fire. As Nathaniel approached, he glowered at the frontiersman.

"You knew they were coming," he said. It all made sense now—Nathaniel's abiding interest in their backtrail, the big fire, the bogus late-night search for firewood. "You left me staked out here like a Judas goat!"

"I wasn't certain that they were coming until a little while ago, when I heard them crashing around in the brush."

"Crashing around!" Jonathan grimaced. He had heard absolutely nothing.

"I figured the word might get around the Chickasaws who tarry at Colbert's crossing and Buzzard's Roost," said Nathaniel. "Remember, since they knew you were a soldier of the White Father they had to figure you were carrying a lot of hard money. The temptation was too great for them."

"Still, you used me for bait."

"Well, they wouldn't have come in if they'd seen an empty camp. Now we don't have to worry about them anymore. They won't return."

"How can you be sure?"

Nathaniel smiled. "Pretty sure," he replied, and rolled up in his blankets to sleep.

"*Pretty* sure," grumbled Jonathan.

Edgy and disgruntled, he stayed up, stirring the fire to keep it alive as long as possible, peering into the darkness, listening as hard as he could—and glancing behind him at least a hundred times. He slept precious little that night.

The next day they passed Tokshish, or McIntoshville, a small and picturesque settlement of five or six farms and a missionary school. They were in Choctaw country now. The next few days they passed through several Indian villages, and in every case were treated courteously. Without mishap, they arrived in Natchez after twelve days and over four hundred miles on the Trace.

In 1713, the French explorer D'Iberville had established a trading post on the banks of the Mississippi at the present site of Natchez. This was followed three years later by the erection of Fort Rosalie, the sight of the infamous massacre in which 250 Frenchmen had been killed, and 300 women and children hauled off into slavery.

Natchez had survived this catastrophe, and later passed into Spanish control, then back into French hands and, finally, with the Louisiana Purchase, had become American domain. Many Kaintuck boatmen preferred to sell their goods at Natchez rather than float on down the river to New Orleans, and the Natchez riverfront was infested with merchants and middlemen who made their living off the Kaintucks.

So did the denizens of the area along Silver Street called "Natchez Under-the-Hill." "On" the hill were the homes of the merchants and lawyers, built on a high bluff overlooking the riverfront district. At the base of the bluff was a neighborhood populated by confidence men, prostitutes, and purveyors of rotgut whiskey. Many were the hapless Kaintucks who carelessly lost their hard-earned profits to this riffraff. Hardly a night passed that a murder or thugging or brawl did not occur on notorious Silver Street.

Nathaniel and Jonathan went directly to the riverfront and asked questions. They found a merchant in his cluttered dockside office who informed them that, indeed, Aaron Burr had arrived the day before. What business did they have with him? They were looking to join his expedition, said Jonathan. The merchant gave him a strange look.

"Then I suppose that makes you a traitor to that uniform you wear, sir."

Jonathan didn't know what to say. He had the sense that some new development, of which he knew nothing, had complicated the situation.

"Apparently you haven't heard the news," remarked the merchant.

"We've been nearly a fortnight on the Trace," said Nathaniel.

"It was by the mail which preceded you down the Trace that we received the president's proclamation. It was printed in the newspaper. Alas, I don't seem to have a copy . . ."

"Just tell us," said Nathaniel.

"President Jefferson has declared that Aaron Burr is engaged in a criminal conspiracy. When Burr arrived here and heard the news he dispersed his followers. Jefferson called for his arrest."

Nathaniel glanced at Jonathan. "Sounds like the president gave up on you, Lieutenant."

"Where did Burr go?" asked Jonathan curtly. He was tired of the hunt. He had lost all patience with this affair.

"Go? He didn't go anywhere, as far as I know. He remains in Natchez."

"No one has tried to arrest him?"

"Certainly not. He has five or six ruffians with him. They've sworn to kill anyone who tries to take Colonel Burr into custody."

"Where can he be found?" asked Jonathan.

The merchant peered at Jonathan's travel-stained uniform. "You two didn't come here to join up with Burr."

"No, we didn't," said Nathaniel.

"Well," sighed the merchant, and shrugged. "If you want to get killed it's none of my affair."

"Where is Burr?" snapped Jonathan.

"You'll find Aaron Burr at King's Tavern."

Without so much as a thank-you Jonathan took his leave, followed by Nathaniel.

"And may God have mercy on your souls," murmured the Natchez merchant.

Chapter 32

King's Tavern was one of the oldest structures in Natchez. The land and building had been granted to one Prosper King by the Spanish back in 1789. Nowadays, it was the favorite meeting place for individuals planning to travel up the Trace in groups, the better to protect themselves from robbers. It was also the delivery point on the United States mail route. The mail was distributed from the tavern to the citizens of Natchez. It was a three-story structure, facing the Trace, constructed of brick on the ground level, with the upper levels of cypress clapboard and poplar wood.

As they drew near the tavern, riding side by side down the street, Nathaniel abruptly leaned forward and grabbed Rosinante's bridle cheekstrap. The sorrel gave a whicker and jerked away, but the frontiersman held fast, stopping the horse. Then he placed his own mount broadside in Jonathan's path.

"What do you intend to do, Lieutenant?"

"Arrest Aaron Burr, of course."

"Just march right into that tavern and grab him, is that it?"

"The game is up," said Jonathan. "I hope you're not suggesting that we carry through with your plan—pretending to be volunteers. That would scarcely work at this point."

"Probably not. By now everyone knows about the president's proclamation."

Thought of Jefferson's proclamation did not improve Jonathan's mood. "I am ashamed to think that the president gave up all hope of hearing from me," he said. "Though I suppose I can't blame him."

"I wouldn't take it as a personal affront."

"The president depended on me to do a job, and I intend to do it."

"That uniform of yours is what concerns me," said Nathaniel. "Or rather, their reaction to it. You'll get yourself killed, Lieutenant."

"Perhaps. What do you suggest?"

"I'll go in alone," said Nathaniel.

"You most certainly will not."

"I don't aim to get killed. I'll be going home to my wife and daughter. I'm going in alone, Lieutenant. You do a little scouting. See how many men Burr's got with him, and what their disposition might be. Wait out here until I return, out of sight."

Jonathan thought it over. From the way Flintlock Jones spoke, Jonathan knew that the frontiersman was *telling* him how it was going to be—not just making a suggestion.

"You'll not try to take Burr into custody yourself?"

"I'll leave that to you."

Jonathan nodded. "Don't take long. I won't wait forever."

Nathaniel rode on.

Jonathan sat his horse in the middle of the street, watching, as the frontiersman dismounted in front of King's Tavern and tethered his horse to an iron ring in one of the hitching posts. With a last glance down the street at Jonathan, Nathaniel entered the tavern.

As soon as Nathaniel was out of sight, Jonathan dismounted and led his horse to the nearest post, which happened to be in front of a mercantile. He whipped his longcoat aside and drew the flintlock pistol from his belt in order to check its priming. A man in town clothes emerged from the store at that instant. Jonathan looked up sharply. The man took note of Jonathan's pistol, and the Tripolitan cutlass at his side—as well as the expression on the lieutenant's face. Then he performed an abrupt about-face and hastened back into the store.

Jonathan swallowed the lump in his throat and started for the tavern.

Reaching the mouth of the alley that lay between King's Tavern and an adjacent building, he paused and gave the tavern a long and careful scrutiny. He noticed stairs clinging to the side of the tavern, providing means by which a person could enter or exit through a second-story door and reach the back corner of the structure. Jonathan made up his mind. He would give Flintlock Jones five minutes. Then he would enter King's Tavern by yonder stairs and do what he had come so far to do.

When Nathaniel entered the common room of King's Tavern a wave of nostalgia swept over him. This place reminded him strongly of his father's Virginia inn. The trestle tables, the big stone hearth, the heady aroma of a variety of liquors. He tried to shake it off and attend to the dangerous business at hand.

There were six men in the common room. Four were seated at a table in the back corner, near stairs that provided access to the second floor. Two men stood at the counter—heavy planks laid across big hogshead casks, one on either side. The man on the far side of the counter was clearly the tavernkeeper or one of his hired help. He was handing a demijohn across the counter to the other man. This one turned to go back to the table occupied by the quartet. He and two of the men at the table wore grimy buckskins. The other two wore good cloaks of pilot-cloth and tricorner hats.

The man with the demijohn stopped dead in his tracks when he saw Nathaniel's long and lanky frame in the doorway.

The four at the table had been conversing in subdued tones. Now they fell suddenly silent and watched the frontiersman. The tension in the room was a tangible thing. For a moment no one spoke.

"I'm looking for Colonel Aaron Burr," said Nathaniel.

The man with the demijohn glanced across the common room at the table. Then he looked back at Nathaniel and asked, "What do you want him for?"

"Name's Nathaniel Jones. I'm in search of a friend of mine. A young man named Stephen Cooper."

"You the one they call Flintlock Jones up Kaintuck way?"

"I am."

"Don't know nobody named Stephen Cooper."

"You're not Burr."

Again the man looked across the table.

Nathaniel started across the room. "I've come to speak to the colonel," he said.

"Close enough," warned one of the buckskin-clad characters at the table.

"No," said one of the men clad in cloak and tricorner. He rose to his feet. "You are welcome at our table, Mr. Jones."

"Colonel Burr?"

The man bowed slightly at the waist. "At your service, sir."

"Would you mind telling your friend to bring his pistol out where I can see it?"

Burr smiled. He was a singularly handsome man, with dark hair pulled back neatly in a queue, and lively blue-green eyes. His was a strong face, full of character, and his frame was compact and athletic.

"You have sharp eyes," he complimented. "Daltrey,

dispense with the pistol, if you please. Now, what may I do for you, Mr. Jones?"

"I'm looking for a young friend named Stephen Cooper. I was given to understand that he joined your expedition, Colonel."

"I fear you have been misinformed. My . . . expedition has been dispersed. This is all that remains of it. But I am certain that no one by that name enlisted."

Nathaniel got a good look at all the men with Burr except for the one who was dressed like the colonel. This one kept his tricorner pulled down low over his face. Clearly he did not care for Nathaniel to identify him, and under the circumstances, Nathaniel couldn't fault him.

"I am curious," said Burr. "Why were you looking for your friend?"

"To fetch him home to his family."

"He expressed a desire to join my expedition?"

"He'd talked about it. Then one day he just up and disappeared."

"And you did not approve?"

"Don't know much about it."

"I think you know more than you are willing to admit."

"Well, I do know that the president has branded you a traitor."

"President Jefferson is a fair and honest man. But he has been grievously misled as to my true intentions. He has fallen prey to the lies and calum-

nies which my mortal enemies had leveled against
me."

"I wouldn't know about all that," said Nathaniel.
"But I am a little curious about why you're sitting
here if you know the president has ordered your arrest."

Burr shrugged. "I have not yet made up my mind
what to do about the situation."

"Seems to me you could run or give yourself
up."

At that moment Jonathan appeared at the top of
the stairs, almost directly above the table that Burr
and his cohorts occupied.

"Colonel Burr! In the name of the republic I arrest
you!"

The man named Daltrey reached for the flintlock
pistol on the table in front of him.

Nathaniel heard the man who had been standing
behind him, the one carrying the demijohn, rush forward.

The frontiersman had been standing with the
flintlock rifle cradled in his arms. Now he whirled,
swinging his rifle, so that the long barrel struck the
man squarely on the side of the head, dropping him
cold. The demijohn shattered on the floor. Nathaniel
turned back toward the table just as Daltrey fired up
at Jonathan. The young lieutenant shot at the same
instant. Daltrey's bullet splintered the staircase ban-
nister. Jonathan's hit home. Clutching at his chest,
Daltrey wheeled and stumbled toward the tavern
door. He didn't make it, falling first to his knees and

then, with a horrible sound, pitching forward on his face.

Aaron Burr tried to run. He could either attempt to get past Nathaniel and reach the tavern door, or go up the stairs past Jonathan. He chose the latter, aware that Jonathan's pistol was empty, while the frontiersman's rifle was still loaded. As he pounded up the stairs he reached under his cloak and brandished a pistol. But Jonathan had dropped his empty pistol and drew the Tripolitan cutlass. A quick downward stroke knocked the pistol from Burr's grasp. It clattered down the stairs. Jonathan slammed into Burr, driving him into the wall, and then stepped back, raising the cutlass, and pinning Burr with the point of the curved blade against his chest.

"The chase is over," rasped Jonathan.

Burr raised his arms away from his sides, palms turned upwards. With a tight smile he said, "I see that it is so."

Nathaniel leveled his long rifle on the two men at the table. The one in buckskins had begun to rise out of his chair and turn for his own rifle, which was leaning against the wall behind him.

"Don't," was all Nathaniel said.

It was all he had to say. The man sat back down, glowering.

"Are we too under arrest?" inquired the man whose face was hidden from Nathaniel by his pulled-low tricorner.

His was a faintly British accent, and Nathaniel

thought there was something familiar about it—it struck a chord of memory, but a memory too dim to recall.

"Do I know you from somewhere?" asked the frontiersman.

"I don't believe I've had the pleasure of your acquaintance before today, sir."

"Burr's the one we came for," said Nathaniel. "I suggest the rest of you go home."

"I have no home."

"Come on, Lieutenant," urged Nathaniel.

Jonathan escorted a docile Burr out the front door, stepping over Daltrey and sparing the dead man a bleak glance. Nathaniel kept the other two men covered until Jonathan and his prisoner were safely outside.

As soon as the frontiersman was gone, the buckskin-clad man at the table shot to his feet and grabbed his rifle.

Peter McLeod grabbed his arm. "What do you intend?"

"I promised the colonel I wouldn't let them take him against his will. We all did. And I aim to keep my word."

"Very commendable," said McLeod dryly. "But this is neither the time nor the place."

"They've got to be stopped."

"Oh, they will be. Especially Lieutenant Jonathan Groves, damn his eyes."

"Who?"

"The fellow who shot your friend, Mr. Daltrey."

"You know him?"

"We had not met before today. But I am certain we will meet again."

Chapter 33

They found a horse for Burr at the edge of town. A man who operated a livery and blacksmith shop gave it to them gratis when he learned that their intention was to haul Burr off to trial. He harbored nothing but contempt for the former vice president. "I've lost a wife and a son," he growled, "one to the pox and the other to Injuns. My own flesh and blood—and for what? To make this country part and parcel of the United States, that's what. And now this two-legged snake wants to carve his own little kingdom out of it. Over my dead body."

Burr remained composed in the face of this hostility. As they were riding out of Natchez, Jonathan couldn't refrain from making a comment.

"Doesn't look like you're all that popular out here after all, Colonel."

"Lies," said Burr, with disdain. "I never intended what that man said."

"What about the men, the guns, the boats?"

"You must not be aware that I was given title to 350,000 acres along the Washita."

"I heard."

"My expedition was for the sole purpose of colonizing that grant."

"What about the women and children?"

"They were to be sent for at a later date, when it was safe to do so. The Indians in that region are notorious."

Jonathan shook his head. "You're a smooth talker, Colonel Burr. You seem to have a plausible answer for everything."

"I'm telling the truth."

"Reckon you'll have your chance to tell that story to a jury," said Nathaniel.

"It won't be the first time I have been required to do so, sir. How many times must a man be proven innocent in a court of law?"

"You don't sound too worried," observed Jonathan.

"I am not at all."

"The president has evidence. I've seen it."

Burr kept his gaze fixed on the trail ahead. "Manufactured by my enemies. Justice will prevail. Mark my words, gentlemen. I shall be exonerated. No charge brought against me can be proven. Least of all the charge of treason."

That night they camped in the woods. Burr rolled up in his blanket and went to sleep immediately. Nathaniel and Jonathan sat around the fire. Burr's unflappable confidence clearly disturbed Jonathan.

"You think he's really asleep?" he asked Nathaniel. "Or just playing possum?"

Nathaniel listened a moment to Burr's breathing. At length he said, "He's asleep."

"He's got nerves of steel. Do you think he *will* go free?"

Nathaniel shrugged.

"Well, it doesn't really matter to me, I guess," said the young lieutenant.

"You did your job. Of course, I ought to mention that you almost got us both killed."

Jonathan grimaced. "I couldn't wait any longer. What were you doing in there?"

"I was thinking about asking the colonel if he'd like to save us all a lot of trouble and just give up."

"Burr? Surrender? I doubt that."

"Well, we'll never know."

They did not speak for a while, lost in their own thoughts, gazing into the fire.

"I guess you can't wait to get home," said Jonathan.

Nathaniel nodded. It was exactly what he had been thinking. "I promised Amanda a long time ago that I wouldn't leave her alone. Sometimes I just couldn't help it. But those times were few and far between. Lately, though, it seems like I've been gone for a coon's age."

Jonathan didn't say anything.

"What about you?" asked the frontiersman. "Back to the sea, I reckon."

"I don't know."

"You've got a home and family back east?"

"A family. Not a home."

Nathaniel studied the lieutenant's face. Jonathan was staring morosely into the fire.

"You know," said the frontiersman, "it struck me as peculiar at the time, but my daughter asked me to promise her that I wouldn't let anything befall you."

"She did? When?"

Nathaniel suppressed a smile. "Before we left home."

"I . . . she . . ." Jonathan felt heat in his cheeks, and it wasn't from the fire.

"A puzzlement to me," continued Nathaniel, "but then I put it together with the two of you sitting up in front of the fireplace all that night before we left, and it started to—"

"You know about that?"

"Well, I wasn't trying to spy. But I'm a mighty light sleeper. Got the Shawnees to thank for that."

"I assure you, Mr. Jones, that nothing—"

"I know as much, Lieutenant. You don't have to say it."

"She was afraid. She imagined Indians at her window."

Nathaniel nodded sadly. "It'll take time for her to get over that completely. You could be a help to her."

"Me?"

"She's kind of taken to you, I think."

"And I . . ." Jonathan gulped at the lump in his throat. "I like her, too, sir."

Nathaniel yawned and stretched, and in an off-handed way said, "Well, then, I reckon you'd best go home with me. Since you like to stay up nights, you can take the first watch."

"Yes, sir!"

That suited Jonathan just fine. He didn't think he could sleep a wink anyway. Not now. Suddenly he was no longer tired, no longer despondent. All he could think about was Rebecca, and how she would come running down that long bluegrass slope to greet him as he came home.

Peter McLeod and his two buckskin-clad accomplices struck without warning.

They slipped past the camp that night, and proceeded along the Trace about a mile, to a spot which McLeod deemed perfect for ambush. Here the Trace was flanked on either side by cutbanks thick with brush. He positioned his two associates on either side of the trail, directly across from one another, while he proceeded uptrail approximately fifty yards. Dismounting, he led his horse into a persimmon thicket. He stood there, reins clenched tightly in his hands, in a spot where he had a clear view down the trail to the ambush site, and yet was effectively concealed.

He did not have long to wait.

The trail was narrow here, so that his victims were forced to ride single file. The frontiersman, Flintlock Jones, was in the lead. Aaron Burr was behind him, with the lieutenant bringing up the rear.

The instant before one of McLeod's fellow ambushers fired, the frontiersman checked his horse sharply and, turning in the saddle, shouted a warning to Jonathan. McLeod had mere seconds to wonder how Nathaniel had known he was riding into a trap—and then an ambusher broke through the brush on the rim of the cutbank, raised his rifle, and fired. The impact of the bullet at such close range knocked Nathaniel right out of the saddle.

Aaron Burr kicked his horse into a gallop. The horse jumped the body of the fallen frontiersman and thundered up the trail towards McLeod's position, with Burr bent low in the saddle.

McLeod was pleased. Things were working out just as he had planned. Best of all, Flintlock Jones had fallen with the first shot. He was, thought McLeod, the most dangerous of the two adversaries.

But Jonathan proved himself dangerous enough, as the second ambusher appeared at the top of the cutbank, leveling his rifle at the naval lieutenant. Jonathan drew the pistol from his belt and fired first. He hit his mark—no easy task on a plunging horse. The ambusher cried out and pitched forward, somersaulting as he toppled off the cutbank and fell to the trail below.

The man who had shot Nathaniel discarded his rifle. A hunting knife brandished, he launched himself off the cutbank at Jonathan, who was almost directly below him.

Nathaniel's rifle roared. The frontiersman, sprawled on the trail, fired from a half-prone position, but his aim was true. The bullet struck the ambusher in mid-air and hurled him to the ground.

Jonathan managed to get Rosinante under control, and made as though to dismount. He was more concerned with Nathaniel's condition than the pursuit of Burr.

"No!" yelled Nathaniel. He struggled to his feet, clutching a shoulder.

Jonathan was shocked to see blood leaking through the frontiersman's fingers. For some reason he had thought Flintlock Jones invincible.

"Get Burr!" barked Nathaniel.

Jonathan settled back in the saddle and kicked Rosinante into a gallop.

As Burr rode past his place of concealment, McLeod leaped astride his horse and emerged from the thicket, placing himself between Burr and Jonathan. Raising his pistol, he fired. Missing his intended target, he killed Jonathan's horse instead. Rosinante died in midstride. Front legs buckling, the horse plowed headfirst into the dirt, throwing Jonathan.

McLeod glanced over his shoulder, to see that Burr had stopped on a short distance uptrail.

"Ride on," shouted McLeod.

He looked back in the direction of the ambush and was surprised to see Jonathan on his feet and running straight at him, brandishing the wicked-looking cutlass.

Surprised, but not displeased.

McLeod tossed away his empty pistol, drew his own saber, and rode to meet the hard-charging lieutenant.

The fact that one of his arms was in a sling put

Jonathan at a disadvantage. He tried to parry Mc-
Leod's sweeping saber stroke. Steel rang against
steel. Sparks showered Jonathan as the impact
knocked the cutlass from his grasp. He lost his balance and fell backward. McLeod savagely checked
and wheeled his horse. With a cry of triumph he
bore down on Jonathan again. Stunned, the lieutenant managed to pick himself up and dive for the cutlass. McLeod's saber stroke missed him by inches.
Jonathan came up with the cutlass as McLeod thundered past, turned his horse again, and once more
charged forward.

This time Jonathan feinted as though he were going for McLeod's body. At the last possible moment
he dodged downward and slashed at McLeod, opening a deep gash in the Tory's thigh. McLeod pulled
so hard on the reins that his horse almost sat down.
He spared his injury a disdainful glance, then leered
at Jonathan.

"You will have to do better," he said.

In a blur of buckskin, Nathaniel caught him on
the blindside—a running leap that carried McLeod
clean out of the saddle. But the frontiersman landed
poorly, and nearly blacked out. The agile McLeod recovered quickly. Bouncing to his feet, he raised the
saber for a killing stroke.

"Damn you," rasped McLeod, eyes ablaze. "Damn
you all."

Nathaniel could only raise an arm—a feeble
defense—and watch the saber coming down.

Steel met steel again, as Jonathan blocked the saber stroke with his cutlass. Lashing out blindly, Jonathan struck the saber from McLeod's grasp, and they fell in a tangle of arms and legs. Jonathan was the first to his feet. Unarmed now, McLeod also rose. Jonathan placed the point of the cutlass to his chest.

"Go ahead," snarled McLeod. "Run me through."

Jonathan hesitated, blinded by a sudden, vivid image of the woman on the Fairfax road, and of the expression on her face as he ran her through with the saber . . .

McLeod smirked. "You bloody coward."

He turned and ran to his horse, standing nearby, vaulting into the saddle. The horse reared, but could not unseat him.

"We'll meet again, Lieutenant Groves!" laughed McLeod, and galloped away, back down the road toward Natchez in the opposite direction Burr had taken.

As far as Peter McLeod was concerned, that coward Burr was on his own.

Jonathan rushed to Nathaniel's side.

"I reckon he misjudged you," said Nathaniel. "You're a brave fool, but no bloody coward, that's certain."

"How did he know me?"

Nathaniel shook his head. "I would have slept better had you killed him."

"Are you bad hurt?"

"I've suffered worse. Don't worry about me. Go after Burr. He must not escape."

Jonathan nodded grimly. "He won't."

Nathaniel's horse stood nearby. Jonathan gathered the reins and heaved himself up into the saddle, no easy task for a man with one arm in a sling.

"I'll be back with Burr," he promised, and rode on up the trail in the direction their prisoner had taken in flight.

"I don't doubt that," breathed Nathaniel. He stretched out on his back with a weary, pain-wracked sigh. Laying there across the Trace, he stared up through a canopy of winter-bare treetops at a sky as blue as Amanda's eyes.

Epilogue

Nathaniel found Jonathan down by the spring, sitting on the big log near the pool beneath the rocks from which the water flowed. The lieutenant was wearing his uniform, the fabric brushed clean and the brass buttons polished. The woods were alive with birdsong, and the air was sweet with the fragrance of the wildflowers growing profusely in the grass. It was the kind of day, mused the frontiersman, when everything seemed right with the world. So he might have wondered why Jonathan looked so solemn. Might have, but didn't. He had a good idea why.

"Thought I might find you here," said Nathaniel.

Jonathan jumped at the sound of his voice. So wrapped up was he in his own thoughts that the young lieutenant hadn't heard Nathaniel coming through the woods. But then, Flintlock Jones moved quiet, like an Indian.

"I'm sorry," said Jonathan. "Are they looking for me? Is it time?"

"Not yet. Ol' Brashears hasn't made it. But he'll be

along, don't fret. He's a little crazy, but always on time."

Jonathan nodded.

"Nervous?" asked Nathaniel. Leaning on his long rifle, he tried to suppress a smile, but the effort was in vain. No harm done, though—Jonathan was back to staring at the spring.

"No, not really. I . . . this is where it happened."

Now it was Nathaniel's turn to nod without speaking. The smile was gone from his face.

"Rebecca came down here with me yesterday," said Jonathan.

"Did she?" The frontiersman was surprised. "I didn't know."

"It's a good sign, don't you think?"

"Reckon so. She's getting over it. Thanks to you."

"Do you think . . . did she love Stephen Cooper?"

Nathaniel chose his words carefully. "I don't think she knew what love was until she met you, Jonathan."

"Has anyone heard from him lately?"

Nathaniel shook his head. Stephen Cooper had recovered slowly from his wounds. At least, he had recovered physically. But a couple of months back he had up and disappeared. Tom Cooper, his father, claimed it was when Stephen learned that Rebecca and Jonathan were to be married.

"I doubt if we'll ever see him around these parts again," said Nathaniel. "By the way, some of the folks from Boonesboro brought news of Burr."

"What has happened?"

"He was put on trial for treason, over in Richmond. None other than John Marshall was the judge presiding."

"The chief justice!" Jefferson's worst fears had been realized, then.

As he had promised Nathaniel, Jonathan had caught Burr on the Natchez Trace. They had delivered him to Nashville, where a squad of soldiers had taken Burr into custody. Jonathan had assumed that Burr would hang—or at least spend the rest of his days in prison.

"Burr was right," he said, bitterly. "He got off scot-free."

Jonathan was stunned. "How can that be? The president had evidence?"

"Politics, I reckon."

"Is there no justice in our laws?"

"Sometimes not."

"Then it was all for nothing."

"I wouldn't say that. Burr's on a ship bound for Europe. He knows he has no future here. There's talk that he's going to ask Bonaparte for a commission. Important thing is, his scheme out here has failed. He's no longer a threat to the republic. In fact, he's a man without a country."

Jonathan stood up. "Well, I guess we had better be getting back."

They walked through the woods in silence. Jonathan couldn't get that damned Aaron Burr off his mind. He felt thoroughly dissatisfied with the affair's outcome.

But when they emerged from the woods, and he saw the people gathered in front of the cabin, amongst an array of wagons and horses that had conveyed them here from Boonesboro and other homesteads, Jonathan forgot all about Aaron Burr. He saw Rebecca, looking like an angel in a white dress she and her mother had spent weeks making, with the sunlight in her golden hair. She had been watching for him, and now she waved.

Jonathan waved back and quickened his stride, leaving his smiling, buckskin-clad, future father-in-law behind.